Written in Water

Heir to the Firstborn, Volume 1

Elizabeth Schechter

Published by Elizabeth Schechter, 2020.

Published by Raven's Wing Books

Previously published as **Written in Water** (Elizabeth Schechter, 2019)

Editor: Michael Schechter
Cover design by GetCovers

Raven's Wing Books

ravens-wing-books.com
ISBN: 978-0578444833

Table of Contents

To Corey, for joining me on Patreon for the wild ride that is creating fiction in real time.

And to M and J. Always.

Prologue

THE FIRSTBORN WAS DEAD.

Since the world began, the tribes of Adavar had been ruled by the Firstborn, chosen by the Mother Goddess to take up the reins of power once held by Axia, Firstborn Daughter of the Goddess. The ritual to choose the Heir had been handed down since Axia's daughter Alaine had taken on the mantle of rule – each candidate went alone into the crypt in the Mother's temple where Axia and her Companions were entombed. It didn't matter how many claimants entered – only the true Heir would find Axia's Diadem, and be named Heir. And when the time came for the Heir to become the Firstborn, only they would find Axia's Crown.

It had been just five years since Firstborn Tirine had brought the Crown from the crypt, and her rule had been welcomed with great acclaim. She'd served as Heir for fifteen years, and throughout it all, her affection and respect for her people were clear to anyone who cared to look, and they had loved and respected her in return. She was, in truth, a generous and loving person, a fair and impartial judge when necessary, and completely implacable in times of need. Her Companions had grown from young men and women alongside her, and each of the tribes knew and trusted that their representative on the Council would serve them well, and support their Firstborn as the first Companions had done to Axia.

And now she was dead. Murdered, along with her Companions. It was unthinkable. Unimaginable. And yet....

If, perhaps, it *could* have been imagined, could even have been conceived of, then perhaps it could have been prevented. There had never before been one who dared to say the Goddess was wrong, and who then somehow managed to convince others to follow him and take up arms against the Firstborn. The very idea was absurd! And so there were no guards in the Palace, no precautions against attack. When Mannon and his men struck in the dark hours before dawn, there was no warning. By the time the sun rose, where once the halls of the Palace that overlooked the sea had been filled with light, the scent of flowers, and the sounds of laughter, now they were filled with smoke, the stench of blood, and the moans of the dying.

And the soft, repetitive swearing of a young woman leading a small group of survivors. There were four of them: first came the woman. She went before the others, and was armed with a pair of traditional Water Tribe hook swords. Behind her were three young men — one of them unconscious, covered in blood, and being carried by the other two.

"There. That door isn't broken. Check there." She gestured toward a door. One of the young men surrendered his burden to the other and darted forward. He peered inside the room, then nodded.

"It's empty. And the lock is intact. Mem, bring him in here." He got out of the way as the other man carried their wounded friend inside, then closed and barred the door. He glanced at the woman, who nodded.

"Do what you can, Jehan," she said softly. "I'll guard."

"You're the only one armed," Jehan replied, just as softly. "I'm not sure what I can do, Aleia."

"Do something," she said, her voice cracking slightly. He nodded and turned away, moving to kneel next to the other men.

"Jehan, tell me you can do something?" The one Jehan had called Mem whispered, his eyes never leaving the unnatural pallor of their wounded friend's face.

"Let me see." Jehan knelt next to the wounded man. He rested one hand on his chest, the other on his forehead, and closed his eyes, tried to push back the sick feeling of terror that had been near constant since the screams had woken him from a sound sleep. He had to focus. Milon needed him.

And they needed Milon. With Tirine dead, he was the next Firstborn. They needed him to put everything right.

ALEIA LISTENED AT THE door, trying to force herself to relax. She could hear nothing outside the door, but she knew that didn't mean anything. She'd heard nothing before the screams started. She closed her eyes, feeling her stomach churn. The swords she held had been her mother's, and her grandmother's. The stories in her family said the swords had been made for their distant ancestor, Abin, the first Companion from the Water tribe. As far as Aleia knew, the swords had only ever been used for dancing. They'd never been used against another person. Not until today.

She swallowed and looked over her shoulder. Jehan was in profile to her, his head bowed as he attempted to save Milon's life. Memfis was across from him, but she knew the big man wasn't seeing anything but Milon.

Milon. What weird currents had brought the Heir to the Firstborn to her mother's canoe? What had made him choose *her* to wear the Water gem, out of all of her sisters, all of her cousins? She'd never thought to leave the sea, never thought that she'd ever live on land. Never thought she'd come to love anyone as much as she loved these men. To lose Milon—

No. No, they were not going to lose Milon. Jehan was an excellent healer — all of his teachers said so. He hadn't finished his training, but it was only another year. He'd put Milon to rights, and then...

And then what? She tensed as she heard shouting from the corridor, but the voices faded away after a moment, and she let out a shaky breath. What were they supposed to do now? She closed her eyes for a moment, trying to think. To plan, the way she'd been taught.

First things first! They needed to get out of the Palace. They needed to get to safety. Where would be safe?

Someplace inaccessible to Mannon and his land-based troops. Which meant not the Earth tribe lands, nor the Fire tribe. They'd probably be safe with the Air tribe, but she doubted that they'd be able to get any further than the Solstice Fair village before they were taken.

That meant she needed to take them home with her, back to the sea. If they went out to the deep waters, Mannon would never find them. They could plan further once they were safe. She nodded slowly, and looked back at the men. Memfis had taken Milon's hand, and it had to be the angle, or the shadows.

Memfis couldn't be crying.

"I don't know what else I can do," Jehan said, his voice just barely audible to Aleia. "Every time I fix something, two other things go wrong. At least two things. He needs a real healer, not a half-trained one!"

"You're all we have, Jehan," Memfis insisted.

"And I'm making it worse!" Jehan's voice was filled with despair, and at the sound, Milon groaned. From where she stood, Aleia saw Jehan's olive skin go ashen. But his voice was steady when he leaned over Milon. "Milon, easy. Don't try to move."

To Aleia's shock, she heard a weak chuckle. "Not..." Milon wheezed. "Hurts... hurts too much. Block it? Please?"

Jehan licked his lips. Then he nodded. A moment later, Milon sighed. "Thank you. Mem?"

"I'm here," Memfis said. He reached out and brushed back Milon's dark hair. Milon smiled slightly. He blinked, looked up, and frowned.

"Oh. Here," he murmured. "Mem, we're here."

"We're where?" Memfis asked. Then he moaned softly. "No. No, we are not here. We're not. You're not leaving me, Milon."

Milon coughed. "Saw it. Saw it in the smoke. You know."

"No!"

"Don't shout!" Aleia hissed. "They'll hear you!"

"Aleia?" Milon raised his voice slightly. "C'mere, Guppy."

Aleia left the door and joined the others, kneeling down and laying her swords aside so that she could lean over to kiss Milon's forehead. "Don't call me Guppy," she whispered. She sat up and looked at Memfis. "What did he see?" Memfis and Milon had known each other the longest — they'd been boys together in the Fire tribe city of Forge, training to be prophetic Smoke Dancers. Milon's visions had never been wrong. "What is he talking about?"

Memfis swallowed and blinked, his pale amber eyes filling again with tears. "His death. It's one of the first things we see when we start to dance in the smoke. We see our end."

Jehan looked up. "You never told me that!"

"You may be part Fire—"

"Maybe," Jehan muttered. Memfis shook his head.

"But you're not a Smoke Dancer," he finished. "You didn't need to know."

"Mem, promise me," Milon said, his voice quiet. "Get them out. Promise me."

"Milon—"

"Guppy is pregnant. You need to see them safe," Milon continued. He frowned. "Liara... never see her again. Never see the baby. Babies."

"How did you know?" Jehan demanded. "I only just confirmed it this morning. Yesterday." He looked at Aleia. "I don't even know when I am anymore."

"Jehan, focus," Memfis murmured. "Don't panic."

"I'm not panicking!" Jehan snapped. Then he swallowed and let out a soft huff. "Okay. A little bit."

Aleia looked down, and realized that Milon's eyes were closed. "Is he—"

"No," Jehan answered. "Milon, stay with us. We'll get out of this."

"Mem." Milon's voice was softer. "Get them out. You know how."

Memfis nodded. "I know. But I can't leave you!"

Milon smiled slightly. "That's an order," he said. "From your Firstborn. Go."

Memfis looked at if he'd been slapped. "Milon—"

"Go, Mem. They're coming." Milon swallowed. "Send word to Liara. Tell her to be safe. That I love her." He smiled. "Love you all."

Aleia leaned down and kissed Milon gently. Then she picked up her swords and moved away, going back to the door so that the others could say their goodbyes. She heard a step behind her, then Jehan came to stand on her left.

"Did you tell him?" he asked. Aleia looked up at him and shook her head.

"You know he always knew more than he should have," she answered. She shifted both swords to her right hand so that she could take Jehan's hand. "Jehan—"

"Don't ask me how I am," he said quickly. "I couldn't even tell you."

Aleia nodded, squeezing his fingers. Behind her, she heard Memfis whispering something, but couldn't make out the words. She heard Milon's voice whispering something in response, then Memfis raised his voice. "Jehan, he wants the block removed."

"I don't have to," Jehan said as he turned back. "I can leave it." He went back to kneel once more next to Milon. Aleia followed him, resting her hand on his shoulder as Jehan looked down at his hands, then took one of Milon's hands in his. "I can leave the block, and I can put you to sleep. You... you won't wake."

"Do that," Memfis said, his voice cracking. "Give him that much."

Jehan looked up at Memfis, then back at Milon. Milon nodded, closing his eyes once more. "Please."

Jehan sat very still for a moment, then reached out and rested his free hand on Milon's forehead. Milon sighed softly, and his body went limp. Jehan laid Milon's hand on his chest, then wiped his face. "Where—?" he started, and his voice cracked. He stopped, cleared his throat, then started again, "Mem, where are we going?"

Memfis didn't answer immediately. Slowly, he laid Milon's hand down. He leaned down and kissed Milon's lips gently, then paused with his forehead touching Milon's. He straightened and looked at Jehan. Then he looked up at Aleia. "Pregnant?"

Aleia swallowed. "Yes."

"Is Milon the father, or Jehan?"

"Jehan," Aleia answered. "The timing is wrong for Milon."

Memfis nodded slowly. He got to his feet and took a deep breath. "Where are we going?" he repeated. "Down the servant's way. You two ever been in the corridors?"

Jehan shook his head. "No. Have you?"

Memfis nodded. "Milon showed me. There are tunnels that lead right down to the water. It's how they bring supplies up to the palace. Milon and I, we'd go down to the docks and watch the ships come in." He got up and crossed the room to a tapestry in the corner, shifting it aside to reveal a door. "Come on. They'll start searching the rooms soon, when they realize we're not among the dead."

ALEIA COULD SMELL THE sea long before they were out of the tunnels – the smell of home. Then they were at the mouth of the tunnels, and she could see the sunlight glittering on the water. They stopped, and she stood between Jehan and Memfis, taking their hands in hers.

"You're coming back with me," she said. "The both of you. We'll be safe—"

"I'm going back to Forge," Memfis interrupted. "That's where my path runs."

"Mannon will find you," Jehan said. "He'll look for you, for all of us. Once he knows we're alive, he'll hunt for us."

Memfis snorted. "He won't find me. Remember, I know my end. It's a long time from now. And to get there, I need to go back to Forge. There are things I need to do there." He looked down at Aleia and smiled. "I'll be all right. Your road is on the waves, Guppy. Take Jehan and go back to your family."

"I can't go yet," Jehan said softly. "I need to go back to the healing center. I need to finish my training, so that... so I don't fail again. So that when I need to, I can save the people I love." He swallowed, then looked at Aleia. "Will you come with me?"

"Jehan!"

"I..." Jehan blushed. "I love you. I love you both. I loved Milon, too. I can't lose you all. Memfis knows his road. Say you'll take my road with me? It will be only until I finish my training, and then we'll go to the sea. I... I'm a lousy carpenter. I'll build a canoe with you, if you want, but it might sink."

Aleia felt her throat tighten. She slipped her hand from Jehan's, slid her arm around his back and leaned in to him, mindful of the sword case that she wore strapped to her back. "I won't let you drown, Jehan."

He slipped his arm around her. "And I won't call you Guppy."

"Let's go," Memfis murmured. "I have money. We can bribe one of the merchants to take us south, and head inland from there. I'll leave you at the healing center."

"You don't have to see us there, Mem," Aleia protested.

"I promised him I'd see you safe," Memfis replied. "I'm keeping that promise. Come on."

CHAPTER ONE

AVEN'S WORLD CONSISTED of four constants — his parents, their canoe, his water-cat, and the sea. Occasionally, there might be visits to his extended family, but they were so infrequent that they might as well never have happened at all. Truly, when his mother did insist on those rare visits, Aven couldn't wait to leave. His grandmother, his aunts, and his cousins all tended to look down their noses at him, and he'd heard the whispered epithets more than once — Mudborn, they called him, because his father wasn't Water tribe, but Earth. Their disdain made no sense to Aven, and it completely infuriated his mother. So they lived away from the rest of the tribe, sailing to meet them perhaps twice a year, mostly for trade.

Sometime soon, Aven hoped, one of the women of the Water tribe might look past his bloodline and speak to his mother about him. Then she would ask him to build a canoe with her, to be her husband and start a family of his own. It was past time, really. He was, after all, nearly twenty-five, and if you ignored his father, his bloodline was one of the oldest in the Water tribe. He could trace his descent back to the man he'd been named for: Abin, one of the husbands of Axia, the first Firstborn.

But Abin had been one of the first of the Water tribe, favored of the daughter of a goddess. His distant grandson Aven was Mudborn — beneath the waves, Aven had his mother's Waterborn gills, and silver-and-pearl scales from his hips to his dorsal fins. But he also had his father's Earthborn hazel eyes, and his father's Earthborn healing abilities. He was as much a part of the land as he was of the sea, and so had no real place in either.

Were the Earth tribe lands anything at all like the little shelter island where their canoe currently rested, waiting for him to return with the long seaweed ropes they needed for repairs? Were the storms there like the ones on the water? The one that had driven them to the beach had lasted three days — the worst storm he could remember. Aven considered what a storm inland might be like, and finally decided that he really had no idea. Their island took ten minutes to walk across, from the rocky beach to the cliffs overlooking the sea. Twice that to walk the length of it, and an hour to walk all the way around the perimeter. Surely storms inland must be different? How? He shrugged, adjusting the coils of long seaweed he had already cut where they crossed his chest. Enough to repair the deck and the shelter? He thought so. And, he thought as he looked toward the light dappling the surface above him, he'd been down here a long time. His father would be worrying. He flipped his tail, and shot like an arrow toward the surface, through ever-brightening waters until he breached the surface, arcing through the air, and diving back down into the water. He surfaced again, and swam toward the rocks that jutted out into the deep water.

There was a place where the rocks had worn into natural handholds, and he grabbed onto them, pulling himself out of the water, and sprawling on the warm, water-worn rocks. He felt his gills closing, the first sign of his change back. For a moment, his chest felt tight, until his body remembered that he could breathe air as well as water. He took a long, deep breath and let it out, slipped the coil of seaweed over his head, then pillowed his head on it as he lay back and looked up at the clouds. He closed his eyes and sighed, listening to the wind and the water. And footsteps, coming closer.

"So. Deep thinking in deep waters?"

Aven opened his eyes to see his father, upside down from his angle. He smiled and nodded, but couldn't answer. Speaking would take him another minute or two. His father smiled in response and came over to sit down on the rocks next to Aven. He looked at home in the traditional Water tribe kilt and vest, but there was grizzled hair on his chest where no Waterborn male would have hair, and his throat was bare of gill slits. The pendant he never removed rested in the hollow of his throat — a brown and gold stone carved into an elaborate design. Aven's mother had a similar one, carved from some kind of blue stone, but Aven had never seen her wear it.

"Think you have enough?"

Aven shrugged one shoulder, then tried to talk, croaking out, "Maybe."

His father grinned. "Give it another minute. Where's Melody?"

Aven nodded toward the water, then whistled, high and shrill. The water in front of the rocks rippled as a long, dark-gray, diamond-shaped head popped out of the water. The water-cat trilled in response, then disappeared underwater again.

"She's found a friend," Aven said, his voice closer to normal. "She'll be back."

"A friend?" his father repeated. "Or a meal?"

Aven laughed. "Sometimes it's hard to tell with her. Is Ama back?"

His father nodded. "She brought back a string of moon-fish. She's cooking them up, and we'll work on the canoe after we eat. Did you hunt while you were below?"

Aven shook his head, propping himself up on his elbows and looked down at himself. His dorsal fins had retracted, and his scales were smaller. He'd have legs again soon. "No," he answered. "Fa, tell me about storms when you live on land?"

His father coughed. "Is *that* what you were thinking about?"

"Not all of it," Aven admitted. "What would the storm have been like there? Would it have lasted for days?"

"Probably not, no," his father answered slowly. "Going over land slows a storm, weakens it. The more land, the more it breaks the storm down. Now, that's the way it was. I'm not sure how it is now. The storms have been getting worse, and I've not been in Earth tribe lands since you were born." He reached out and poked Aven in the shoulder. "That's not really what you were thinking about for all that time, was it?"

"It's where I ended up," Aven said. He looked up at the clouds. "I was wondering about the Earth tribe. About the rest of me, I guess."

"You're more Water than anything else. A little Earth. Possibly a little Fire."

Aven blinked. "Fire?"

"My mother was a Healer. Same as me, same as you. And Healers in the Earth tribe sometimes do their healing horizontally. My mother thought my father might have been Fireborn, but she might have been wrong."

Aven glanced at his father, saw the scowl cross his face. "That bothers you?"

"If it's true, then..." His father stopped. "It makes no difference. Not to me. Nor to your mother." He paused, then softly murmured, "Oh. I see. Your grandmother was at you again when we were there last?"

"Aunt Jisa, actually." Aven sat up, resting his hands on his thighs as he flexed his feet, rotating his ankles. The change was finished, and he turned to face his father, folding his legs and resting his elbows on his knees. "And the cousins. Fa, I'm never going to be a part of them."

"Because they're closed-minded idiots."

Aven looked up and smiled. "Ama!"

His mother smiled as she moved to stand behind his father, resting her hand on his shoulder. "I was wondering where you both were. Supper is ready."

"I only just came back up, Ama." Aven answered. "I had to change."

She nodded. Then she frowned, looking out to sea. "Jehan? Stand up."

Jehan and Aven both scrambled to their feet. "What?" Jehan asked. "Aleia, what?"

In answer, Aleia pointed. Aven turned and looked, and saw... "Is that... Ama, is that a ship?" he asked slowly. Not a canoe. A *ship*.

"Yes," Jehan answered, his voice cold. "And it shouldn't be there." He tugged on Aven's arm. "Come on. Don't forget the ropes. We have work to do. And I want my glass."

"I thought you said that ships like that didn't sail this far out to sea," Aven asked, following his father as they hurried along the rocks and back toward the beach. "That they couldn't navigate like we do."

"They can't," Aleia called from behind him. She hurried to catch up with him. "Trading ships like that aren't built for deep water. They never leave sight of land. Your father is right. It shouldn't be here."

Jehan was ahead of them, already rummaging through one of the storage compartments built into the decking of their canoe. He pulled out a box, and took out a viewing glass. He frowned down at it, then looked at them. "Start the repairs. I'll see what I can see, and we can decide which way we're sailing."

Aven didn't say anything as his father ran back the way they'd come. Instead he tossed the coils of seaweed onto the deck and started to work. There were places where the storm had weakened the cording that connected the decking, the forward boom, and the hull floats; it all needed to be replaced before the canoe would be safe to launch. Aven cut the old cording free and started to work.

"Ama?" he said, not looking up from his task. "Why would we be sailing away from a ship?"

"Because they're not safe, Ven," she answered. The same old answer. Why didn't they visit the inland harbors for trade the way the rest of the Water tribe did? Why did they stay so far out to sea? Not just to avoid the family. No, it was because it wasn't safe to do otherwise.

"Why isn't it safe?" Aven cinched the cord he was working on and sat back on his heels. "You've never explained it. And I've never asked. But it's something I need to know, isn't it?"

His mother sighed. "It's a conversation your father and I have been putting off for far too long, I think. Can you wait another day? The way you ask questions, we'll need time."

"I can wait," Aven agreed. "Do I need to wait until it's safe?"

She smiled at him, but there was sadness in her eyes. "Ven, if they're sailing this far out, we're not going to be safe. And it's time you knew why." She finished with the cord she was working on. "What do you know about the fall of the Firstborn?"

Aven frowned. "Not much. I know it happened before I was born. I know that the man who rules now isn't the Firstborn. But when we were with the family, and the cousins were having their lessons, the elders would always stop talking when I was close enough to hear."

Aleia arched a brow. "You never said."

Aven shrugged. "It didn't seem to be worth the fight, Ama. So what am I missing?"

Aleia looked thoughtful. She took a deep breath, then sat up and looked past Aven. "Jehan?"

Aven turned to see his father coming toward them, a frown on his face. "It's dead in the water," he said. "The mast is gone, and it's listing badly. They must have been caught in the storm."

"Any survivors?" Aleia asked.

"Not that I could see, but that doesn't mean anything." Jehan collapsed the viewing glass and put it back into the case. "I'm not sure it's not a trick."

"Ama and I can go take a closer look," Aven suggested.

Jehan scowled. "No. I don't want either of you near that ship. Not when you're changed."

"They won't see us, love," Aleia said. Jehan just shook his head.

"You're a fierce fighter on land, Guppy. You've saved my life more than once. And I know you've fought underwater. But it's that few minutes between that will get you killed, and you're not taking that risk. Not you, and not our boy."

Aven blinked, shocked. His mother had fought, had saved his father's life? He turned to look at his mother, and saw the look on her face — she'd gone pale.

"You said you wouldn't call me that," she said softly.

"I wanted to be sure you were listening to me," Jehan answered. "Because you're as stubborn as the sea is deep, and I won't lose you, too."

"Too?" Aven repeated.

"That's part of what we need to explain to you, Ven," Aleia said. "But not now. Let's finish the canoe, and go take a look at this ship."

BY THE TIME THEY'D finished repairing their canoe, the tide was going out and the sun was starting to sink toward the horizon.

"We won't have much time," Aleia murmured.

"It shouldn't take too long, and if there is someone on that ship, we'll be able to get away in the dark," Jehan answered. "If we wait until morning, it'll be gone. Either taken by the current, or sunken."

"I prefer sunken." Aleia stepped up onto the deck and took hold of the sail lines. "If it sinks, we can examine it underwater without being disturbed. We're ready. I've wet down the sand, so we need to get going."

Aven didn't say anything. He stood by the hull float and stared out to sea. He could see Melody playing in the waves, and wished that he could go join her. He heard a step behind him, and his father's hand closed on his shoulder.

"Come help me launch," Jehan said. "And call Melody in. We'll want her with us."

"Why?" Aven said, following his father around to the rear of the canoe. He took his place behind the port float, ready to push.

"Because she'll rip the throat out of anyone who looks cross-eyed at you," Jehan answered calmly.

"What?"

"Just push, Ven."

Together, they pushed the canoe out into the water, splashing up and onto the deck as the wind caught the sail. Jehan took the steering paddle and laid it on the deck next to his knees. They didn't need it yet — under Aleia's steady guidance, the canoe was quickly headed away from the island. Aven leaned over the side of the decking and slapped the water twice, then twice again. He heard a distant squeal and nodded.

"Melody will catch up," he called.

"Good," his mother called back. "Eat something. And serve your father."

Aven nodded and found the pot in one of the storage compartments, nestled in a bed of cloth scraps so that it stayed warm. He ladled out a bowl of the fragrant fish and seaweed mix, brought it to his father, then served himself.

"So tell me what else you were thinking about for so long," Jehan said. Aven swallowed, looked down at his bowl.

"Now?" he asked.

"When else?" Jehan took another bite, gesturing with his free hand.

Aven frowned slightly, then nodded. "Wondering, really. I'm never going to fit in with the cousins. Or the rest of the Water tribe, I don't think—"

"You've only met the part of the tribe you're related to," Aleia called.

"Still. I'm twenty-five. I'm starting to wonder if there's ever going to be a girl who'll ask me to build a canoe with her." Aven took another bite of his stew, then looked up to see his father frowning. "Fa?"

"You've been thinking about this for a while?" Jehan asked.

"No. Only since we left the family the last time. Marsin is nineteen, and Iara of Tarscana's canoe has offered for him. Trevi is twenty-two, and he has two daughters already. When will it be me?"

Jehan nodded. He looked thoughtful, then turned. "Remember what we were talking about?"

"And the answer is still no," Aleia answered, her voice crisp.

"If I'm with you, there's no hiding—"

"There's no hiding it anyway, Jehan!" Aleia interrupted. "He has your eyes, and he's a healer."

"And if we went south, it wouldn't matter!"

"Going south won't change who he is. Who we are. Going south opens us up to more risk. It's too close—"

Aven slammed his empty bowl down with a hard thump. "Could you not talk about me like I'm not here?" he demanded. "What are you talking about? What's in the south?"

Jehan sighed. "There are places on the coast, south of here. Earth tribe lands, but there are fishing harbors mostly inhabited by Waterborn. There's a lot of intermarriage." He finished his own food and set his bowl aside. "You wouldn't stand out there—"

"But it wouldn't be safe," Aven finished, and his voice sounded harsh even to his own ears. Certainly to his father's, who looked shocked at Aven's tone. "You're both terrified of something, and you're not telling me what or why! Is it me you're afraid for, and that's why you're not saying anything?" An odd thought occurred to him, and he frowned. "Or is it me you're afraid of?"

"We're not afraid of you, Ven," Jehan said. "For you, yes. And because of us." He gestured to himself, to Aleia. "Because of who we are. Who we were." He took a deep breath absently playing with his pendant. "Aleia? Now?"

"Once we're done with the ship," Aleia answered. "I told Ven that we'd explain everything, but it will take time to answer his questions and dealing with this ship needs to come first."

Aven swallowed, trying to make sense of what he was feeling. Too many conflicting emotions, and none that he could really put a name to. "I'm finished eating," he called, and got to his feet. "I'll take the sails. Come and eat, Ama."

A few minutes later, Aven was holding the lines controlling the sails, easing them on their way across the waves. He had to concentrate on what he was doing, which meant that he didn't have to think about what he was feeling. He studied their destination instead. The ship was growing closer, and he could clearly see the splintered mast, the tattered sail.

"If it is a dead ship, what do we do?" he called over his shoulder.

"We see if there's anything that we can use. Then we burn the corpse," his father answered. "I don't want the wreck drifting back to shore." He came up next to Aven. "You know, you broke your bowl."

Aven blinked, but he didn't turn from his task. "I did?"

"Cracked it clean across. It fell apart when your mother picked it up." Jehan sighed and put his hand on Aven's shoulder. "We should never have kept this from you, Ven. We thought it was for the best, but we were wrong. I'm sorry."

Aven nodded. "You still haven't told me anything."

"Once we're done."

MOORING THE CANOE TO the listing ship proved to be a challenge, one solved by Aleia taking the lines and bringing the canoe alongside, holding it there until Jehan and Aven could throw hooked cables over the railings.

"Aleia, stay on the steering paddle," Jehan said. "You're better than I am with it."

"Aven can—"

"No, I'm taking him with me," Jehan said. "Aleia, he needs to know. And he's involved, just because he's breathing. Time for us to own that."

Aleia scowled. Then she nodded once and turned to face Aven. "Take your club."

"What?" Aven gasped. "I..."

"You might need it. Jehan—"

"I'll take mine. And we've both got our knives." Jehan scowled at the ship. "She's running low. Either a heavy cargo, or she's taken on water. Either way, it'll be easier for us to board. Ven, get the weapons."

Aven went to the long compartment and took out the two heavy clubs, each of them edged with double rows of shark's teeth. He handed one to his father, looked down at the other one. "Fa, are you sure you want me with you?" he asked. "I've never actually used this outside of dancing and practice with Ama."

Jehan moved to stand in front of him, resting one hand on Aven's shoulder. "Aven, if you need to use that, it's because I've already gone down. And if I go down, then you are going to use that club to get yourself off the ship and into deep water. Aleia, be ready to cut those lines and get out."

"I'm not leaving you, Jehan."

Jehan growled softly. He turned and looked at Aleia. "Love, if you have to cut those lines, I'm already gone." He looked back at the ship. "But I don't think it will come to that."

Jehan went first, balancing on the hull float closest to the ship until he could get his hands on the railing and hoist himself up onto the deck. He crouched there for a moment, then shook his head. "There's no one here. Come on, Ven. Toss the clubs up and come over."

Aven did as he was bid, tossing one club to his father, then the other. He followed Jehan's example, pulling himself up onto the deck of what was easily the largest vessel he'd ever been aboard. And once on board, it was clear that the ship had been abandoned — casks were smashed open and the deck was littered with debris. He walked away from his father, looking around curiously as he picked his way through the trash.

"They don't sail away from shore?" he called.

"They need to be able to see the shore so they know where they are. They must have been caught in the storm and blown out to sea," Jehan answered. Aven turned to see his father kneeling, going through a cask. "We'll salvage what we can, but it looks like a lot of the supplies were ruined." He stood up and looked around. "There's a hold—"

"A what?"

"Storage underneath the deck. Like our compartments, but under the entire deck," Jehan said, pointing down. "There should be hatches, raised up from the deck. Probably covered in trash. You start over there."

Aven walked to the stern of the ship and started forward, studying the decking. He spotted the raised hatch just as he heard his father call, "Found one!"

"So did I!" Aven called back, moving smashed timber and revealing crossing leather straps that had been nailed into the decking, sealing the hatch closed. "Mine is strapped shut."

"What?" Jehan came trotting across the deck. "That's not right."

Aven frowned. "Why not?"

"There's no need," Jehan said. He frowned. Then he shook his head. "Well, do we open this one first, or the other one?"

Aven looked down at the straps. There was a tug, an insistence that there was something here, something he needed to see. "They don't usually seal the hatches?" he asked slowly.

"No."

"Then we need to look here first," Aven suggested. "See what they're trying to keep safe."

Jehan nodded, drawing his knife. Aven drew his as well, and they started sawing at the heavy straps. They parted slowly, and Aven could hear his mother calling, asking what was going on. Jehan left for a moment, going back to the railing to reassure her. Aven kept cutting, and had just finished his strap when Jehan came back. Together, they cut through the other strap. Jehan grabbed the handle in the center of the hatch and lifted it. Aven peered through the hole, then cursed and jumped down into the hold, ignoring the ladder. He heard a heavy thump overhead – the hatch hitting the deck, he assumed.

"Ven!" Jehan shouted.

"There's a girl in a cage down here!" Aven shouted back. "A girl with wings!" He dropped to his knees in the dirty water, reaching through the bars to touch the girl's throat. "And she's alive!"

CHAPTER TWO

IT TOOK SOME DOING to get the cage open — Jehan left Aven to watch over the girl while he searched for tools. He came back with a heavy sledgehammer, directing Aven to stand on the far side of the cage and hold it still. It took two strikes with the hammer to break the lock.

"I'll take her to your mother," Jehan said. "Look around. If you see anything that you think would be useful to us, take it up on deck."

Aven nodded, watching as his father gathered the girl up in his arms, carrying her carefully up the ladder and out into the air. Then he looked around. Jehan had told him that the hold was beneath the entire deck, but there was a wall separating this part from the rest. The wall was new, the wood still so raw that Aven could smell it even over the muck sloshing around his knees. Erected to separate the prisoner from the cargo, he assumed. But why? The girl had been in a cage. Why go to the extra effort of creating a cell around that cage, and then sealing the hatch?

Unless the girl hadn't been the only thing sealed in the hold? He turned, looking around. The light coming through the hatch wasn't enough to illuminate the shadows; with the hatch closed, it must have been as dark as the deep caves where no light ever shone, where the fish and crabs were blind and hunted by smell. The idea made him shudder, and he looked around again, searching through the stinking water. He wanted to be out of here, but this was important.

What else was hidden down here? What was so valuable that it had to be guarded like this?

He tripped on it, stumbling and almost stretching his length in the bilge. Backtracking, he kicked it, and pulled from the water a square chest as long as his arm, and a hand-span deep. It hadn't been underwater for long — the wood was barely damaged, the lock still bright. The chest in his hands was surprisingly light.

"Ven!" His father appeared in the open hatch. "What are you doing?"

"I found something else!" Aven called back. "I'm coming up." He tucked the chest under his arm and clambered up the ladder.

"What's that?" Jehan asked.

"I don't know," Aven answered. "But it's locked, and they had it down there with her. So that means it must be important, doesn't it?" He glanced at the railing and the canoe beyond it. "How is she?"

"She's in a healing sleep right now," Jehan answered. "She'll live, but she won't fly again for a while. The bastards clipped her wings." Jehan looked around. "Let's see what we can salvage."

Aven set the chest down next to the railing. He waved to his mother, then took a moment to study the girl lying in the deck shelter on the canoe. He'd never seen an Airborn before. He wondered what it meant that her wings had been clipped. How long it would take before she'd fly again. What seeing her in flight would be like. A trill interrupted his thoughts, and Melody surfaced next to the canoe. He whistled a greeting to her, stopped, then trilled back at her. The water cat disappeared beneath the waves, then resurfaced and jumped lightly onto the canoe. She greeted Aleia with a sniff and a head-bump, then went to the unconscious girl. Melody sniffed the girl's dirty hair, sneezed, then coiled her long, sinuous body protectively around the girl. She raised her head, clicked at Aven, then rested her muzzle on her front legs.

"Ven?" Aleia sounded shocked. "When did you teach her to do that?"

"Just now," Aven answered. "I wasn't sure it would work. I'll be back." He turned from the railing, hearing his mother sputtering behind him. The sound was enough to make him grin in spite of everything that had happened. It wasn't often that he could get that reaction from her anymore.

They searched the far side of the hold, and the chest was soon joined by a cask of salted meat, and another of something Jehan called 'hardtack.' There was a variety of metal tools, bundles of sailcloth and silk, a small chest of finely carved gemstones that Jehan pronounced Earth tribe work, and a large number of casks containing something that had made Jehan's eyes widen, and that he forbade Aven to go near. It was dangerous, he said, and he'd explain more later.

Once Jehan finally declared them finished, Aven jumped down to the canoe, taking things as Jehan passed them down, securing the smaller items in storage compartments, and tying the larger bundles down for safety.

"Now what?" he asked as he took the last item — the chest. He held it close as he looked up at Jehan.

"Now? We deal with the ship," Jehan answered. "Hide that." He pointed at the chest, then turned and disappeared. Aven looked down at the box in his arms, then took it to a compartment near where his mother stood. He put the chest inside, then went to stand next to her.

"When we're clear," he said quietly. "I want to know why."

She looked up at him and nodded. "When we're clear, I'll tell you."

All at once, they heard Jehan shouting, "Cut the lines! Cut the lines!" Aven froze, staring at the ship. His mother didn't; she shoved the sail lines into Aven's hands, drew her knife, and dove toward the closest line. As it parted, Jehan appeared, running toward the railing. He vaulted over it, landing hard on the deck and rolling to break his fall before he broke his bones. He came up at once, grabbing the steering paddle and plunging it into the water, pushing them away from the ship as Aleia cut the second line.

"Get us away, Ven!" Jehan ordered.

Aven looked over at the dangling ropes. "We'll lose the hooks!"

"Aven, now!"

Aven had never heard that tone from his father before, and did as he was bid, tugging on the lines and pulling the sail into position to catch the winds. The canoe shot away from the ship, a heartbeat before the entire vessel burst into flames that rocketed toward the night skies.

"Mother of us all!" Aleia gasped. "Jehan, what did you do?"

Jehan drew the paddle back onto the canoe and leaned on it, looking back at the burning ship. "They were carrying inferno oil. Casks and casks of it. I saw them. I warned Aven to stay away from them. I was going to use that to burn the ship. I took some and poured some on the deck. But when I lit it, a spark fell into the hold and caught. One of the casks must have leaked. I saw the bilge start to burn, and ran."

"What's inferno oil?" Aven asked. "And where are we going?"

"Back to the island," Aleia said. "We'll spend the night there. And you and your father are both scrubbing yourselves and this deck with sand and sweet water before we leave again. I don't want to have to replace the decking, but we will if we have to."

Aven gaped at his mother. "What *is* this stuff?"

"It sticks to whatever it touches, and it burns without stopping until it's exhausted. If you pour water onto it, it'll spread and keep burning," Aleia answered.

"The Fire tribe invented it, and has regretted it ever since," Jehan added. "They've tried to bury the knowledge, but you can't sweep back the tide."

"Then our Airborn girl is going to have to scrub, too," Aven said. "She was lying in the stuff. Did she drink it, do you think? Will it poison her?"

"That's a good question. Jehan, how is she?" Aleia asked.

"She'll be fine," Jehan answered. "Inferno oil... it won't kill you. I don't know what's in the stuff, but it won't kill you." He crossed to kneel next to her, absently scratching Melody's head as he held one hand open over the girl's chest. "Where's that chest, Ven?"

Aven tapped his foot on the deck. "Here. Are we going to open it?"

"Not yet," Jehan answered. He sat down, rested his elbows on his knees, and steepled his fingers. "I want to talk to her first. Once she wakes."

"Where were they taking her?" Aven asked. "And why? Did you see anything that might have said?"

"There should have been a log book. Trading records. I looked, but I didn't see them." Jehan frowned. "There also should have been skiffs. Now, they could have broken off in the storm—"

"Or the crew might have escaped," Aleia finished.

"We didn't see any bodies," Aven said softly.

Jehan scowled. Then he shrugged. "Makes no difference. If they got away on the skiffs, they wouldn't have survived the storm. And even if they did, they won't survive out here. Not for long."

"Not unless they find help," Aleia murmured. "You know there are some canoes that support him."

Aven turned his attention back to the sails, judging angles and the speed of the wind, studying the stars on the horizon, then tacking carefully so that they were heading back toward the island. He felt his mother's hand on his back.

"Explanations?" she asked.

He smiled and glanced at her. "It's waited this long. It can wait until we come to land and get scrubbed."

She smiled and hugged him, then took the lines from him. "Go help your father. It'll be good practice. You've never worked on an Airborn before."

Aven nodded and went to sit next to his father. Jehan acknowledged his presence with a nod, then gestured. His meaning was clear — *examine your patient, Healer.* So Aven held his hand out over the girl's chest, the tips of his fingers just touching her collarbone. He closed his eyes and concentrated, letting the healing power flow from his hand. Surface first — bruises and abrasions. No head wounds. Nothing serious. Go deeper, examine the bones...

"Fa, her bones are wrong!" Aven gasped.

"Her bones are hollow," Jehan answered, sounding amused. "Like a bird. So she can fly. That's normal for Airborn." He chuckled. "I had the same reaction the first time I met one."

Aven nodded, refocusing and going deeper. No damage to organs, no corruption in her blood. But there was something there, something sour.

"Fa, was she drugged?" he asked.

"I think so," Jehan said. "I don't recognize what it might be, but she hasn't been injured. There's no reason for her to be unconscious like this, unless she was drugged."

"It's not that inferno oil, is it?"

"No. It doesn't have those properties. Anything else?"

Aven did one final sweep, then focused on her wings. How the muscles and bones joined her shoulders, and how the breadth of her shoulders supported their weight. "Can she really fly, Fa?"

"They're the most beautiful of the Mother's children in the air," Jehan answered. "Just as the Waterborn are in the sea."

Aven smiled. "You're biased, Fa."

"I'm not." Jehan stretched and groaned. "How much longer, love?"

"It'll be well after dark by the time we come to shore."

"Once we're on land, we'll light a fire. After we scrub." Jehan ran a hand over his face. "Definitely after. Then, we'll talk. And maybe she'll wake by the time we get there."

"Can we flush the drug out of her blood?" Aven asked. "The way we do with poisons?"

Jehan nodded slowly. "I know I've taught you how, but you're missing one thing. One big thing. Don't make this mistake when it counts, Ven."

"What am I– oh." Aven looked around. "Sweet water."

"We don't have enough sweet water to replace what we flush out of her blood," Jehan confirmed. "So we'll just let her sleep." He reached over and poked Aven in the shoulder. "You should sleep, too. We'll be busy."

"I'm not tired." Aven turned and looked back at the burning ship. "Will they be able to see that from shore?"

"We're too far," Aleia answered. "Other canoes might see it."

Aven nodded, watching the flames reach to touch the stars. "When the ship sinks, will it keep burning all the way to the bottom?" he asked, and yawned. He heard his father chuckle.

"Not tired, hm?"

"Maybe a little."

"Sleep, Ven." Jehan's hand closed on his shoulder. "I'll wake you when we get to land."

Aven smiled. He got up and walked around to Melody's far side, curling up against her and closing his eyes.

Jehan waited until Aven's breathing had grown deep and regular before getting to his feet and going to stand next to Aleia.

"It's over, isn't it?" he murmured softly. "The life we've made. It's over. We're going back."

"We don't know, Jehan," Aleia answered. She held one arm out, angled so that her thumb seemed to touch the horizon. Jehan couldn't see the tattoos on the back of her hand, but he knew they were there. They were his constants, guiding him home.

"She looks like him," Jehan said.

"Who him?"

"Milon. She's got his cheekbones."

Aleia looked up. "You think that she is Liara's?"

Jehan nodded. Then he sighed. "Who else would Mannon want so badly?"

Aleia shook her head. "You can't be sure. It's been twenty-five years."

"And I remember his face as well as I remember yours, Aleia." He nodded toward the sleeping girl. "That's Milon's daughter. And things have just gotten very complicated."

"How so?"

"Because I think I know what might be in that chest."

CHAPTER THREE

AVEN WOKE UP AS THE canoe slid to a stop on the beach. He blinked, shook his head, then rolled off the side of the canoe, standing in water up to his knees. Without being told, he grabbed onto the forward boom and pushed. His father was on the other side of the canoe, doing the same, and they pushed the canoe further up onto the sands and out of reach of the tides.

"Go and scrub, the pair of you," Aleia called. "I'll start a fire."

Aven straightened and looked over at the girl. "How is she?"

"She's starting to come out of it, I think. We need to hurry. I want to be here when she wakes," Jehan answered. He beckoned Aven over, and they headed inland. There were two reasons that they used this island as a shelter — there was a deep cave where they could shelter in very bad storms and where they could store supplies. And, more importantly for Jehan, there was a spring of sweet water, one that supplied Jehan with ample drinking water, and that spilled into a natural bathing pool.

Aven stripped his kilt and vest off at the water's edge, then dove in, swimming down to the bottom of the pool. It was dark underwater, cool in the depths, and Aven rose to the surface and flipped onto his back to float and look up at the stars. Sweet water didn't trigger the change the way that salt water did, so he could bathe without having to wait to resume his human form. But he couldn't breathe underwater without the change, and the feeling of being submerged and yet not being able to breathe was very odd and very uncomfortable.

"Remember to scrub."

Aven turned to look at Jehan, who was standing near the edge of the pool, rubbing his skin with sand.

"All over?" Aven asked. "Or just where the water touched."

"All over. We can't be careless."

Aven nodded and swam to join his father, scooping up handfuls of fine sand from the bottom of the pool and scrubbing his skin until it tingled. "What about my clothes?" he asked. "Can they be cleaned? I like this vest."

"I'm afraid not," Jehan answered. "Once the oil has sunk into the fibers, it won't come out. Everything we're wearing needs to be burned."

"We'll need clothes for her, then." Aven frowned. "How about feathers?"

In the dim light of the moon, Aven saw his father's eyes widen. "I have no idea. That's a terrifying thought, though. Let's go back. She'll be waking up soon."

Aven fell in next to his father, carrying his clothes in a bundle in one hand. Jehan paused, looked around as if he was expecting someone to appear, then turned to Aven. "Ven, don't tell her we have the chest."

"What?"

"Don't tell her that we have the chest. Not yet. I'm not sure who she is, or what's going on, but I have a theory." Jehan ran one hand through his hair. "Your mother thinks I'm insane. Seeing ghosts. Maybe I am. But for now, humor your father and don't mention the chest."

"If that's what you want, Fa," Aven agreed, fighting down an unfamiliar wave of resentment. He was getting wholly tired of being so confused.

His father sighed and reached out to cup Aven's cheek. "That's a look that I never thought I'd see on your face, Ven."

"I... I have a look?" Aven stammered. "What look?"

"Angry. Resentful," Jehan answered. "I'm sorry, Ven. Truly. We probably should have told you, but your mother thought you too young until only just recently. Then we just... never..." He paused. "Aven, I need you to understand—"

"That's kind of difficult, when you won't tell me anything!" Aven snapped, then felt his face grow warm. "Fa, I'm sorry."

"Don't be. I think we deserve that, your mother and I. Let me tell you this. The day I found out that your mother was pregnant? That was one of the happiest days of my life. And two days later, everything changed. My world was ripped apart, and I lost someone I loved as much as I love your mother. I won't go through that again. I will do anything I have to in order to keep from losing her, and you. And if that includes not telling you everything, then that is what I will do. So yes, I'm sorry. But not much."

Aven stared at his father. "Fa, what... *who*?"

"Long story, Ven. Let's go check on our Airborn girl, then we'll see how much I can tell you before I fall asleep."

They walked in silence back to the canoe. Aleia had lit a fire, and Aven could smell something cooking. He surrendered his bundle of clothes to his father, and went to the canoe, taking a fresh kilt out of a compartment. As he wrapped it around his waist, he heard a soft *pop* from behind him.

"What was that?" he called, turning and seeing that the fire was burning higher than before.

"Inferno oil," Jehan called back. "On our clothes. We're going to need to be careful with the decking."

"We're going to redo the decking," his mother corrected. "Every bit of it. We'll start felling trees tomorrow."

Melody trilled, and when Aven turned to look at her, he realized why. The girl's eyes were open, and she was regarding him with an oddly calm gaze.

"Fa," he called. "We have a guest." He went over to the girl and crouched next to her. He smiled gently and asked, "Are you going to stay awake?"

She blinked, studied him for a moment, then looked thoughtful. "I don't know you. But I should." She looked around. "Or am I dreaming?"

"You're not dreaming," Aven answered. "You're awake. And you're safe."

"I don't think that the last one will ever be true," she murmured. She sat up, then groaned, "Oh, my head!"

"Do you know what they gave you?" Jehan asked, wrapping a kilt around his waist. "Did they tell you?"

She looked up, and her eyes widened. "I know you. You're Jehan." She smiled broadly. "I've seen you before."

Jehan looked startled. "That's not possible."

"In dreams," the girl added. "Visions. I described you, and my mother told me your name. I knew I would see you someday."

Jehan sat down and closed his eyes. "I knew it," he murmured. "I knew it had to be... what's your name?"

"Aria," she answered. She looked around. "Aleia. Is she here?"

"I am." Aleia said as she came closer. To Aven's surprise, she was carrying her knife in one hand, and a torch in the other. "Aria, you said?"

"Aria, daughter of Liara and Milon," Aria answered. She looked around. "Where are we?"

"First, answer my question," Jehan said. "Did they tell you what they gave you?"

Aria frowned. "I... I think they said it was Euphoria?"

Jehan sighed. "That explains it. You're not going to be awake long, Aria. Let's get some food into you, and some sweet water. Then you need to scrub. You were locked in with—"

"Inferno oil. I know," Aria finished. "They told me that the ship was bound for Forge, and they were going to burn the city to the ground."

Aleia swore softly. Jehan just looked stunned. "Forge? Burn Forge? But…"

"I don't know why," Aria said. "No one said anything where I could hear." She turned toward Aven. "I don't know you."

"You said that," Aven said. "Why would you, though?"

"Ven, let your father see to her. Come with me," Aleia said. There was a tone to her voice that put a stop to any arguments, and Aven nodded and got to his feet. He followed her back to the fire, where she tossed the torch onto the blaze.

"Do you know the name Milon?" Aleia asked.

Aven frowned, thinking. Then he shook his head. "I don't think so. Why?"

Aleia sighed and sat down, gesturing for Aven to sit with her. She stared at the fire for a long time, then spoke without looking at Aven.

"I never knew why he chose me. Out of all of my sisters, all of the cousins, what made me special?"

"You mean Fa?"

She smiled slightly. Sadly. "I mean Milon. Milon was the Heir, Aven. Heir to the Firstborn. After Firstborn Tirine took her place on Axia's Throne, Milon was the one who the Mother entrusted with the Diadem. He was the Heir, and he came on progress. He came to the Water tribe first. They always do, since Abin was the first of Axia's Companions. He came to my mother's canoe, and he chose me. Then we went ashore at the Palace and went north to the Solstice Fair village, where the Air mountains spill into the Earth tribe lands. That's where we found Liara. She was as close as a sister to me. We went further south into the Earth tribe lands and we met with them. And Milon chose this awkward, skinny, half-trained healer boy—"

"Fa."

Aleia looked at him and nodded, then laughed. "He was so clumsy, when I first met him. He hadn't yet come into his growth, and he was all hands and feet—"

"Ama, how old were you?"

"Sixteen, when I took the Water gem from Milon's hand," Aleia answered. "Your father was fifteen. We went south next, to Forge. Milon already knew who he'd be giving the Fire gem to. That was Memfis. We were his Companions. We were the ones who'd be with him when he became the Firstborn, to speak for our tribes. You understand?"

"I know the lore, yes," Aven said.

"We had five years together. Five years of learning and growing, and loving each other. I came back to the Water tribe once a year, for a season, and every time, I couldn't wait to go back on land, back to the Palace. Back to them. Milon..." she paused, and took a deep breath. "Milon had a way about him. He loved everyone, and everyone loved him. But he had a special place in his heart for Memfis, and for Liara."

"And Aria is their daughter."

Aleia nodded. "Liara was spending her season with her flock –"

"Flock?" Aven interrupted.

"Oh," Aleia murmured. "Oh, of course. The Airborn, they call their family groups flocks. Like we call ours canoes. Liara was with her flock, and wasn't in the Palace when the attack happened. Milon—" Her voice cracked. "He died that night. He made Memfis promise to get us out, and he died."

Aven stared into the fire, watching the dancing flames and the rising sparks. He heard footsteps behind them, and his father's voice, "May we join you?"

"Aria shouldn't," Aven said, turning in place to face them. "She's been lying in inferno oil for we don't know how long. It's in her hair and her clothes, and her feathers. She needs to bathe first."

"I'll take you," Aleia said. She got to her feet and dusted sand off her skirt. "You can tell me about how Liara is. We'll have to find a way to get word to her. She must be frantic."

Aria shook her head. "My mother is dead. They killed her when they took me."

"Oh, Aria!" Aleia breathed. She put her arm around the girl's waist. "Come on. You can bathe, then you can eat. We'll hear your story after. And if you fall asleep, we'll hear your story in the morning." She led Aria away from the fire, leaving Aven alone with Jehan.

"Your mother told you?" Jehan asked.

"Yes," Aven answered. "Up to the point when you got out."

Jehan nodded, touching his pendant. "I asked your mother to come with me. We went to the healing center where I was born, and I finished my training. If I'd finished it before, if I'd known then what I know now, maybe I could have saved him. Milon, I mean. Once I was finished with my training, we came here."

Aven nodded. "And it's not safe—"

"Because Mannon will kill us on sight," Jehan answered. "Because we're proof that his rule is illegitimate. He'll kill us, and he might kill you. He'll probably kill you, because he can't be sure that you're not Milon's child."

Aven gaped at Jehan. "What?"

"You're not," Jehan answered. "You're mine. We're certain of that. Milon was in Forge visiting his grandmother when Aleia came back from her season with the tribe. So he wasn't there for her welcome home. Memfis never slept with the girls. He was completely devoted to Milon. No, Ven. You're mine to your fingertips."

"And Ama's to my fins," Aven finished the old joke. Jehan grinned.

"But because you're mine, because you're Aleia's, you're automatically in danger, if ever Mannon got his hands on you. He might kill you out of hand. Or he might not. Mannon is... unpredictable."

"And Aria?" Aven asked. "How'd she stay safe?"

"What do you know about the Air tribe, and where they live?" Jehan answered.

"They live in the mountains, I know that. And that's all I really know."

"Their mountains are impossible to reach if you don't have wings," Jehan answered. "As long as Liara kept to her home aerie, no one would have been able to reach her. Memfis was supposed to try and get word to her. I assume that he did, since she didn't go back to the Palace at the end of her season. Or maybe it was just that word of the fall reached them. Doesn't much matter now. The question that I have is how did they get Aria?" He reached out and stirred the contents of the cook-pot, then frowned. "Ven, go fetch some of that hardtack we took from the ship."

"That stuff is food?" Aven asked as he got to his feet.

Jehan blinked, looking startled. "Yes, it's food. Why? What did you think it was?"

Aven grinned, thinking of the hard, coarse squares that had filled the cask. "Ballast," he called over his shoulder. Jehan's echoing laughter followed him down to the canoe.

BY THE TIME AVEN RETURNED to the fireside, Jehan had started ladling the soup into bowls. He put a piece of hardtack at the bottom of Aria's bowl, and set it aside.

"It'll soften as it heats, and it will dissolve and thicken the broth," he'd explained to Aven. "It'll be closer to what she's used to eating. Do you want to try it?"

Aven had considered it, then refused. He wasn't entirely certain that the brick-like things were food, no matter what his father said.

"Fa, you said they clipped her wings. What does that mean?"

"It means they cut the feathers she needs to fly. They'll grow back in, but it will take time." Jehan passed a bowl to Aven. "So, what are you thinking?"

"I really don't know," Aven admitted. "It's a lot to take in."

"There's more," Jehan said. "You know how the storms have been getting worse? That's part of it."

"How?"

"Mannon is not the rightful ruler. He murdered the Firstborn and her Heir. He's an affront to the Mother and to Adavar itself." He frowned. "He's the grit inside the oyster, Aven."

"It doesn't sound as if Adavar is making a pearl," Aven replied. He saw something moving in the dark, and sat up. It was Aleia, and she was alone.

"I'd forgotten that Air folk have a nudity taboo," she explained. She went to the canoe, took out some clothes, and went back into the darkness.

"Nudity taboo?" Aven asked.

"It's cold in the mountains, Ven," Jehan said. "So they cover up, all over. Took Liara almost a year to get used to Milon, Memfis and Aleia walking around bare."

Aven nodded. Then he frowned. "But, their wings? Don't they get in the way? How do they wear... well, vests? Or anything up top?"

Jehan turned, and nodded at the shadows. "You're about to find out."

Aleia approached the fire first, then stopped and held her hand out. "It's all right. You can come closer."

"But—" Aria's voice came out of the darkness.

"This is how we dress," Aleia said, her voice firm. "It's normal here. I know it's not what you're used to, but we don't have what you're used to. Your choices are wear it, or go bare."

"It's... strange," Aria said, and came into the light. She was wearing one of Aleia's wrapped skirts, and a red top that Aven recognized as being part of Aleia's formal dance costume. He understood why Aleia had chosen it — it wrapped around the chest, covering the wearer's breasts. It was, Aven thought, the only piece of clothing on this island that would accommodate Aria's wings.

"It suits you," he offered. "You look very nice. The red is a good color for you."

Aria's eyes widened, and her cheeks colored. "Thank you," she murmured, and moved to sit near the fire. Jehan handed her the bowl of soup that he'd prepared for her.

"It's not quite what you're used to, and it's probably not spiced enough. I know you probably like some heat to it."

She smiled and nodded. "I do, but I will not complain. Hunger is the best spice, no?"

Jehan laughed. "Your mother used to say that."

"She taught me, when she taught me to cook," Aria said. She sipped the hardtack-thickened broth and smiled. "It is good. Thank you."

"Once you've eaten, will you tell us your story?" Aleia asked, taking another bowl from Jehan. "What happened?"

Aria frowned slightly. "Mother told me that my father was a Smoke Dancer. That his blood in me is what give me visions. I saw you both, in one." She smiled shyly at Aven. "I did not see you."

"I'm nothing special," Aven answered, and Aria blushed again. "Go on."

"I had other visions. And one in particular came several times over the years. I saw..." She shook her head. "I will not say what I saw.

But after the last time, my mother took me from our flock and we left our aerie. We went to the Temple—"

"You went *where*?" Jehan interrupted.

"We went to the Temple at the Mother's Womb," Aria said. "We flew in under cover of darkness. No one saw us. Mother took me to the Crypt—"

"Jehan," Aleia interrupted. "Go get it."

Jehan stood without speaking and disappeared into the darkness. He came back a few minutes later carrying the chest that Aven had found in the hold.

"This holds what I think it holds, doesn't it?" he asked, his voice harsh.

Aria didn't answer. No one spoke, until finally the silence grew too much for Aven. "Fa? What's in there?"

Jehan looked at Aleia, then set the chest down. He drew his knife, and smashed the hilt against the lock until it shattered. Aven shifted around so that he could see inside when the lid flipped open.

Inside the chest was a diadem, and four ornately carved stones — one clear, one brown and gold, one shades of blue mingled with white, and one all reds and oranges. The brown and blue ones Aven knew. Had known his entire life.

Jehan sat down, his eyes never leaving the contents of the chest. "Mother of us all," he murmured. "I never thought I'd see this again. And... what happened then?"

"When we left the Temple, we were seen. They came for us, and Mother tried to divert them. She told me to go back to our flock, and to take the diadem and the gems." She paused, and her voice was strained when she continued. "I didn't get far. They had nets. They brought me down. Mother tried to save me, but—" She stopped, and Aven could see tears on her face. "They were bringing me to Mannon. I don't know why they didn't kill me outright. But by now, he surely knows that there's a true Heir to the Firstborn in the world again."

"The only way he'd know is if someone survived that ship," Aleia said. "Which means there's a chance he doesn't know. Not after that storm."

"I don't know what I'm supposed to do now," Aria said. "I haven't had a vision since the one that sent us to the Temple. I don't know what my next step is supposed to be." She looked down at the chest, and its contents. For a moment, she looked puzzled. She looked up, briefly, then back down. It was, Aven thought, as if she was having a silent conversation with someone. She turned the chest toward her, took something out, and closed the chest before getting to her feet. Her right hand was clasped around something, but Aven could see the cord hanging down as she walked toward him

No.

He stumbled to his feet, knowing that he could not be sitting when she reached him. He was taller than she was, and loomed over her as she stopped, so close that they were almost touching. She held her hand out, her palm to the sky, the sea-blue gem shining against her skin.

"This is yours," she said softly. "If you'll have it. If you'll stand by me." She paused, took a breath. "Stand with me, as Abin stood by Axia. Be my Companion."

CHAPTER FOUR

THERE WERE MORE WORDS, ritual words that Aven thought that he should be paying attention to. But he didn't hear a single one of them. Instead, what imprinted on his memory were the looks on his parent's faces. The complete devastation on his father's face. The horror in his mother's eyes.

Silence, and he realized that Aria had stopped speaking. She stood there, her hand held out, the blue gem shining in the firelight.

"Why me?" Aven croaked. "I'm not anything special. I told you that. We could take you to the rest of the tribe, find you someone better—"

"There's no one else," Aria said. "I knew from the moment I saw you."

"But I'm not the right one. I can't be the right one!" Aven insisted. "I don't know anything. I've never been anywhere. I'm not even entirely Water!"

"And I'm not entirely Air," Aria pointed out. "The Mother doesn't care, Aven. She sent the Diadem to me, and the gems. The first one is yours."

Aven swallowed around the boulder in his throat, then looked past Aria to his parents. "Ama? Fa? What do I do?"

"We can't make this choice for you, Ven," his mother said. "But you don't have to make it now, either. We're not going anywhere. Not without a plan. So sleep on it."

For a moment, Aria looked stunned. Then she scowled and started to turn. She stopped, closed her eyes, and took a deep breath. "Yes. Yes, let it be. I will still be here in the morning." She went back to the chest, put the water gem back into its place, and sat down near the fire, picking up her bowl and starting to eat again. Aven got the distinct feeling that she was angry at him for not immediately accepting the gem, and that she was now ignoring him.

"I... I'm going to go get some sleep," he stammered, and turned away from the fire. He knew the way down to the beach in the dark, and he was certain that he could find the sheltered inlet where he preferred to pass his nights in his sleep. Tonight, though, it seemed as if every rock and root on the island was attempting to find a place under his feet. Halfway down the trail, he stopped, sitting down on a rock, trying to get his thoughts in order.

If he did this, if he took the Water gem from Aria and accepted his place as her Companion, his days were numbered.

But they already had been. He had just never known it before. Because of who his parents had been before he was even born, he was marked for death. Refusing the gem wouldn't change that. But taking the gem might mean that he *could* change it. If he took the gem, if he stood by Aria and helped her to take her place as Firstborn, maybe they could stop Mannon.

And maybe he could sprout wings and fly like Aria.

He growled softly, and heard an answering growl from the shadows. Melody came up the trail toward him, planted her front legs on either side of his feet, and growled at him.

"Melody?" Aven said. "What's wrong?" He got up, and looked out over the water. To his surprise, he could still see the distant fire, a bright spot on the horizon. The burning ship seemed to be truly disturbing to the water-cat. She pressed against Aven's side and crooned discordantly, a sound that he'd never heard from her. He went to one knee and draped his arm over her back. "Melody, it's all right. It's a long way away, and it will be gone by morning." He rested his hand on the water-cat's head. "Come on. Let's go swim. I've got some thinking to do."

He gently urged Melody down the path toward the inlet. Once they were out of sight of the flames, Melody calmed down, running ahead and diving into the water. Aven followed more slowly, and stopped at the edge to take off his kilt. He folded it and laid it aside, wondering if there'd be time to make new taipa cloth to replace his other kilt before they left the island. If not, he'd make a new kilt from some of the sail cloth, he decided, and dove into the water. The cold was a shock, as always, and as the salt water surrounded him, he felt his gills opening, and his body starting to change. His legs merged together, and he felt the tickling sensation that always accompanied the unfurling of his fins. He closed his eyes and sank to the bottom of the pool, watching as Melody swam in circles above him, then came down to settle next to him, nudging his arm with her nose. He smiled and clicked at her, and she streaked off, flicking her long tail at him.

Aven grinned. Oh, so it was to be stalk and pounce before bed, hm? He flexed his tail, checking his transformation, then swam after Melody. To his surprise, she led him out of the inlet and into open waters. He whistled for her to come back, but she ignored him. He growled and chased her, following her through the forest of kelp, hearing her crooning and clicking in her excitement. Aven circled and stopped, looking back for a moment. He shouldn't swim out too far. If his parents came looking for him, they'd worry. He should go back...

Melody charged at him, swimming around him in fast circles before streaking off once more. He growled once more and followed, kicking hard to make up speed. For a while, he could ignore the world above the waves.

ALEIA PACED AROUND the fire, looking off into the darkness.

"He'll be fine," Jehan said gently. "He has a lot to think about. You know he thinks best when he's off in the deep."

"That's where wisdom lies," Aleia answered, almost automatically. "In deep places." She glanced over toward where Aria was curled up asleep. "Jehan—"

"It's his choice, Aleia. We can't make it for him."

Aleia nodded. Then, to Jehan's surprise, she smiled. "He sounded like you. He reminded me so much of you."

"I had the same thoughts, I think," Jehan said. "Why me? There were others who would have been much better choices. Why choose a half-trained healer with no bloodlines to speak of?"

"Because you were the right choice," Aleia answered. She moved to sit down next to Jehan, leaning against his arm. She sighed. "And so is he. Jehan, he's not ready—"

"Were we?" Jehan countered. "Right now, it's our job to prepare him. Prepare the both of them. Just... what are we preparing them for? What's next?"

Aleia straightened, wrapping her arms around her knees. She scowled at the fire. Jehan studied her for a moment, but said nothing. He knew this look. They'd all been trained in tactics, but Aleia had taken to it with breathtaking ease, to the point that Milon had taken to calling her 'the little General.' She had a way of taking what they knew, guessing at what they didn't know, and coming up with plans. So Jehan knew that when she spoke again, she'd have an answer. He might not like it, but it would be an answer.

"We need to go south," she said slowly. "We need Memfis."

"South," Jehan repeated. "Oh, of course. We'll just slip past all of Mannon's ships and go ashore outside Forge. March right up to the gates and find him waiting for us. Aleia, we don't even know if he's still alive!"

"We need to go on land. She needs her other Companions," Aleia said. "South gives us a direction, at least. And possibly an ally."

"And possibly gets us caught!" Jehan insisted. "Aleia, any ship captain worth his salt is going to see a canoe with two Waterborn, an Earthborn and an Airborn, and know something isn't right. We'll never make it."

Aleia didn't answer. She shifted, stretching her legs out and combing her fingers through the sand. Jehan let her think, stretching out on his back and staring up at the stars.

"It might work," Aleia said after a long time.

"What might?"

"We'd have to go quickly, in case there were survivors. Leave as soon as we possibly can. Tomorrow. We'd have to get ahead of them."

"What about replacing the decking?" Jehan asked. Aleia ignored him.

"We'll have to dive for pearls as we go. We'll need quite a few, I think, but not immediately."

"Aleia—"

"Do you think she knows how to swim?"

"Guppy!" Jehan sat up. "Will you finish a blasted thought?"

She looked at him and smiled. "Now you sound like Milon did."

"For the same reason! You need to explain the whole thing for those of us who can't think the way you do. By which I mean your long-suffering husband. Now, please."

She explained. And as he'd expected, he didn't like it.

"This is going to get us killed," he muttered, stretching back out on the sand. She chuckled and lay down next to him, her head pillowed on his shoulder.

"Do you have a better idea?" she asked.

"No. But it's going to get us killed."

"You have until morning to come up with something different."

AFTER A LONG CHASE, Aven finally managed to get Melody to swim back to the inlet. He surfaced, wondering if anyone had come after him. To his surprise, there was someone standing on the rocks overlooking the water where he'd left his kilt — Aria. He swam closer, splashing so that she'd hear him, and pulled himself up to rest his arms on a rock near where she was standing. She saw him and came over to sit on the rock facing him.

"Your parents are asleep," she said. "I woke up, and you had not come back. I thought I would come and find you."

Aven smiled and gestured to the water, tipping his head and closing his eyes. She frowned, clearly puzzled. Then she laughed.

"Can you not speak when you are in the water?" she asked. When Aven shook his head, she nodded. "I see. Do you sleep here?" He nodded, and she smiled. "I understand. I will go back to the fire, then. I wanted to talk to you. But I don't want to talk at you. It will wait until morning."

Aven shook his head, rested his hands on the rock, and pulled himself out of the water. Aria's eyes widened when she saw him.

"Oh, you're so beautiful!" she gasped. "You're out of the water. Does this mean you'll change back?"

Aven swallowed, feeling the tightness in his chest as his gills closed. He nodded, then took a tentative breath. Then another. Remembering what his mother had said about Airborn and nudity, he reached past Aria and picked up his kilt, draping it over his midsection as the change started. She watched him, and he saw her cheeks darken in the moonlight.

"Thank you," she murmured. "I...I have much to learn, I think."

Aven nodded and decided to try his voice, "We both do."

She grimaced. "You do not sound like you yet," she proclaimed, and Aven laughed. He leaned back on his elbows and looked up at the sky, and at her.

"Why me?" he asked, his voice still not sounding right to his ears. It didn't matter. He needed to know.

She looked thoughtful for a moment, then sighed. "I do not know?" she answered. "It is, I think, the best answer I can give you. I do not know who will wear the gems. I will not know until I see them. But they will know me. I know this. My mother told me that she knew from the moment that she saw my father that she was meant to stand with him."

Aven swallowed, remembering the tug he'd felt before they'd even cut the straps that held the hatch closed, the need to find whatever was hidden in the hold. "I knew before I even saw you," he said softly. "I knew before we got into the hold that there was something in there that I needed."

She looked startled. "You knew? And still you did not take the gem?"

"I didn't understand," Aven answered. "I still don't." He glanced down at himself, seeing his legs and feet had returned. "I knew nothing about Milon, or about who my parents were before I was born. They never told me. Now? Well, like you said, I've a lot to learn."

"We will learn together," Aria said, resting her hand on his shoulder, her skin warm and soft against his. He tipped his head back to look at her, and was shocked when she leaned down and kissed him. It was a fleeting thing, her lips brushing against his, leaving behind a barest hint of warmth. Before he could react, she'd scrambled to her feet.

"I should go back," she stammered. "You should sleep. I... I will see you in the morning."

"Aria—"

Too late. She was gone, hurrying back up the trail. He watched her go, then sighed, laying aside his kilt and slipping back into the water.

How was he supposed to sleep now?

CHAPTER FIVE

AVEN WOKE UP WHEN THE sun filtered down through the waters, and only then realized that he'd actually slept. He drifted up to the surface and rolled onto his back, floating like an otter and studying the sky. There were a few high clouds drifting across the clear blue expanse, looking more than a little like the white banding in the gem that Aria had offered to him.

He was going to do it. He was going to take the gem. He'd decided that at some point before he'd fallen asleep. He had no idea what it would mean for his future, but he already had no idea what his future held. This, at least, was a choice that he could make. By taking the gem, he was choosing his future, not merely accepting whatever happened. At least, that was what he was going to tell his parents.

He reached the top of the trail, and heard the raised voices coming from the beach. One he recognized as his mother, although he rarely heard her voice raised when it was just them. Usually, that was reserved for when they visited his grandmother, and heralded the immediate end to the visit. As his father once told him, when Aleia's patience was frayed enough that she reached the point of yelling to get her point across, it was time to leave.

The other voice was Aria's, and Aven quickly made his way down toward the beach. He saw his father first, and stopped next to him, looking down at the canoe, and at the two women facing each other. It was the first time that he'd seen Aria in full light, and the sight of her took his breath away. Her long hair was as dark as his own, and fell over her shoulders in rippling waves. Her skin was paler than his, and he already knew how soft it was. He still wasn't certain of the color of her eyes, and found himself eager to find out. And finally, her wings— banded gray and white like those of a sea eagle, she had them spread wide. To intimidate, he guessed, having seen similar displays in sea birds. But his mother wasn't going to be intimidated by a girl who could have been her daughter.

"What's happened?" Aven asked his father. "Why are they yelling?"

"Aria can't swim," Jehan answered. "And she's refusing to learn."

As if she'd heard him, Aria raised her voice, her tone one of strident derision. "I am a bird!" she proclaimed. "Birds do not swim!"

Aven coughed, and spoke without thinking, "Cormorants swim."

Aria's head whipped around, and she stared at him. "What?"

"Cormorants swim," Aven repeated, hearing his father chuckle. "And sea eagles. There are birds that swim."

She looked almost betrayed. "You're supposed to support me!"

"Not when you're trying to do something stupid," Aven answered, and saw his mother's approving nod. "And since the only way off this island is by canoe, at least until your feathers grow back, you need to learn to swim. Because going on a long voyage on a canoe when you can't swim is stupid. Doing it during storm season is suicidal. You need to learn."

"He's right," Jehan added. "Your Companions aren't going to just blindly support you. They're supposed to argue with you, and make sure that you're doing the best for your people. They're supposed to tell you when you're wrong. It's their entire purpose."

"So, one of us is going to teach you how to swim," Aleia finished, her voice very firm. "Who?"

Aria gaped at them, then shrieked and stormed off. Aven watched her go, then turned to his father.

"What's wrong with her?" he asked.

"There's nothing wrong with her that having someone telling her no won't fix," Jehan answered. "Think of your cousin."

"Oh, Neera?" Aven nodded. Neera was his next oldest cousin, the only daughter of his mother's youngest sister. Aunt Jisa was heir to the family canoe, and eventually, she'd be Clan Mother, the head of their family, and Neera was her heir. So, her mother had indulged her outrageously, and it had left Neera with a definite opinion that if she wasn't able to swim under the waves, she'd definitely be able to walk on them. She tried to lord her eventual position over Aven's head once too many times. "Aria's spoiled like that?"

"She appears to be. She was raised knowing that she was Milon's daughter," Aleia said as she joined them. "From the sounds of her, she was treated as if she was the Heir long before she went to the Temple."

"I can see Liara doing that," Jehan groaned. "So, how do we proceed?"

Aleia smiled slightly. "You compared her to Neera? Ven, remember how you took the wind out of Neera's sails?"

Aven nodded. "Yes, but—"

"You're not going to get in trouble for it now," Jehan said. "It will drive the point home. And it won't hurt her."

"It'll make her mad at me," Aven said, looking off in the direction that Aria had gone. "Fa, she came down to the pool last night."

Jehan looked momentarily shocked, then schooled his face to careful neutrality. "Did she?"

"We talked," Aven said. 'And... she kissed me. Then she ran off."

Jehan and Aleia shared a glance, then Jehan asked, "And have you decided?"

"I'm taking the gem," Aven answered. "And not because she kissed me. Because if I'm on Mannon's better- off- dead list regardless, then I'm not going to drift toward my future. I'm setting my own course, and maybe changing the outcome."

Jehan nodded, putting one arm around Aleia's shoulders. "That makes sense. All right. Go teach the Heir to swim."

THERE WEREN'T MANY places that Aria could have gone — Aven found her sitting on the rock that overlooked the pool where he slept. The rock where they'd been sitting when she kissed him. He was certain that she knew he was coming, but she didn't turn to see who was coming. He sat down on the rock next to her, and listened to the wind and the water.

Finally, she spoke, "That was unkind. You called me stupid."

"No, I said you were going to do something stupid. Stupid and suicidal," Aven corrected. "You need to learn to swim."

She sniffed. "I do not."

"And if you fall in the sea?" Aven asked. She turned to him and smiled.

"I know you will save me."

There was such faith, such trust in her answer that for a moment, Aven wasn't sure that he wanted to go through with this. But her refusal endangered her life, and he couldn't allow that. So he sighed, and shoved her off the rock and into the water. She screamed, the sound swallowed by the splash as she hit the water. Then she surfaced, and there was more splashing, more screaming and sputtering as she flailed wildly.

"Grab onto the rock," he called.

She didn't hear him. She didn't stop fighting, and Aven realized that she was panicking. He swore softly and scrambled to his feet, diving off the rock, angling away from Aria to avoid her struggling.

He twisted, using his arms to swim toward Aria as his gills opened and the change began. He broke the surface close to her — too close, and her flailing fist caught him across the cheek. He hissed, dove, and resurfaced behind her, only to be hit by one of her wings. He dove once more, surfacing in front of her, grabbing one of her wrists and pulling her close, pinning her arms to her sides with his own arms. He kicked as hard as he could, driving them across the pool toward the shallows and beaching himself on the sand, releasing Aria so she could crawl away. He rolled onto his back, already feeling the backlash of aborting his change in the middle. He couldn't breathe, and his bones from the hips down felt as if they were splintering. He closed his eyes, waiting for it to pass. Perhaps it was a good thing that he couldn't breathe. It meant he couldn't scream.

He heard splashing, and Aria gasping his name. Before he could open his eyes, she was kneeling over him, beating against his chest with her fists, hard enough that he was certain it should hurt. It just didn't hurt enough to drown out the pain he was already in.

"Why did you do that?" she wailed. "I thought I was going to die!"

He raised his arms to try and protect himself, only to let them fall back to his sides as the pain in his bones grew worse, far worse than the last time this had happened. Aria stopped hitting him, resting her hand on his chest.

"Aven?" her voice cracked. "What is it? What's wrong?" She touched his face. "It... it wasn't like this last night. I... this is something I did. I... Jehan! Aleia!" She got to her feet and ran, shouting for his parents. Then she came back. "I can't leave you. I can't leave you like this. What did I *do*?"

"Aria!" Aven heard his father's voice. "Aria!" A moment later, there was splashing, and Jehan was dropping to his knees in the water. "Ven? Ven, can you talk yet?"

Aven shook his head, felt his father's hand on his forehead, the warmth of his healing power. "Oh, Ven. Been a long time. I'm putting you out for the rest."

Dimly, Aven heard his father saying something else. He didn't hear what Jehan was saying, nor Aria's answer, as the warmth grew deeper, darker, drowning out both pain and awareness.

JEHAN WATCHED AS AVEN'S eyes closed, then rested his hand on his son's chest. He spoke without looking up. "What happened?"

"I don't know!" Aria whimpered. "He pushed me into the water. I got frightened, and he jumped in after me. I... I think I hit him. And he pulled me out of the water. Then he was like this and I don't know what I did to hurt him!"

Jehan looked at her, and saw the tears on her face. "It wasn't anything you did to him. He did it to himself, getting you out of the water. It takes time for him to change."

"I saw it happen last night, when he changed back. It didn't hurt him last night. Why is it hurting him now?"

"It looks like he wasn't fully changed from land to sea when he pulled you out of the water," Jehan said. "Breaking the cycle of the change hurts."

Aria looked distraught. "He pushed me into the water when I told him I would not learn to swim. I told him I knew that he would save me if I fell in. He pushed me in... and he saved me. I knew that he would. I didn't know that doing it would hurt him."

Jehan looked up, saw Aleia standing on the other side of the pool, near the top of the trail down to the beach. "Go down to the beach with Aleia. You can help her get things ready to leave. I'll bring Aven back to the canoe once he wakes up."

"I should stay. Help you. Watch him." Aria twisted her hands in her lap. "I didn't know it would hurt him!"

"It's not something that Waterborn tell people, Aria," Jehan said gently. "And there's not much you can do here. He'll be in a healing sleep for an hour or so. It'll be long and boring. Go help Aleia. I promise you, he'll be fine."

"Can you lift him?" Aria asked. "I could help. He shouldn't lie in the water... oh. Oh, that was stupid. He sleeps in the water—"

Jehan smiled. "Thank you, but it'll be easier and more comfortable for him if he sleeps it off here," Jehan answered. "Trust me, he'll be fine."

Aria nodded. She reached out and touched Aven's shoulder, then got to her feet. She walked out of the water, skirted around the pool, then stopped by Aleia. Her wet wings drooped, and Jehan heard her clearly. "I'm sorry. If I hadn't argued, Aven would not be hurting. I will learn to swim."

"You can tell him when he wakes up," Aleia said. "Come with me. We've got some work to do." She put her arm around Aria and led her away. Once they were gone, Jehan looked down at his sleeping son.

"You're going to have your hands full with her, Ven," he murmured. "She's not as bad as Neera, but she's every bit as stubborn as Milon was."

AVEN COULD ALWAYS TELL when he'd been in a healing sleep. His father told him all healers could tell. There was a definite feeling of having his head stuffed with sea-foam. The last time had been when he'd broken his arm diving into a rock. What had happened this time?

All at once, he remembered the pool, and Aria. He jerked, coming awake all at once and pushing himself up onto his elbows. He was lying on his back on the sand at the far side of his pool, his legs still mostly submerged. He sat up, rubbing his thighs.

"Feeling better?"

Aven turned and saw his father sitting on a rock. "I think so," he answered. "Where's Aria?"

"With your mother. She's fine. You scared the pinfeathers off of her, but she's fine now."

Aven slowly got to his feet. "I scared me, and I don't have pinfeathers. What happened? It wasn't nearly that bad the last time I stopped the change."

"You're older. The last time you were, what? Twelve?" Jehan got to his feet. "The last time, it was before you came into your full growth. Your bones were more malleable. Now, you're an adult. Adult bones aren't as forgiving. And I should have told you that when we had that 'what's happening to me?' conversation back then, but since I only had the theory class on being a Waterborn, and your mother is the one that had the practicum, I didn't even think of it."

Aven twisted from the waist. "I feel fine now."

"Good. Come on. We've got a lot of work ahead of us, and we're behind." Jehan sighed and shook his head. "Maybe telling you to shove her into the deep water wasn't the brightest thing I've ever done."

"I think it was Ama's idea, actually." Aven said, falling in next to his father as they walked around the pool and started toward the beach.

"Still wasn't the smartest idea either of us have ever had. Or, it might have been. I'm not sure. But Aria has already apologized to your mother, and promised that she'd learn to swim." Jehan glanced over at his son. "I'm not sure she'll ask you to teach her, though. I think she's afraid she'll break you."

Aven chuckled. "She's stronger than I thought she was. She punched me, when I was trying to get her to shore. And she tried to stove in my chest."

"Is that where those bruises came from?" Jehan asked, and whistled. "I'd wondered. I thought you might have been wrestling with Melody. Speaking of, you'll want to call her in. We're leaving soon."

"Leaving?" Aven asked. "To go where?"

"Your mother has a plan." Jehan answered. They crested the last rise and started down toward the beach. There were piles and bundles all around the canoe, and Aven could see Aleia and Aria packing things into the canoe's storage compartments.

"What about the decking?" Aven asked.

"We're going to be very careful," Jehan answered.

Aleia looked up from her packing, saw them and waved. Then she said something to Aria, who looked up and got to her feet, her wings flared out. Then, to Aven's shock, she launched herself into the air, wings beating furiously as she flew toward him. She landed ahead of him on the path, and ran straight at him, throwing her arms around his neck and hitting him hard enough to drive him back several steps and almost knock him over. She was laughing and crying all at once, and it took a moment before Aven could understand what she was saying.

"...sorry, I'm sorry! I didn't know it would hurt you! I didn't mean for you to get hurt!" She clung to him, and the only thing he could think to do was put his arms around her.

"I'm fine," he said. "I'm all right. And I'm sorry. I shouldn't have pushed you in." He closed his eyes, marveling at the smell of her. She smelled like the wind and the sea combined. "Are you all right?"

"I am fine. If I hadn't panicked, I'd know how to swim by now!" She laughed and pulled back slightly, enough that they were nose to nose. Her eyes, he could see now, were a pale gold, a color that he'd never seen before. He couldn't think — she was in his arms, body pressed against his, warm and smelling like fresh wind and sea-salt, and Aven didn't think that he could put two words together if he tried.

"You flew," Jehan said, breaking into Aven's reverie and reminding him that there were others on the beach. "I didn't think you could with your feathers clipped."

Aria loosened her arms around Aven, a clear signal that he should let her go. He did, only then realizing that he'd been holding her off the ground. He set her on her feet, and felt ridiculously pleased when she took his hand. "I cannot fly high or far like this," Aria said. "Short flights, close to the ground? That I can do. I cannot touch the sky until my feathers grow in."

"Fa, what are we doing?" Aven asked.

"We're leaving," Aleia answered, coming up the slope. "As soon as we're able."

"What about the decking?" Aven asked. Aleia shook her head.

"We don't have the time to wait," she said. "I want us heading south as soon as we're ready, to get ahead of the news from any survivors. We're going to Forge."

"We're going where?" Aven gasped. "But, that's where they were taking Aria. Isn't Mannon there?"

"No, Mannon would be at the Palace," Jehan said. "Forge is where we'll find Memfis, and we'll start finding the rest of Aria's Companions."

"I should give Aven the water gem," Aria said.

"Not yet," Jehan stopped Aria before she could run down the slope. "Not until we're in Forge. We've a long way to go, and we'll probably be challenged at least once. We don't want it stolen, or worse, recognized." He reached up and touched his own gem. "Which means I should take this off."

"Jehan, if everything goes according to plan, they'll never see you," Aleia said. "Aven, go call Melody in. You'll need to explain to her that she can't come with us."

Aven blinked, shaking his head. "You're going too fast. Yesterday, you didn't want to take me south. Now, we're leaving immediately. And Melody can't come with us?"

"The waters near Forge wouldn't be good for her," Jehan answered. "It'll be easier if she stays behind now, and she's less likely to get hurt if we run into trouble." He squeezed Aven's shoulder. "I know you'll miss her, and I'm sorry."

"Who is Melody?" Aria asked.

"I'll introduce you," Aven told her. "Fa, do you need me?"

"Not at the moment. I'll help your mother. Go start teaching Aria to swim, and introduce her to Melody."

CHAPTER SIX

AVEN LED ARIA AWAY from the canoe, and down to the water's edge. He waded out to his knees and slapped the water twice, then twice again.

"What are you doing?" Aria asked.

"The sound carries underwater," Aven answered. "For miles. That tells Melody to come in."

Aria smiled, moving into the water up to her ankles. "You still haven't told me what a Melody is."

Aven grinned. "Besides what you sing, if you're not singing the harmony? Melody is a water-cat. She's been with me since she and I were both kits."

Aria looked around. She looked down at the water swirling around her feet, then asked, "How are you going to teach me to swim, when you can't speak when you've got a tail?"

"We could start in the sweet water pool, where you bathed last night. That won't trigger my change," Aven answered. "And if I don't go all the way under in salt, I won't change." He tapped the side of his throat. "I have to be up to the gills."

"Oh." Aria took another few steps, moving deeper into the water. She looked back over her shoulder, then at Aven. "I have another question."

Aven nodded. "Go ahead."

"You call your mother Ama. Why?"

Aven burst out laughing. "Oh, that?" He waved Aria closer. "Come on. You need to be deeper to swim. I'll make a bargain with you. If you float, all alone, then I'll tell you."

Aria looked skeptical. "Float?"

"It's the first part of swimming. And you're light, so you should have no trouble. It's easy. You just lie here. Come on." Aven held his hand out. "I won't let you get hurt."

"If I lie there, what do I do with my wings?" Aria asked. She took Aven's hand, and he led her into deeper water, up to his waist. He didn't ask her to take her clothes off, nor did he take off his kilt. They were both ruined anyway from their disastrous swimming lesson, so there didn't seem to be a need. He considered her question, then shrugged. "I'm not sure. I've never taught anyone with wings to swim before. We'll see what works for you." He put his hands on her shoulders, turned her sideways, then placed one hand on her back, below her wings. "Lie back. You're going to start with resting on my arms. And relax. I won't let you go."

Aria shivered, then looked up at him. "I trust you," she said softly. She leaned back into his hand, and he eased her down until she was lying on his arms, her wings outspread.

"You're too stiff," he said. "Relax. This is just like lying on the ground."

"I won't go under when I'm on the ground," Aria protested.

"You won't go under here. Your body wants to float." He spoke gently to her, softly, and slowly she softened, relaxing until all of the tension was gone from her limbs. "Good. Very good. I have you. I'm taking one arm away. You're doing just fine."

Slowly, he drew his right arm back, watching Aria closely. She simply sighed and took a soft breath.

"I think you're ready to fly, little bird," he murmured, and took his left hand away. She bobbed gently with the waves for a moment, then must have realized what he'd said and that his hand was gone.

She jerked, started to sink, and put her feet down with a splash. She stared at him for a moment, then laughed.

"I did it?"

"You did it," Aven agreed. "Very good for a first time."

She giggled, splashing over to him. "Now tell me the story!"

Aven blinked, then remembered what he'd promised. "Oh, that. Yes. When I was little, I had trouble with the word Mama. I don't know if I heard it wrong, or if I couldn't say the first 'm', but I called my mother Ama."

Aria made a soft cooing sound. "That's so sweet!"

Aven snorted. "Got teased for it by my cousins when I was older, and I tried to change it. The first time I called my mother Mama, she looked at me. Just...looked." He shook his head. "She looked sad. When I asked her why, she told me that it was because everyone else called their mothers Mama. She was the only Ama she'd ever heard of, and that made it special. I've never called her anything else since."

Aria smiled and rested her hand on his chest. "That's beautiful. You're so lucky to have such parents."

Aven nodded. "I know. Thanks." He looked up when a high trill sounded, louder than he'd expected. "Come up on the beach. That's Melody. You should meet her on land. She's less intimidating that way."

"Intimidating?" Aria followed him out of the water. "I've known cats, Aven. They're not intimidating."

"They're not? I've never seen a land cat," Aven said as he reached the shore. He turned, and saw motion in the water. "There she is."

A moment later, Melody surfaced, and he heard Aria gasp.

"Aven," she said slowly. "That is not a cat!"

Aven studied Melody for a moment – her dark-gray skin, soft as fine leather. Her diamond-shaped head and large, dark eyes. Her long, sleek body and powerful legs, and the sinuous tail that was longer than her body, longer than he was tall. She trilled as she came up the beach, then cocked her head to the side.

Aven held his hand out to her. "Come on, Melody. I want you to properly meet Aria." As Melody came to his side, he turned to Aria. "How are land cats different?" he asked.

"Cats are small!" Aria blurted.

"I'd wondered," Aven admitted. "Fa says that if he'd been around at the beginning of the world, he'd never have named them water-cats, because they don't look anything like cats. But he never really explained." He knelt down and slung his arm over Melody's shoulders. "Aria, she won't hurt you. And to be honest, she's met you already. She watched over you while you slept, after we got you out of that ship."

"She did?" Aria stepped forward, then went to her knees, holding her hands out. Melody stretched toward her, sniffing her hands. Then she shoved her head against Aria's hands, crooning and purring as she left Aven's side to curl around Aria, rubbing against her. Aria's laughter was like bells.

"She's so soft!" Aria draped one arm around Melody's shoulders, as Aven had, and scratched Melody under the chin with the nails of her other hand. Melody's crooning grew louder, and she flopped onto her side, almost knocking Aria over. Aven laughed and moved closer, stroking Melody's flank as Aria whispered soft nonsense to the water-cat.

"She likes you," Aven said. "That's good."

"Will she stay here, Aven?" Aria asked. "If you tell her to stay, will she?"

"She won't like it," Aven answered. "And I'm not sure if she'll listen to me. Fa says that she will, because I've got what Earthborn call an animal sense. Not enough that I can understand them, but they seem to understand me pretty well. Melody certainly does. But she's got her own mind, and she doesn't always do what I want her to do."

"That's very much like a land cat," Aria said. "They're willful."

"That's a good way of describing her." Aven clicked at Melody, who raised her head languorously and looked at him. "If I could bother you?" Aven teased. "Melody, we're leaving the island. You can't come with us." Melody's eyes flared, and she snorted. Aven nodded. "I know. You don't like it. I don't like it either. But where we're going, you could get hurt. I want you safe. We'll be back. I don't know when, but we'll be back."

Melody shook off Aria's hands and rose, shaking herself all over before twining around Aven, coiling around him twice before resting her head on his chest. He wrapped his arms around her, suddenly sad and scared, and feeling very much alone.

"I'll miss you, too," he mumbled. "I don't want to leave you behind. But it's not safe where we're going, and I don't want you hurt."

She *whuffed* into his hair, crooned in his ear, then uncoiled herself from around him. She nudged his chest, rubbed her face against his, then turned and walked slowly into the water. The last sign of her was the slight wake that followed her passing.

Aria shifted on the sand, moving to sit next to him, taking his hand.

"Do you think she understood?"

Aven didn't look at her, watching the water where the wake had already vanished. "I think so."

"Do you think she'll follow us?"

"Mother of us all, I hope not." Aven swallowed. "I couldn't do this again. And if she got hurt—" He rubbed his face with his free hand. "Let's go help my parents. We need to get started with whatever this plan is."

"You don't know?"

"I've asked, but I haven't really gotten a full answer yet," Aven said. "We're going south, when yesterday going south was too dangerous."

"Yesterday, I wasn't with you," Aria pointed out. "Well, not until late yesterday. Things have changed."

Aven nodded. "This much change this quickly is... uncomfortable."

"I'm sorry, Aven," she said, hugging his arm. He looked at her and smiled.

"I know. Thank you. Let's go finish getting ready." He got to his feet, pulled Aria to hers. "While we go, you can learn to sail."

Aria looked down at their linked hands. "Your mother has marks on her hand. You don't."

"Ama is a navigator," Aven said, leading her up the beach and toward the canoe. "I just know how to sail. Someday, I might earn navigator's tattoos."

"Who decides if you do?" Aria asked. "Is there a school, or someplace you learn?"

"You learn by doing. And by not dying." Aven shrugged. "The head of the family is the one who decides, usually. Which would be my grandmother, and she wouldn't pour sweet water on me if I was on fire, so I know she won't ever recognize me as a navigator."

Aria stopped so abruptly that Aven almost pulled her off her feet. "She doesn't like you? Whyever not?"

Aven shrugged again. "Because she doesn't like my father. She doesn't think Water blood should marry outside the tribe. So when my mother asked my father to build a canoe with her—"

"I'm sorry?"

Aven grinned. "She asked him to marry her. Before the wedding, a woman and her man have to build a canoe. The families provide the materials, but they have to build it, all without help. If their relationship survives the building, they're ready to marry. So when a woman asks a man to build a canoe with her—"

"She's asking him to marry her. I see. And I imagine that there are a number who do not last through the building?"

"I imagine not, but I don't actually know." Aven tugged Aria into motion again. "To go back to my grandmother, she was furious when Ama took Fa as her husband. And she really doesn't like me, because she doesn't think I should have happened." He shook his head, trying to decide how much to tell Aria. He glanced at her, and saw that she was studying him.

"There is something you are not saying," she said. "I can see it."

He smiled. "You met me yesterday. You're not supposed to be able to do that."

"Do what?" She laughed and hugged his arm. "I met you yesterday, but we've known each other since before we were born. We're meant to be. You, me, and the others who will wear the other gems w hen we find them. Now, tell me?"

Aven considered, then sighed. She'd find out if they met any of the rest of the Water tribe. "When you reach twenty, you're considered an adult in the tribe. And the head of your family marks that by giving you the family tattoo."

Aria frowned. "You're the same age as I am. You have no tattoos."

"Because my grandmother refused to allow it," Aven finished. "That's why I know she won't give me navigator tattoos."

Aria stopped again, and Aven laughed. "I'm going to pull you over if you keep doing that!"

"She refused you?" Aria sounded outraged. More than sounded — her anger was written in every line of her body, from her stiff legs to her flared wings. "You're an adult of your people, and she won't recognize that?"

"Aria, I appreciate that you're angry on my behalf, but please, don't be," Aven said gently. "I don't care what she thinks. And it doesn't matter, does it?" He waited until Aria looked quizzically at him. "What matters is what you think," he finished. "And what I think of myself. Not necessarily in that order, of course."

Aria smiled. "Of course." She moved in closer, then slipped her arms around Aven's waist. "And I think you're perfect. And wonderful. And if I knew how to give you a tattoo, I would."

Aven put his arms around her shoulders, holding her close. "You don't have to," he murmured into her hair.

"I don't?"

"You gave me the Water gem."

He felt her shiver against him, a sensation that did the most amazing things to him. "And if we want to find the others, we need to go. Which means that we need to go and help your parents."

By the time they reached the canoe, almost everything was stowed away.

"Fa, where's that sailcloth we took from the ship?" Aven called, looking around. The only things that were still on the beach were the sweet water casks that they carried for Jehan.

"What we didn't pack for a spare sail is stowed in the cave," Jehan called. "Why?"

"I was going to cut some for new kilts, since mine were ruined. And something else for Aria. She can't keep wearing your clothes, and there's no time to make new taipa."

Aleia nodded, looking thoughtful. "That's a good thought. Cut enough to make for your father, too. Two each. And cut twice as much in the silk. Silk packs small. We can't trade it without explaining where we got it, but we can wear it. While you do that, Aria can help us fill the water casks."

Aven fetched his knife and headed inland, following the trail through the trees toward the cave where they stored supplies and where they took shelter during the worst of the storms. He had to duck underneath the low opening at the cave mouth, but it opened up three paces inside, and he could stand straight up. There was a ledge there, where they kept a flint and steel, and an oil lamp. With practiced ease, he lit the lamp, then carried it further into the cave. Their supplies were stacked near the rear, wrapped up against weather and animals. He found the bundles of canvas and of silk and measured the lengths that he would need, then cut them and laid them aside to rummage through the other bundles and baskets. He found an extra sewing kit, a spare knife, and another flint and steel. And, to his surprise, his mother's swords, well-wrapped in oilcloth.

"Why leave them here?" he murmured.

"Why leave what here?"

Aven turned to see his mother had come into the cave. For some reason, she was wearing his canvas carry-bag, the one that he used when he was collecting oysters and shellfish. "Ama, why are you leaving your swords here?"

Aleia came and crouched next to him. "Jehan and Aria are filling the casks. I thought we might need another one, since we've another person who can only drink sweet water. So I came to get it. And why am I leaving the swords? Because... I don't know. If I bring them, that means I'm going to use them."

"But isn't it going to be dangerous?" Aven asked. "Shouldn't we have them?"

Aleia frowned slightly. Then she nodded. "Bring them. Don't forget to put out the lamp. I'll get the cask." She handed his bag to him. "And wear this. Aven, I'm serious about this. I want you to keep this to hand from the minute we leave until we reach Forge."

Aven took the bag from her, feeling the weight of it. "What... Ama, there's something in here?"

"Yes. Think about it."

Aven frowned, hefted the bag, then blinked. "The Diadem? And the gems?"

"Don't let Aria know you have them," Aleia said. "I don't want her to know where they're hidden."

"They're hers, though," Aven said. He slung the bag over his head and across his body, settling it on his hip. "Why not tell her?"

"Because if things go badly, it'll be on you to keep her, and those, safe." Aleia folded her arms over her chest. "And she's got a good heart. She has to, or she'd not wear the Diadem. If things go badly, and she thought for an instant that she'd be able to save you by giving Mannon the Diadem, she'd do it."

"And she can't," Aven said. He smoothed his hand over the strap on his chest.

"He can't have the Diadem, and he cannot have her," Aleia said softly. "Aven, the only reason that we left Milon behind was that he was dying. If Mannon had gotten his hands on the Heir... no. No, Milon wasn't the Heir at that point. He was the Firstborn. If Mannon had gotten his hands on the Firstborn... I don't know. I don't want to know. You're her Companion now, Aven. It's on you to keep her safe." She sighed. "And that's another reason to bring the swords. You'll need them."

"Me?" Aven said. No, he didn't say it, he *squeaked* it, and felt his face grow hot. "Ama—"

"I've taught you all of the sword dances, and you're very good with sword and club."

"But that's just dancing!" Aven protested. "Ama—"

"You have the skills," Aleia cut him off. "You'll know what to do when the time comes."

"If—"

Aleia shook her head. "I've no doubt that the time is coming, Aven. Don't deny that. You'll be fighting. We'll all be fighting." She bent, picking up the oilcloth bundle. "These were Abin's, you know."

"You told me the story," Aven said, but his mother didn't seem to hear him.

"I brought them with me to the Palace, because my mother insisted. She gave them to me before I left, telling me to bear them with pride. She was proud of me then, proud that I was going to be Companion to the Firstborn, the same as our distant father. I'd only ever used them to dance. I never used them on another person until the morning Mannon attacked the palace." She cradled the swords like a baby. "I would dance with these, for Milon. He was a dancer, too. I was teaching him sword dancing, and he was teaching me smoke blades." She smiled, softly. "It's fitting that you should have them, that you should use them to protect his daughter." She looked up. "Do you want to carry these, or the cask?"

"I'll carry the cask, Ama." He packed the cask with the canvas and the silk, and the other supplies he'd collected, then hoisted it under his arm. It wasn't heavy. Not nearly as heavy as the meaning of the weight of the bag that rested on his hip.

CHAPTER SEVEN

CASKS WERE FILLED WITH sweet water and lashed to the mast. Supplies were packed and repacked into compartments built into the deck. The deck shelter was inspected and repaired, and the sails unfurled, inspected, and deemed ready. Aven had been sailing with his parents for his entire life, but he couldn't remember ever before having gone over the canoe with such meticulous care. Finally, Aleia stood back, folded her arms over her chest, and nodded.

"We're ready."

Then there was nothing else to do but push the canoe into the water, scramble aboard, and stay out of the way as Aleia took the lines. She held her hand out, studying the horizon, and set their course.

South. Aven stared out at the water, watching as the island slowly faded into the distance. Never before had setting out on a journey seemed so ominous.

"How long will we be at sea?" Aria asked, sitting down next to him and taking his hand.

"I don't know," Aven answered. "It'll be a long trip, I think. When we go visit Ama's family, we're usually sailing for three or four days. And they're not near land at all."

"If we keep a good wind, we'll probably start seeing ships in fourteen or fifteen days," Jehan added. "Once we see our first ship, we'll be about four or five days from Forge."

"It's that far?" Aria gasped. She looked around, then frowned. "I... Aleia, may I ask you a question?" She got up and walked across the deck to where Aleia stood.

"I think Aria just noticed that there's no privacy," Jehan murmured to Aven. Aven frowned, looked at his father, then realized what Jehan meant.

"Oh, I... Fa—"

"We'll look away, son. We'll look away." Jehan answered. "She's going to have to get used to other customs. When she finds her Earthborn... well, if she finds another Healer, she's going to get an education." He grinned. "You will, too."

"Fa!"

"Take it from someone who knows, Ven. Healers tend to be much more open-minded about..." Jehan's voice trailed off, then he shrugged. "Everything. So when you finally meet a healer who's actually been trained in a Healing center in Earth tribe lands—"

"Other than you," Aven interjected.

"Other than me," Jehan agreed. "You're going to find yourself shocked at least once. Possibly more than once. I know I regularly shocked the fins off of your mother and Liara."

"But not Milon or... what was his name?"

"Memfis. And no, not them. They were both born and raised in Forge, and there's enough intermingling of blood between Fire and Earth that there was a healing center in Forge. I don't know if it's still there. But it was, so Milon and Memfis knew what to expect." He grinned. "You'll get your feet kicked out from under you, Ven. And about time, too."

"Fa!" Aven felt his face growing warmer. "That's... I don't really want to talk about that."

Jehan looked puzzled. "You never had an issue before." Then he glanced back over his shoulder. "Oh. Lack of privacy?"

Aven nodded. "Fa, if I'm her Companion, that means that at some point she'll want me to share her bed."

Jehan nudged Aven's arm and got up, leading his son to the far side of the canoe, as far from the women as it was possible to be. "Is that a problem, Ven?" Jehan asked, very serious. "I know you don't have a lot of experience—"

"Any," Aven interrupted. "Any experience."

"Oh?" Jehan breathed. "Oh, and here I was assuming because you'd gone swimming with that girl from Chiandre's canoe. The last time that we were with the family."

"Mera?" Aven shook his head. "No, after that first time, Aunt Jisa spoke to Mera's mother, and Mera's mother told Mera that she didn't want her spending any more time with me."

Jehan's jaw dropped. "I... you never said a word!"

"And you were going to do what?" Aven asked. "Go to Mera's mother? How would that have helped?"

Jehan opened his mouth, closed it again, then let out a long breath. "Good point. What about that young man? What was his name?"

"Heshi? He vanished the minute he realized who I really was." Aven shook his head. "When we go to the family and the rest of the tribe, the only time I get looked over by anyone is when they don't know who I am. And Aunt Jisa watches like a spy-hopping whale. The minute anyone tries to get close, she interferes."

Jehan was silent for a moment. "I wish you'd told us. That's above and beyond what I thought was happening. For that, I'd go argue with your grandmother."

"Fa, it's not worth it." Aven stared out at the horizon. "If someone can't see beyond my bloodline to see me, then I really don't want them in my bed. Why would I?" He glanced back at Aria and Aleia. "And... Aria doesn't really see me yet, does she? It's been a day. But the way she looks at me..."

"It's a little strange at first," Jehan said. "The first few months we were all together, the only people sharing beds were Milon and Memfis. And that was because they'd been lovers before. It was almost a year before anyone else was sharing space. So yes, Aria might ask you to her bed, but it won't be until she knows you better. Accepting the gem doesn't mean you're automatically on your back."

"She already kissed me," Aven murmured. "It wasn't a big thing, but..."

"Different?"

"Yes. Very." Aven felt his face growing warm again. "It wasn't like kissing Mera. Or Heshi. That was play. This was *real*."

Jehan nodded, looking off into the distance. He didn't say anything for a long time. Then he cleared his throat. "You remember what we taught you?"

Aven nodded. "I remember. The first move is hers."

Jehan draped his arm over Aven's shoulders. "You and she will be fine. And you'll meet the others, and you'll all be fine."

"Assuming that we all survive," Aven added. "Fa, are you going to tell me the plan now?"

"Your mother will explain," Jehan said. He turned and raised his voice. "You are going to explain now, aren't you?"

"If you come closer," Aleia called. Jehan and Aven both got up and crossed to sit with Aria.

Aleia didn't speak for a minute, then sighed. "We'll be challenged once we get further south and east. So we'll have to have a cover story. Some reason we're sailing. So we'll be making a stop before we keep sailing." She glanced over at them. "We're spending a few days at the pearl fields."

"We're pearl diving?" Aven asked with a grin. "All right. Why?"

"Because our story is that we're going to Fire tribe waters to trade pearls for metal tools." Aleia adjusted the lines. "We'll probably lose some of them as bribes. Can't be helped."

"Wait," Jehan said. "If we're stopped, we're going to be caught."

Aleia smiled at him. "Not if you and Aria aren't here."

"Where will we be?" Aria asked. "I cannot carry Jehan."

"Guppy, are you honestly suggesting—" Jehan started. He swore briefly, then dragged his fingers through his hair. "Yes. Yes, you are. And it's the only way to do this, isn't it?"

"Fa?"

"Aria and I will be under the canoe," Jehan said. "In the carry-net."

Aria's eyes widened. "I do not like this plan."

"You have about ten days after we leave the pearl fields to come up with a better one," Aleia said.

THEY SPENT FOUR DAYS at the pearl fields, with Aven and Aleia spending most of it in their sea forms, collecting the pearl-bearing oysters that had been farmed here by the Water Tribes for generations. Aria sewed kilts and dresses, and learned to open oysters without slicing off her fingers as they filled three flat baskets to the top with pearls in various shades of white, gray, pink and blue. The oyster meat was packed away in a cask of fruit juice to marinate for later eating.

"I had no idea they came in so many colors!" Aria gasped, running her fingers through one of the baskets. "They're so pretty!"

Aven grinned at her, resting his forearms on the hull float. With his mother's blessing, he'd taken an especially nice dark-gray pearl and put it aside to give to Aria as a gift after their first night in her bed. He no longer doubted it would happen. It was just a question of when. He slung his carry bag over the float and tapped her leg, then gestured toward the water.

"Do we have time to swim?" she asked, looking at the sky. Aven followed her gaze, looking at the position of the sun and the high clouds. He nodded and reached out to tug on her ankle. She laughed and pulled her leg back, standing up and reaching behind her neck to untie the neck of the wrapped silk dress that she wore, blushing a little as she let it fall. Swimming naked, she'd decided, was much more comfortable than sitting around in wet clothes afterward. But she still blushed.

She slipped into the water, holding on to the hull float with one hand as Aven swam around to join her, placing one hand on her waist as she started to tread water the way that Jehan had showed her. Once she was ready, she nodded, and Aven swam a short distance from the canoe. He slapped the water until she located him, then waited. She took a deep breath and let go, sinking slightly before she started paddling, started kicking. Started moving, closing the short distance between the canoe and Aven. He could feel the grin growing on his face as she got closer, until she was close enough that he could reach out and touch her hand. She grabbed on to him, and he pulled her into a hug, laughing with her.

"I did it!" she crowed. "I swam!" She giggled and hugged him tightly, then kissed him. It wasn't the sort of kiss that they'd shared over the past few days — quick brushes of the lips, barely there before they were gone. This was deep. Passionate. Possessive, as she wound her fingers into his hair and tugged. Coiled her legs around his tail and clung to him. It felt as if every inch of her skin was touching his, and it was maddening. He wanted more, but of what, he wasn't sure.

He heard a splash, and a raised voice. His father's voice. It was enough to cool his ardor.

Barely.

Aria heard it, too. She tensed in his arms, and when she pulled back, every bit of her that he could see was the brilliant pink of embarrassment.

"I'm sorry," she whispered. "I... I got carried away." Aven smiled. He couldn't say anything to reassure her, so he leaned in and kissed her on the tip of her nose. She giggled and hugged him. "I want to try to swim back," she said. Aven nodded and let her go, and she splashed and foundered a little before setting out for the canoe. Aven swam alongside her, silently encouraging her until she reached the hull float. Jehan was standing on the deck, clapping.

"Well done!" he called, and offered Aria a hand. Once she was back on the canoe, Aven lifted himself out of the water and flopped onto his back on the deck, staring up at the sky as his chest tightened and his gills closed. He took a deep breath, then closed his eyes.

"Once you're able to talk, we need to discuss plans," Jehan said. "And we'll eat."

Aven nodded, lacing his fingers together over his stomach and waiting for the change to finish. Only to jump when fingers started combing through his hair. He opened his eyes to see Aria sitting next to him, bare and beautiful, running her fingers through his long hair.

"I can braid this, if you like," she offered. "It's one of the ways we wear it, so it doesn't get in the way when we fly."

Aven smiled and nodded. She continued finger combing his hair. The gentle preening was soothing, relaxing in a way that Aven hadn't expected, and he sighed in contentment.

Something nudged him in the thigh. "Ven, wake up."

"I'm not sleeping," Aven answered. His voice sounded normal to his ears. He'd finished changing? He opened his eyes and blinked. The skies were darker, the clouds painted with the pinks and golds of sunset. "I was asleep?"

"Snoring, too," Jehan answered with a chuckle. "Come and eat." He dropped Aven's kilt onto his chest and walked away. Aven rolled over and got to his knees, seeing Aria sitting with his mother across the canoe.

"I brought up some more oysters," Aven called. He wrapped his kilt around his waist. "I left my bag hanging in the water. Why didn't you wake me?"

"We can't set out until morning anyway," Aleia answered. "So you get first watch."

"That's fair," Aven got to his feet and went to the edge of the canoe, kneeling down and reaching out to the float to grab the strap of his bag. He carried it over to the others and took out several handfuls of oysters, putting them into a bowl that Jehan held out. "Here. We can add these to the meal."

He sat down next to Aria, who smiled at him. "Did you sleep well?"

"I didn't even realize that I was asleep, so I think so." He picked an oyster out of the bowl and drew his knife. Deftly, he opened the oyster, sliced the meat free, then offered it to Aria. She looked at it, clearly puzzled.

"Is there a pearl?" she asked.

"This one is for eating," Aven said. He looked down at the half-shell. "You just... well, eat it."

"We preserved the others, Ven. Aria hasn't had one raw yet," Jehan pointed out. "I didn't show her how to eat them like that."

"And you didn't sneak any yourself?" Aleia asked.

"Well, I didn't say that..."

Aven grinned. "It's good," he said to Aria. "It's sweet, a little. And it tastes like the sea."

"Show me?" she asked. Aven nodded, put the half shell to his lips and poured the oyster into his mouth, chewing the briny, chewy morsel before swallowing it. When he looked back at Aria, her eyes were wide. "All right," she said slowly. "If it's that simple."

Aven cut open two more oysters, and handed one to Aria. She looked skeptical for a moment. "Do I need to check for pearls before I eat it?" she asked.

"I already did," Aven assured her.

She nodded again, copying Aven's movements. She put the half-shell to her lips, poured the oyster into her mouth, chewed and swallowed. She licked her lips and made a face. "I'm not sure if I liked that."

"Try another?" Jehan suggested. "It was your first time, after all."

They shared the rest of the oysters and the bowl of cut seaweed and thin slices of moonfish as the skies grew darker and the stars started to appear. When the bowls were empty, Aleia looked up at the skies.

"We'll start south tomorrow morning," she said. "If we have good winds, we'll be in Forge in fourteen or fifteen days."

"And then what?" Aven asked. "What do we do once we're in Forge?"

His parents both looked at him. There was a long silence, then Jehan sighed. "We'll find out once we get there?" he offered. "We don't know what the next step will be. We won't know until we find Memfis."

"And what if he is no longer there?" Aria asked. "If he is gone, or if he is dead? What do we do then?"

Jehan glanced at Aleia. "You have to have thought about that."

Aleia nodded. "If we can't find Memfis, then we find your Fire companion, and we move on to the Earth tribe lands. We'll go to the healing center. Earth companions are almost always healers. It seems like a good place to start."

Aven nodded. "And what about Air? How do we get there?"

Aleia shook her head. "Haven't gotten that far yet. There are too many variables. Once we reach the healing center, then I'll be able to answer that question."

Conversation ceased at that point, and Aleia and Jehan took Aria with them when they went to the deck shelter to sleep. Aven rinsed out the bowls and packed them into their storage space, then took from another compartment a bundle of fibers. He sat down with his back to the mast and combed the fibers with his fingers, looking for where he'd left off. The braided and knotted pattern in the cords was intricate, but his fingers knew the motions well enough that he could do this in the dark. The braid was about as wide as two of his fingers together, a mesh of lacy knotwork that resembled the patterns in some of the coral that grew near their island. He'd started this weeks ago, thinking that it would be something added to their trade goods. Now, he knew better. This was for Aria, and would hold the gray pearl that he'd kept to give to her.

He heard the decking creak, and looked up to see that Aria wasn't asleep. She came over and curled up next to him on the deck.

"What are you doing?" she asked.

"Knotwork," he answered, putting down the fibers. "It passes the time."

She nodded, her face ghostly in the moonlight. "Will you show me?"

"When we have enough light," Aven answered. "I can do it in the dark, but I can't teach in the dark. You need to see what you're doing."

She sighed. "I wish I could see what I was doing," she said softly.

It took Aven a moment to realize that she wasn't talking about the night. "You had visions," he said, remembering her story.

"And I have not had one since the one that took my mother and I to the Temple," Aria said. "I don't know what my next step should be. And I'm worried." She shook her head. "No. No, I'm not worried. I'm frightened." She turned and looked at Aven. "For you. For them. I'm the Heir. I'm supposed to stop Mannon, and I don't know what to do."

"None of us do," Aven said. "So we do the best we can, and hope that the Mother will guide us." He reached out and took Aria's hand. "She brought you this far."

Aria smiled slightly, and squeezed Aven's fingers. "She brought me to you." She moved closer and rested her cheek on Aven's shoulder. "We'll be all right."

Aven rubbed his cheek against her hair, breathing in her scent of sea-salt and wind. "We'll be all right in the end," he said, remembering something his father had told him once. "It might take a while. It might seem like it's all sunk to the bottom of the sea. But that's not the end. If it's not all right, it's not the end."

CHAPTER EIGHT

THE DAYS FLOWED ONE into the next as they sailed south and east. Aven spent part of each day sailing, learning more about navigation. He spent part of each evening hunting and collecting edible seaweed. And he spent a portion of the rest of the time that he was awake practicing swords with his mother. With only the one set of swords between them, Aleia used long wooden rods that they had stored for repairs. They were about as long as the swords, and would do less damage when she bested Aven in a bout.

Which seemed to happen constantly.

"I always thought I was good at this," he grumbled as Aleia disarmed him once again. He could feel Aria watching him, which only made his failures worse.

"You are good," Aleia assured him. "You can be better. Now, guard again."

"Before you start, Aleia," Jehan called from where he was manning the lines. "I want your eyes."

Aleia turned and joined Jehan at the lines. Aven followed her, scanning the horizon. "Sails," he murmured.

"We can see them. They should be able to see us," Aleia said. "Jehan, it's time."

Jehan leaned down and kissed Aleia, then nodded to Aria. "Ready?"

"No," Aria answered, but she reached up behind her neck and untied her dress. Jehan stripped as well, handing his kilt and vest to

Aven, who put them and Aria's dress into a basket. When he turned back, Jehan had moved to sit on one of the hull floats, and was holding his hand out to Aria.

"Come on," he said. "I'll help you. Keep your wings close to your back."

"I will do my best," she answered. She looked up at Aven and gave a weak smile. "Be safe," she said.

"You, too." Aven looked off at the sail, then back at Aria. He stepped closer and kissed her on the cheek. "Go on."

She went and joined Jehan, sitting next to him on the float. Aven shifted to the other side of the canoe to balance their weight, and watched as Jehan reached down and did something. Aven knew what was happening — there were nets underneath the deck, where they could store things that wouldn't be damaged by exposure to water. Jehan was holding the nets that ran underneath the deck open so that Aria could crawl in. Then he'd join her. Once Aleia and Aven were done with the Fire ship, and were on their way, Jehan and Aria would be able to crawl out the other side of the net, and onto the hull float on the other side.

Once Jehan and Aria were out of sight, Aleia looked at Aven.

"Put the swords away," she said. "When they stop us, let me do the talking. Be as polite as you would be to your grandmother. Understood?"

"Yes, Ama."

The ship grew closer quickly, and Aven could soon clearly see the men onboard. Many of them seemed to be pointing at the canoe. A small boat was lowered into the water, and men started to row. Aleia guided the canoe toward them, and let out the sail as they drew alongside. One of the men rose, rocking with the small boat, then stepped onto the canoe. He wore more insignia on his coat than the others, more shiny emblems, which seemed to indicate that he was in command.

"You're in strange waters," he said. "Where are you from, and where are you going?"

"Good passage, Commander. I am Jisa, from Arana's canoe," Aleia answered. "This is my son, Othi. We're sailing to Forge to trade pearls for metal tools and cooking gear." She looked back at Aven. "It's past time to see this one wed. Metal tools might bait the line."

"Ama!" Aven groaned, and the men in the boat laughed.

"He's pretty enough," one of them called. "I'll take him!"

Aven turned and stared in shock at his mother. She folded her arms and looked coolly at the man. "I don't think you'd be able to give me granddaughters," she finally answered. The laughter got louder, more raucous, and the man who'd made the comment laughed the loudest.

"Free passage isn't free," the commander said, his voice mild.

Aleia nodded, looking up at him and smiling. "Of course not," she agreed. "What price do you set, Commander?"

For a moment, the commander looked thoughtful. Then he looked Aleia up and down, a predatory expression on his face that made Aven nervous. Finally, he waved one hand. "Show me these pearls you'll be trading."

"Of course," Aleia repeated. "Othi?"

Aven went to the deck shelter and brought out one of the baskets of pearls. The other two had been hidden away by Jehan, and Aven had no idea where they'd been secreted. He brought the basket to the commander, who arched a brow.

"Beautiful," he murmured, and ran his fingers through the collection of pearls. "Find me a matched set, boy. Dark as you can."

"How many in the set, Commander?" Aven asked, sitting down on the deck.

"Five," the commander answered. "Two for ears, two for rings, one for throat."

Aven nodded, then looked up. "Same color and size, or just same color? Do you want smaller for the ears, and larger for the throat?"

The commander looked startled. "That's... that's a good idea. Yes."

Aven looked down at the basket, sifting through the pearls. "If it's black you're looking for, we didn't bring any of those up. I'd have been surprised if we had — they're hard to find."

"And expensive when you do find them," the commander agreed. "A single black pearl would have cost me more than my commission did."

Aven looked up at him. "I've no idea what that means. Are you giving this as a gift?"

The commander nodded. "My wife just gifted me with twin boys."

Aven smiled, and went back through the pearls, finding what he was looking for. "May I suggest a change in your plans, then?"

The commander came and crouched next to him. "What?"

Aven opened his hand. On his palm lay a pair of dark pearls, green-blue as the night-time sea, and as alike as twins. "These," he said, holding his hand out to the commander. "Twin pearls, for twin boys?"

The commander looked at the two pearls, then at Aven. "You've a good head on you, Othi. I like this." He took the two pearls from Aven's palm and tucked them away. "Good sailing, Water lady. And good luck with finding your son a bride. He'll make a good husband to someone."

"Thank you," Aleia said. She looked pleased. "Othi, once the commander and his men are clear, take us away."

The commander and his men cast off, and rowed back to the ship. Once they were clear, Aven took the lines and guided the canoe past them and away. To his surprise, the commander waved at them as they passed.

"That wasn't so bad," he said. "Should I be worried or relieved?"

Aleia sighed. "You shouldn't expect it to be that good again. Very nice with the pearls, by the way."

Aven smiled. "Thank you. When can Fa and Aria come up?"

"Once we're well clear of the ship. You can be certain they're watching us."

THEY ENCOUNTERED THE next ship with the dawn. Again, Aleia greeted the officer courteously, explaining the reason for their trip south. This commander openly leered at Aleia, then suggested that perhaps they could better discuss the cost of safe passage on board his ship. He took Aleia in his small boat, leaving two of his men on the canoe with Aven.

Aven watched his mother sail away, then turned to the men. "How long do you think they'll be gone?" he asked.

One of the sailors spat over the side. "An hour, maybe?"

Aven's stomach twisted, and he hoped his father wasn't listening. He nodded. "Would you mind if I went into the water, then? To hunt? We hadn't eaten yet."

The sailors looked at each other, then the first one nodded. "Go ahead. What are you hunting, anyway?"

Aven shrugged. "I don't know these waters. I'll have to see what's down there. Unless there's something in particular that's good eating?"

The sailor frowned slightly. "You ever hunt snaps?"

"No."

"They're about so big." The sailor held his hands apart, and Aven whistled. "And they're red."

Aven nodded. "All right. I'll look for snaps. One for us, two for you?" He glanced at the ships. "How many mouths are over there, anyway?"

The sailors looked at each other again. "Three. You'll need three for us, at least."

Aven nodded and went to fetch his short, barbed spear. "All right. I'll see what I can catch." He dove off the canoe without bothering to take his kilt off. He wasn't too worried about the sailors searching the canoe — it was something they'd expected, and they'd planned for it. What was in the deck shelter were things that they could afford to lose, and the compartments were hard to find if you didn't know to look for them.

He resurfaced under the canoe, catching on to the net. His father pointed toward the other ship and arched a brow. Aven nodded, and saw the grim expression on Jehan's face. His father nodded, then made a shooing gesture. Aven grinned, reached out and touched Aria's hand, then dove deep to hunt.

Snaps were easily larger than the sailor had indicated, and surprisingly easy to hunt. Aven brought up five, tossing the large fish onto the deck to the exclamations of the sailors. When Aven pulled himself out of the water, one of the two sailors offered him a hand, taking the spear and putting it back where Aven had taken it from.

"You can't talk yet, right?" he said, coming back and crouching next to Aven. He looked young — no more than fifteen, and as wide-eyed and curious as a young seal. "I remember hearing that. That Waterborn can't talk when they have tails. That they trade their voices for gills." Aven nodded. The sailor looked at him curiously. "I'm Jac," he said. "I've never met a Waterborn before." He studied Aven for a moment. "Do you mind if I watch? Or is it a private thing?"

"Jac, stop pestering!" the other sailor shouted. He was sitting near the edge of the canoe, cleaning one of the snaps.

Jac frowned and looked back over his shoulder. Then he looked at Aven. "Am I pestering?"

Aven shook his head. He smiled, wondering how long it would be before his mother returned. Would she return? He looked past Jac toward the ship. There was no sign of the small boat.

Jac followed his gaze and nodded. "Oh, she'll be fine," he said. "Don't worry. The commander won't hurt her."

Aven swallowed. His change seemed to be taking forever this time. He coughed, and tried his voice. "Thank you. I don't mind you watching."

Jac laughed. "That was quick!"

"Voice comes back first," Aven said. "Doesn't sound right though. Not at first. But once the gills close, the voice starts coming back."

"And the rest follows," Jac said, nodding. "That's really interesting! Hey, may I ask you a question?"

Aven glanced at the other sailor, who shook his head and sighed, looking like a long-suffering older sibling. Aven looked back at Jac. "I might not answer."

"That's fine. It's personal. It's just..." To Aven's surprise, Jac's face turned red. "Your..." his voice pitched lower. "Your thing. Your cock. Does it change, too?"

Aven blinked, for a moment too surprised to answer. "It...no. It doesn't change."

Jac's face grew even more red. "I... I was wondering, see. How do you piss, when you're down there. When you've got a tail. And you didn't take your kilt off, so I couldn't see. And I figured, doesn't hurt to ask, right?"

Aven licked his lips and nodded. "It's still there," he said slowly, noticing that the other sailor now appeared to be listening intently. "It's... there's a pouch, in my tail, when I change."

"So you can just stick it out?" Jac asked, and laughed. "Like in trousers?"

"I've never worn trousers," Aven said. "I wouldn't know."

"It's like trousers," the other sailor said. "Jac, you finished embarrassing yourself yet? They're coming back."

Facing Aven, Jac rolled his eyes. "Yeah, I guess so. Thanks, Othi." He rose, cocked his head to the side. "You've got feet again."

Aven nodded and slowly stood up, feeling the water dripping from his kilt onto his feet. "You're welcome. We're even, by the way. You're the first Fireborn I've met."

"You can change into a fish, though. I can't change into a fire mouse," Jac said. "Can't do anything interesting like you can."

"You are interesting," Aven assured him as the small boat drew alongside the canoe. "Thanks for keeping me company. Enjoy the snaps."

Aleia seemed to be unharmed, and directed Aven to take them away once the boat was clear of the canoe. Jac waved cheerfully as the boat moved off.

"Made a friend?" Aleia asked dryly.

"He was nice enough," Aven answered, taking the lines. "Are you all right, Ama?"

"He was nice enough," she repeated his words. "As bribes go, it wasn't the worst. But I'd rather not have to do that again."

Aven nodded, tugging the lines and angling the sail to catch the wind. The sooner they were away, the better. He looked up, seeing birds overhead.

"Are we near land, Ama?"

"Closer than we were. Why?"

"Birds." Aven nodded upward. "First ones I've seen in a while."

"You'll see more of them as we get closer." Aleia looked around. "I'm going to swim. I want to wash their stink off me. I'll follow the canoe." She dove over without waiting for an answer, leaving Aven alone with his thoughts. Every so often, he glanced back at the ship that was growing smaller by the minute. When could he signal and tell the others that they could come up? How soon?

In the end, it was Aleia who brought them up, climbing back onto the canoe as Jehan and Aria clambered out of the nets and onto the deck. Without a word, Jehan went to Aleia and picked her up, carrying her into the deck shelter. Aria came to join Aven.

"He asked that we leave them alone," she said softly. "We could hear what happened, so he knows."

Aven nodded. "The next time—" He faltered. Shook his head. "What if it's me they want the next time?"

"I wouldn't ask that of you, Aven," Aria said, resting her hand on his back. He nodded.

"I know. You wouldn't have asked that of my mother, either. But if that's the coin we have to pay..." he swallowed. "I'll pay."

THEY SAW NO SHIPS THE entire next day, which left Aven feeling nervous, unable to settle with his knotwork, sitting on the edge of the canoe, watching as the mountains in the distance grew closer, constantly glancing at the horizon, searching for sails that weren't there. He could tell he wasn't the only one. Aleia was unusually quiet, working the lines with a single-minded intensity that wouldn't have been out of place in the middle of a raging storm, but seemed too much for the quiet seas that they sailed. Jehan took up his carving, something he did rarely, mostly because he wasn't very good at it.

It was Aria who broke the silence. She'd spent most of the day sitting near the mast, curled up with her knees drawn to her chest, her wings wrapped around herself. She looked miserable.

"I'm sorry," she said, her voice just loud enough to carry over the sound of the waves and the wind. "I wish you'd never found me."

They all stared at her. Jehan set aside the lumpy piece of wood he'd been poking with his knife. "Aria, it's not your fault—"

"You wouldn't be here if it wasn't for me," she answered. "You would be safe. As safe as you could have been." She looked up, then got to her feet. "How far are we from land?" she asked.

"We'll reach Forge tomorrow, if the wind holds," Aleia answered. She pointed at the horizon. "That's the Smoking Mountain. Forge is at the base."

"I didn't ask how far we were from Forge. I asked how far we were from land. Could I fly that far?" She looked around at them. "I'll take the Diadem and the gems. I'll release Aven from his place as my Companion. You can go home and be safe."

"No," Aven said. "I'm not leaving you. If you fly to land, I'll follow." He got up and went to stand in front of Aria, meeting her eyes. "I'm not leaving you," he repeated.

"I don't want you to get hurt!" she protested. "I don't want any of you to get hurt! Or..." he voice trailed off. "Or killed. You could be killed."

"And if you leave us, do you think they won't hurt you? Kill you?" Aven asked. "Together, we have a chance." He glanced back at his parents, then met Aria's eyes again, resting his hands on her shoulders. "We'll make it through."

"And if we don't?" she asked.

"Then we'll have tried," Aleia said, her voice firm. "Now, you should get some sleep. It's getting late, and tomorrow you'll probably be spending some time under the canoe. Sleep will do us all good."

AVEN SUSPECTED THAT his parents intended to sail all night. He said nothing, though. If he had said something, then Aria would have insisted on staying up and helping. And worrying. So he stayed quiet, taking Aria into the deck shelter and letting her curl up against him, her cheek pillowed on his shoulder. He rubbed her lower back until his arm felt as if it was going to fall off, until he felt her grow subtly heavier as she relaxed into sleep. He wasn't certain when he followed her, but his next awareness was of someone shaking him. He blinked, looking up to see his father looking down at him.

"Sails," he whispered. "Wake Aria."

Aven nodded. As Jehan moved away, Aven gently shook Aria's shoulder. "Wake up, Aria. You need to go into the net."

Aria grumbled, then must have realized what Aven had said because she jerked. "The net?"

"There's a sail. Fa just woke me up."

They rolled out of the shelter together. It was late enough to be early — the air tasted like it was trying to decide if it was still night or if it was time to be morning. They were close enough to shore that Aven could see lights, far in the distance. Closer, far too close, he saw lanterns hanging from a ship.

"That's really close!" he breathed.

"They can't see us. We have no lights," Aleia murmured. "But we can't wait any longer. I may have let it go too long."

Aria hugged Aven's arm, then kissed his cheek and hurried to the hull float where Jehan was waiting. Neither of them stripped; they just slipped into the water. A few minutes later, Aven heard the soft knocking that told them that Jehan and Aria were in place.

"Ama, why did you wait so long?" he asked, going to stand with Aleia.

"I thought we might slip past them in the dark. We're close, Ven. Close enough that I got careless. I should have stayed further out until dawn.

"And they saw us?" Aven looked up at the ship, saw a light lowering down to the water. A lantern on a small boat. "How?"

"I don't know," Aleia admitted. "You know what to do by now?"

"Yes, Ama."

The lantern grew closer, revealing that the boat had only three passengers. One of them was wearing a uniform with shiny braid that glinted in the lantern light, far more braid than any of the officers that they'd seen already.

"Ho, the canoe!" he called. "I am Ursol. Would you be Jisa?"

Aleia went very still, looking up at Aven for a moment before stepping forward. "I am. How do you know my name?"

"Captain Tiran sent messenger birds on ahead, to smooth your journey. My captain would like to meet you, if you'd be so kind? And your son. We've had a wonderful report about your most courteous son." Ursol was close enough that they could see him smiling. "Four snaps for the *Wind Runner*? That was wonderful hunting. My captain was very impressed."

"Thank you," Aven said automatically. "Ama?"

Aleia swallowed, her face looking oddly pale in the lantern light. She nodded. "We shouldn't keep the captain waiting." She looked down. "But what about our canoe?"

"Boni here is half Water. He knows his way around a canoe." Ursol indicated one of the two men in the boat. "He'll keep your craft safe, and we won't keep you long."

Aleia nodded slowly. "Othi," she said softly. "Let out the sail. Tie it down, so it doesn't flap."

"Yes, Ama," Aven said. He hurried to the mast and started doing as he was told. A moment later, a young man was helping him.

"Boni," the stranger said. "Good sailing, cousin. Straps are where?"

"Good sailing," Aven answered automatically. Then, too stunned to try and dissemble, he added. "Basket in the shelter." Boni nodded and went to the shelter, coming back with the handful of cords that they used to tie the sail down.

"Don't worry, Mother," Boni said, bowing slightly. "I'll keep her as neat as my own mother's canoe."

"Mind that you do," Aleia said, her voice crisp. "Othi?"

They stepped down into the little boat. Aven watched as the remaining sailor started rowing, guiding them back to the ship. Close up, it looked very similar to the one where they'd found Aria.

"How long, do you think?" Aleia asked.

"Oh, not long," Ursol answered with a smile. "We were expecting you hours ago, so the captain hasn't slept yet. He'll pay his regards, and you'll be done." He glanced at Aven. "I was hoping you'd come later, myself. Snaps are good eating, and hard to catch from shipboard."

Aven shrugged. "Sorry, but you can't argue with the wind."

"True enough," Ursol agreed. "All right. Here we go. Don't make any sudden movements. You might not mind a swim, but I do." He reached out and grabbed a dangling line, attaching it to the prow of the prow of the boat. Another two lines were attached to the corners of the stern, and the boat lurched as it was raised out of the water, jerking gently until it came level with the deck. Ursol stepped out, then turned and offered Aleia his hand. She stepped on board the ship, and Aven followed her, looking around at the ship. It felt as if there were people everywhere. Was that normal on a ship like this? In the middle of the night? He didn't know.

Ursol led them to a door. He knocked, then knocked again. Then he opened the door and bowed, gesturing for them to enter. Aven followed his mother into a room lit only by a single lamp turned low. When the door closed behind them, he could see barely anything. But he heard a squeak, and a scraping of metal as the screw on the lamp was turned. The light grew, revealing a man behind the table, his features now clearly illuminated. He was taller than Aven, and heavier. He was older by a good deal, and his sandy brown hair was fading to silver in places. His eyes were an odd, pale gold, and there was something familiar about his features. At the sight of him, Aleia stopped in her tracks.

"Hello, Aleia," he said softly. "It's been a very long time, hasn't it?"

Aleia cursed. "You knew. The whole time?"

"I suspected," the man answered. "Which is why I'm here. Now, introduce me to your son, and tell me where to find that brother of mine."

Aven suddenly realized who this man was. Knew, and was terrified.

"You're Mannon," Aven blurted. Then he actually registered the rest of what Mannon had said. "Brother?"

CHAPTER NINE

"HUSH, VEN," ALEIA MURMURED. Mannon just chuckled.

"They never told you?" he asked. He waved toward a pair of chairs. "Sit. Both of you. We can talk like adults." He reached for a bottle on the table, poured two glasses full, then studied Aven for a moment before pouring a third. "Sit, Aleia!"

Aleia angled her head to the side and studied Mannon with a calm, cool gaze. Then she nodded and went to one of the chairs. Lacking anything else he could do, Aven followed her, and sat by her side. Mannon came over with two of the glasses, passing one to each of them.

"Fireberry mead," he said. "I seem to recall you liked it once, Aleia." Mannon returned to the table, leaned back against it, and picked up the third glass. He sipped from his, then nodded. "A fine-looking boy, Aleia."

"I think so," Aleia agreed with a small, chilly smile.

"His name isn't Othi, though." It wasn't a question.

"No, it's Aven," Aven answered.

Mannon nodded slowly. "That's better. Aven suits you better. Now, since your parents haven't bothered to give you your complete bloodline, let me fill in the gaps. Your mother, I presume, has given you the entire lineage on the Water side of your blood?" Aven nodded, and Mannon smiled. "I thought as much. On your father's side, though. That's probably a mystery to you. Did you know you were the great grandson of the Firstborn? Firstborn Riga. His son was Elcam. Elcam sired two sons, a good many years apart. By Airborn Falla, he sired... well, me. And by the Earthborn healer Pirit, he sired a rather scruffy little healer named Jhansri. Who never liked his full name, so he went by Jehan." He sipped his mead. "Fireborn are very good at keeping track of bloodlines. That's the bloodline inscribed in the *Book of Silver*. Jehan was claimed as the son of Elcam—"

"But Healer Pirit swore under oath to Firstborn Tirine that she couldn't be sure of that. She swore that she was never certain of the parentage of any of her children, and among the Earth tribe, bloodlines are counted through the mother line, not the father." Aleia smiled up at Mannon.

"Even the Firstborn yields to the writings of the *Book of Silver*," Mannon countered. "So that's what counts." He looked at their cups. "You've neither of you drunk anything."

Almost automatically, Aven put the cup to his lips and sipped. The liquid was sweet, and burned in his throat and chest. He blinked and looked down at it. "I don't think I like it," he said softly, then looked up at Mannon. "No discourtesy meant, but it's..."

"Nothing you've had before," Mannon finished. "I understand. Set it down, lad." He put his own glass down, folded his arms over his chest, and gave Aven a frank look. "I've heard impressive things about you, Aven."

"Mannon—"

Mannon continued as if Aleia hadn't spoken. "Polite to a fault, even when asked some very impertinent questions. An excellent hunter. No navigator tattoos, though. Is that lack of skill, or some other reason?"

"He's not part of this, Mannon," Aleia snapped. Mannon grinned.

"There's the temper!" he laughed. "I'd wondered. He is part of this, Aleia. Whether you like it or no." He glanced at Aven again, then back at Aleia. "Give him to me."

"What?"

Aleia's shocked voice echoed in the cabin, and Aven heard something moving in the darkness. He tried to see what it might be, but couldn't make out what was beyond the circle of light cast by the lamp. It was important, whatever it was. He could feel it. But he couldn't go looking for it. Not now, not as Mannon raised his hand in a gesture that was meant to be pacifying.

"Not in any sordid way, Aleia. I have everything that I could possibly desire, save one thing." He looked at Aven again. "A proper heir. Think on it. He could follow me to the throne—"

"A throne that was never yours," Aleia interrupted.

"I hold it now. That makes it mine," Mannon said with a shrug. "I continue to hold it. That makes it mine. I intend to continue to hold it. And I'm offering to make your son my heir, so that it can be his when I finally die. Is that so outrageous a request?"

"It's not yours," Aven said, hearing the shiver in his voice. "It was never yours. You can't give something that isn't yours."

"Didn't you hear me, Aven?" Mannon asked. "I hold it. That makes it mine."

"Where's Axia's Crown, then?" Aven asked. Mannon's eyes widened.

"You've taught him well," he said slowly. He looked up at the sounds of a commotion outside the room. "I may not have the crown, but I will shortly have the Diadem." He turned toward the door as it swung open, and armed men escorted Jehan and Aria into the room. Mannon looked at them both, then sniffed. "Where were they?"

"In the storage nets under the canoe," Boni answered. "Took me a bit to figure it out. And there's no signs of any gems other than the one that he's wearing and this one." He held up Aleia's water gem. "No Diadem."

Mannon frowned. "No..." his voice trailed off, and he turned and looked at Aria. "Well, then. Aria, Milon's daughter. Where is it?"

Aria shook her head slowly. "I do not know. They were taken from me when I was caught. They were locked in a box, as I was. What happened to the box, I do not know. Perhaps it was burned?"

"That would be unfortunate," Mannon murmured. "But not impossible to deal with." He looked at Jehan and smiled. "Brother. No kind words for me, Jhansri? It's been a long time."

Aven watched as the color drained from Aria's face, and an angry flush rose in his father's. "You are nothing to me," Jehan growled. "You murdered Milon."

Mannon blinked. He raised his right hand. "I swear, I never did. I did not murder Milon."

"Semantics," Jehan snapped. "You ordered him killed. It's the same thing. Do not call me brother. I'll have none of you."

Mannon just laughed. "The *Book of Silver* says otherwise. Now, Jehan, be reasonable. I know you can be. I had intended to make your son my heir—"

"I refuse," Aven interrupted. He rose and went to Aria's side, took her cold hand in his. "I will not be yours. I'm spoken for."

Mannon's eyes widened, and he nodded. "I see," he said. "Well, it doesn't have to change, you know. You could still have her, if you take your place as my heir." His face went slack, his voice flat as he continued, "Or you and your parents could vanish, and I'll have her make me a new heir."

Aven went cold. He glanced at Aria, who looked terrified. He saw her mouth move, but no sound came out.

"Mannon, it doesn't have to be like this," Aleia said quickly, stepping forward. "You searched the canoe. You saw we don't have the Diadem or the gems. We have no way of proving that Aria went to the Temple. Give us our canoe back, and we'll go out to the deep waters. You'll never see us again." She smiled slightly. "We're not a threat to you. How could we be?"

Mannon shook his head. "You, my dear Aleia, were always a threat to me."

"All we ever wanted was to live our lives, Mannon," Jehan said. He stepped forward. "And that's all we want now. Listen to Aleia. You know she's right. We'll take Aria back out onto the deep waters, and you'll never see us again." He held his hand out. "I give you my word."

Mannon arched a brow. "You expect me to believe that?"

"You haven't heard from us for twenty-five years," Jehan pointed out. "We really were coming south to get metal tools and cookware for wedding gifts. There's a small fortune in pearls on that canoe." He grinned and nodded toward Aven and Aria. He offered his hand again. "You take half the pearls, resupply us for the sail home, and we'll leave. You'll never hear from us again."

Mannon looked skeptical. He studied Jehan for a moment, then Aria and Aven. He sniffed. "So, Aven? Is this true?"

"Ama says it's time I was married," Aven answered. It was true, after all. She'd said it to every sailor they'd met on the trip south. He smiled down at Aria. "We haven't built a canoe yet, but we survived teaching her to swim. I think we'll be all right."

Mannon barked out a laugh. "Teaching her to swim? That's your idea of courtship?"

"It worked," Aria said. She leaned into Aven's side, and he could feel her trembling. "Can we go? I don't have what you want. I just want to go home now."

Mannon looked back at Jehan, who still had his hand out. "You leave. And I never see you again. That's the deal?"

"And a half fortune of pearls," Jehan added.

Mannon frowned. Then he nodded and took Jehan's hand. His eyes widened, and he gasped. His knees buckled; Jehan moved like lightning, catching Mannon before he hit the ground, wrenching his arm up and behind him, and catching the back of his neck in his other hand. Mannon howled in pain.

"Now, brother," Jehan growled. "You're going to do exactly what I say—"

"Jehan!" Aleia gasped, getting to her feet. Aven went cold. He knew what was happening. What his father was doing. He was using his power to cause pain — a complete desecration of the healing arts, but one that might save all their lives.

"Leave it, Guppy!" Jehan snapped. "We're walking out of here, Mannon. You're going to order your men to let us pass. We're all going to go down in that little boat, and you're coming with us on the canoe. Once we're clear of any ranged weapons you might have on this thing, you'll be getting back in your boat. Understand?"

"Yes," Mannon hissed through gritted teeth. Then, he gasped again.

"Incentive," Jehan said. "I can keep you dancing on the edge of agony. Now walk." He pushed Mannon forward, past Aria and Aven. Aven went to follow his father, only to stop with his mother's hand on his arm.

"Once we're out in the air," she said, her voice quiet. "Get off this ship. The both of you. Get to Forge. We'll meet you there."

"Ama!" Aven whispered.

"Do as I say," Aleia said, her voice firm. "Aria, take to the skies. It's dark enough still that they won't be able to see you to shoot. Aven, swim deep and stay there. Do not surface. Do you understand me?"

Aven met her eyes. He nodded, feeling cold and sick all at once. "Yes, Ama," he said, and heard Aria echo his words.

Aleia smiled. She tugged Aven down to kiss his cheek, then kissed Aria. "Now do as I said. As soon as we're clear." She met Aven's eyes. "Don't forget your bag."

Aven nodded, running his hand over the strap that crossed his chest. "Be careful, Ama."

"As we can be," she said. "Now go." She turned and followed Jehan and Mannon to the door, leaving Aven and Aria to follow. Aria clung to Aven's hand, and he looked at her and tried to smile. It didn't work.

"I'll see you at Forge," she whispered.

"Where you fly, I'll follow," he whispered back. She squeezed his hand. Then they were outside, and she let him go. She ran two steps, spread her wings, and launched. Aven ran after her, vaulting over the ship railing and diving deep.

He hit the water hard, feeling his chest ache as the change began. He used his arms to pull himself farther down in the dark water, trying to put some distance and depth between him and the ship. By the time his fins had unfurled, he was far below where a spear or harpoon could reach him, and out of range of arrows. He hoped. He twisted, looking upwards. There were lights playing over the surface of the water above him. Lights that shouldn't have been there. He stared for a moment, then decided that he needed to defy his mother — he had to surface. He had to see. He kicked, and shot upwards toward the light.

He broke the surface into the darkest levels of damnation. Fire flickered and danced on the surface of the water. That had been the lights he'd seen. For a moment, Aven couldn't imagine what was happening. Then he saw the outline at the heart of the flames, and realized what had happened.

The canoe had somehow caught fire. How didn't matter. What did matter was that there had indeed been inferno oil soaked into the deck timbers that they'd had no time to replace. The entire canoe was ablaze, and the fire was spreading over the surface of the water. He could hear sailors shouting as they rushed to get the great ship underway, out of reach of the flames. Aven couldn't make out one figure from the next as they ran around the deck, couldn't see his parents anywhere. Were they away? Were they safe?

Then, over the shouting of the sailors, over the crackling and popping of the flames, over sounds of wind and water, a woman's voice pierced like a blade.

"Ven! Go!"

Aven dove, his mother's voice ringing in his ears. He had no idea where she was, but she had to have still been in her land form, in order to shout at him. That meant...

Mother of them all, she'd still been on the ship! His parents had both still been on the ship — there was no way that Aleia would have remained behind if Jehan had gone. And if the ship was underway, that meant that Mannon had control again.

Mannon had them both.

And there was nothing Aven could do to help them. He had no weapons — those had all been on the canoe. He had only the clothes on his back and the canvas carry-bag that contained a diadem, four gems, and a single dark-gray pearl that suddenly didn't seem nearly as important as it once had been. He knew that he should surface, find Aria. If he waited for dawn, he'd be seen. But he needed to at least wait out the fire. So he stayed deep, watching as the flickering light from the surface faded away. Only then did he rise up once more, and break the surface.

The moon was near the horizon, painting the sea with a silver-gray glow. The water was as calm and smooth as glass, and as unbroken. There was no sign of the ship, or of the canoe. Aven stayed where he was for a moment, turning to search. Then he set out for shore, trying to find a place where he could hide and change without being seen.

He came ashore amidst rocks on a beach that was within sight of the walls of Forge. It was the only cover he could find, and not very good cover at that. He hid behind the largest rock, watching as the sky grew lighter, feeling terrifyingly vulnerable. His father had taught him that this was when he was at the most risk – when he was in the heart of the change, neither sea nor land, but something between. It was something that he'd never really understood before. Now he knew it in his bones and hated it. It seemed to be hours before he could once more stand on his own feet. He climbed out of the rocks and looked up at the sky — it was that not quite light, not quite dark that just preceded the sun rising. He needed to go. He needed to get to Forge.

He started walking, feeling the ground turn from sand to rocks under his feet, then to a smooth surfaced road. After a while, he started feeling as if there was something missing. He looked around, puzzled. He could hear the wind through the trees, and the sound of birdsong. What was missing? He turned in a slow circle, and it was when he looked back the way he'd come that he realized what was missing. He could no longer hear the sea. He swallowed, looking out at the water.

"Aven!"

There was a wild flutter of wings as he turned, and Aria hit him, hard enough to knock him off his feet. They landed in a tangle of arms and legs, and he gasped as the air was knocked out of him. She didn't seem to notice — she clung to him, crying, and he put his arms around her, listening to her until he could make out words in the sobs..

"... I couldn't see and I flew until I found land and I landed and I hid until it was light enough that I could come and find out. I was terrified I wouldn't find you," she gasped and sniffled. Then, to Aven's complete shock, she grabbed him and kissed him solidly on the lips. "You're all right," she whispered. "I'm fine now, now that I know you're all right." She looked down at him, and frowned. "Except that I knocked you down. Are you hurt?"

"I'm fine," Aven said. "Let me up. We need to keep moving."

Aria got off of him and helped him to his feet. "Move where?" she asked, taking his arm. Then she looked around. "Aven, where are they?"

Her words cut like a knife. "I don't know," he said quietly. "I... I don't think they got away. I think he has them."

Aria gaped at him, "No. Oh, no! Aven, what do we do?"

"Get to Forge," Aven answered. "Then... I don't know. Find Memfis." He put his arm around her waist, holding her close. "We do what we were told. Then... we'll figure out the next step then."

She looked up at him. "Aven—"

"I promised to keep you safe," he said. "I'm going to do that." He glanced back at the sea. "I can't think about anything else yet. Not until we're safe."

He turned toward Forge, and they started walking. He couldn't make himself stop touching her, stop looking at her. He kept having to check, to make sure that she was real, even though he could feel her in his arms, her body pressed to his side.

"I'm not going anywhere," she said softly. "We might be faster if you held my hand instead of all of me."

Aven swallowed, looked at her, and nodded; he let her go, and took her hand as they walked. It did help with their progress, and the walls of Forge grew larger as they got closer. Which raised the question of what they were going to do once they were in the city?

"Have you ever been in a city like this?" he asked Aria.

"The Solstice Fair village, once," she answered. "It's not nearly this big."

Aven frowned. He was about to ask Aria if she had any ideas when he heard something rattling and rhythmic. It was getting closer.

"Come on. We need to get off the road," he said. He looked around, saw a stand of small, scrubby trees, and tugged Aria's hand. "We might be able to hide there."

They ran from the road and hid in the trees, just as the source of the noise came into view. To Aven, it looked like a box on wheels, drawn by a gray, furry beast. A horse? He wondered. He'd never seen one, but his father had told him about them. There were two men sitting in the box — a man who looked to be a little younger than Aven, and an older man with dark skin.

"This is it," the older man announced as he did something to make the box stop rolling. "They're here."

"You're sure?" the younger man asked. "I mean, I know you saw it, and you're never wrong about that. But are you sure it's today?"

The older man nodded, handing the lines to the younger one and getting out of the box. He took curved staves from the back and came around, facing the stand of trees. He cocked his head to the side, then raised his voice. "I know you're there. Aven, son of Aleia. Aria, daughter of my Milon. Come out."

Aven looked at Aria, who was staring back at him. Who...?

"Memfis," he whispered. "That's Memfis!"

CHAPTER TEN

ARIA STARED AT HIM. "How can that be Memfis? How can he know we're here?" Then she blinked. "Oh. I am an idiot!"

"Why?" Aven whispered.

"He's a Smoke Dancer!" She sounded almost giddy. "He saw us in the smoke!" She got to her feet before Aven could stop her. So he scrambled up and followed her out of the trees and back toward the road.

Up close, Memfis looked older than he seemed at a distance. He was, Aven thought, older than either of his parents. He looked startled when he saw them. No, when he saw Aria. As she drew closer, he smiled.

"You have his eyes," he said. "You're definitely his daughter." He looked at Aven, and grinned. "Oh, and you're Jehan all over again."

"You're Memfis?" Aven asked. "My parents said you would help us."

"Your parents were right," Memfis said. "Now, we need to get you to a safe place before anyone comes looking to see what the fire was last night. And I don't want anyone knowing you're here, so you two get into the back of the cart. We'll make sure no one sees you, and we'll take you someplace safe."

"And," the young man called out. "Since I'm apparently not worth a mention, hello there. Nice to meet you both. I'm Owyn."

Aven couldn't help it. He laughed. There was something about Owyn, something compelling. Aven could have sworn that he'd known the other man forever, for all that they hadn't even been introduced properly yet. There was something in his smile, in his eyes....

"And that's Owyn," Memfis added, breaking into Aven's reverie. "My apprentice. He's an idiot, but only on special occasions." His voice was very fond, and Owyn hooted with laughter. Memfis shook his head and looked at Aven. "Quickly now. The fire in the harbor. Something to do with you?

Aven nodded. "The ship they were using to bring Aria to Mannon was also carrying inferno oil. They were going to use it here."

"What?" Owyn squawked. Memfis waved him silent.

"Some got into the timbers of the deck of the canoe," Aven continued. "We didn't have time to change them. We thought that we'd been fooling them, but they knew who we were, and they'd been luring us in." Aven looked back out to the sea. "Fa used his healing to hurt Mannon. He forced him to let us out. Ama told me and Aria to get to Forge, and that they'd meet us here. But I don't think they got off the ship. I don't know where the fire came from."

"I've not seen them in the smoke to say one way or the other," Memfis murmured. "Looks like it's just us now. Come on, now." He led them around the back of the cart, flipping back the canvas cover and revealing a sunken bed lined with straw, and filled with bundles of straw. He took the bundles out and laid them on the road. "It'll be a little bumpy, but it'll get us past the gate guards."

Aria went to get into the cart, but Aven stopped her. "How do we know you're really Memfis?" he asked.

Memfis grinned. "We used to call Aleia the Little General, but Milon would call her Guppy. She purely hated that. But she loved him, so she let it pass. She was teaching him sword dancing, and he was teaching her to use the smoke blades." He held up one of the curved staves he carried. This close, Aven could see that they were made from metal, not wood. "That help?"

Aven coughed. "Is that where Guppy came from?" he asked. "Fa calls her that."

Memfis' eyebrows rose. "She lets him?"

"He only does it when he thinks she's doing something insane." Aven looked at the cart. "To get her attention, he says. I think we're going to have to trust you, aren't we?"

"I think you'd better," Memfis agreed. "It's getting late. There will be people on the road if we stay much longer. Folks are curious about what happened in the harbor last night." He shook his head. "You've got Jehan all over your face. Your mind is Aleia all through. Come on."

Aven nodded, and turned to Aria. She smiled at him. "I could have told you we could trust them," she said, and kissed his cheek. She climbed into the back, and he followed, stretching out in the straw next to her. Memfis looked around.

"It'll be a little close in there, but it won't be for long." He tugged the canvas cover over them, and weight that must have been the bundles of straw resettled on their feet and legs.

"How did you know you could trust them?" Aven whispered. He could just barely see Aria in the light filtering through the canvas. The cart lurched, and bumped, and he winced.

"He's mine," she answered back. "Owyn. I knew him the way I knew you."

"Was that what it was?" Aven murmured. Aria pressed her hand to her mouth to cover her giggles.

"You knew him?" she asked. She still sounded giddy. "I didn't know you'd know him, too!"

"You two need to hush back there," Memfis called. "We'll be reaching the gates soon."

The road changed, grew bumpier, and Aven winced again. He reached out and took Aria's hand, and tried not to think. They'd found... well, been found by Memfis. That was as far as his plans had gone. Now what? He was suddenly deeply frightened, even more so than before. He had no idea how to live on land!

The cart swayed and slowed, and Aven heard voices.

"Out early, Fisher?"

"Saw the blaze last night, went to see if anything had washed ashore." Aven recognized Memfis' voice. "Too soon, I think."

"Might take another storm to wash up any salvage," the strange voice agreed. "Any idea what it was?

"Not a damned clue. I was going to ask the same of you."

"And you'd have gotten the same answer. Now, I didn't see you pass through."

"On account of we went out the west gate. It's closer to the shop."

"Ah. All right, go on."

The cart lurched and bumped as it started moving again, much slower than before. Aven could hear voices all around, more than he was used to hearing. More than he'd heard even when they'd gone to visit the family. He turned his head slightly and looked up at the canvas.

"Lots of people," Aria whispered. "A big place." She squeezed his hand. "Relax. We're safe."

He looked back at her. "Not yet, we're not."

By the time the cart stopped again, Aven felt as if his teeth had all been rattled right out of his head. He was also hungry and tired enough to feel his mind fogging. He wasn't sure, but he thought Aria might have fallen asleep.

He heard heavy thumping, and the weight on his legs was slowly removed. Then the canvas flipped back, and Aven blinked in the dim light of a lantern held aloft by Owyn.

"We're here," the young man said softly. "Keep your voices down, and I'll take you to the hole."

"Hole?" Aven whispered, sitting up. He looked around, but couldn't see much of the dark room. Owyn nodded.

"That's what I call it. It's a hidden room, under the forge. No one knows it's there but Mem and me. It's like a rabbit hole, you know?" He frowned. "No, you wouldn't know. It's safe, and there are beds there, and I'll get you some food."

"Where is Memfis?" Aria asked as she sat up.

Owyn nodded. "He's in the forge. People here know him as Fisher. He's a smith. Shoes horses, makes tools, that kind of thing. It's past time we got the fires hot and he does it better than I do, so he's off doing that while I see to you." Owyn grinned. "Come on. I'll show you where to sleep, and get you some food." He led them out of the dark room and into a corridor. The stone floors were cold under Aven's feet, but the lantern light wasn't bright enough for him to see much outside the circle of light.

Owyn stopped and opened a door, stepping out of sight. Then he looked back at them. "Come on. Be careful, there are steps."

It was a tiny room lined with shelves, and with one wall that opened and revealed steps leading down. At the bottom, there was another short corridor that opened into a larger room. Owyn lit a slip from his lantern, and used it to light several lamps that were scattered around the room. There were two narrow beds against the wall, a table and chairs, and another door.

"That's the privy," Owyn said, pointing at the door. "It's not much, but it's functional. I'll bring wash water after I bring the food. Then I'll have to go help Mem in the forge, so you'll be able to sleep in peace for a bit." He looked around, then smiled. "Look, this is going to sound really weird, but it's good to have you here. He's been fretting like mad about the visions. We'll figure out the next step once you're rested. Back in a few minutes with food." He hurried back down the corridor, taking the lantern with him.

"Is your head spinning yet?" Aria asked. "Because mine is spinning. This is all happening so fast!"

"I'm not sure if it's spinning because things are happening, or because I'm tired," Aven answered. He went to the table and sat down, folding his hands and staring at them. "Aria, I dove deep. I couldn't see. What happened up there?"

"To the canoe?" Aria asked. She pulled a chair around so that she could sit next to Aven. She leaned her cheek against his shoulder, and rested her hand on his folded ones. "I'm not sure. I was up high. I heard a lot of shouting once you went over the side. I couldn't see what was happening, but I did see something bright fall. One of the lamps, I think. I think burning the canoe was an accident." All at once, she went rigid. "Aven... the Diadem! The gems! They were on the canoe!" She sat up. "Can we go back? Can you dive that deep and find them?"

"I don't have to," Aven admitted. He touched the strap running across the chest. "I've had them. The whole time. Ama gave them to me before we left the island."

Aria looked both stunned and hurt. "You never told me!"

"Ama was worried you'd trade them for our safety," Aven said. Aria frowned.

"She... might have had a point," she said softly. "I am not to say anything, then?"

"We'll leave them where they are, and hidden. Until we know what our next step will be." Aven looked up at the sound of footsteps on the stairs. Owyn came back in, carrying a tray.

"Here we are. I wasn't sure what you all would eat, and Mem is with a customer, so I brought a bit of everything we had in the kitchen." He set the tray down with a heavy thump. "We've got bread, cheese, roasted eggs, fruit jam, cold roast rock hen, and berry tart. Water here, and there's a pump in the privy for more."

Aven blinked. "No fish?"

Owyn shook his head. "No. Sorry. Not many people fish around here. Try the roast, though. You might like that." He pointed to red and yellow spheres in a bowl. "Those are apples. Ever seen one?"

"No," Aven admitted. "There's nothing I recognize here. But I'll try it."

"I can help him, Owyn," Aria said. "Go help Memfis."

Owyn smiled at her. "Thank you. I'll come back later for the tray." He hurried away once more. Aria rested her chin on her hand and smiled.

"He's very different from you," she said. "I'm not sure how to compare you."

"Don't?" Aven suggested. "He's himself. I'm me. Help me choose what to try?"

"Try the roast, first," she said, and started to make a plate for him.

Aven ate slowly, trying everything that Aria had set onto his plate. The rock hen was sweet and savory, and he enjoyed it, and the eggs. This bread was much better than what he'd had in the past, especially when spread with the fruit jam. Aria ate her cheese with relish, telling Aven that it was very good. He had nothing to compare it to, so he decided to take her word for it. He also decided that it was something that he wasn't sure he'd eat again — it was rich, and coated his mouth in a way that he didn't think he liked. He ate another piece of roast to try and get the taste of the cheese out of his mouth, and drank from the jug of sweet water that Owyn had brought.

"Do you want to try and plan, or try and sleep?" Aria asked as they finished.

"Sleep," Aven answered. "We don't know enough to plan."

Aria turned and looked at the beds. "They're not big enough to share. Do you mind if we don't?"

"I don't mind," Aven said. He grimaced slightly — his stomach felt strange. "Go get some sleep."

Aria smiled and kissed him, then rose and went to one of the two beds. She lay down, her back to him. Aven sat at the table and sipped his water, trying to think. His brains felt like muddy water — he couldn't think. Sleep. He needed to sleep. He got up, feeling dizzy and slightly nauseous. Was he getting sick? If he was sick, Fa would put it right...

No. No, Fa wouldn't be putting anything right. Not now. Maybe not ever. Aven lay down on the bed, buried his face in the pillow, and cried for what felt like hours. It left him feeling drained and even more ill. He tried to settle to sleep, but the bed wasn't right. It was too soft, and it made his body ache when he lay still for too long. He finally took the blankets and put them on the floor, then lay on them, shivering and sick, until he finally fell asleep.

He wasn't sure how long he slept before he heard the clatter, and Owyn's cheerful, "Good morning!" The young man came in and stood by the table. "Well, not really morning. It's nearing dusk, if you want the truth. But you're only just getting up, so good morning!" Aven blinked blearily up at him and sat up. When he did, Owyn's eyes widened. "You don't look so good."

"What?" Aria mumbled. She pushed herself up on the bed and looked around. "Aven, why are you on the floor?"

Aven shook his head; the movement made the room spin around him, and he groaned and lay back down. Owyn stared, then turned and shouted, "Shit. Mem! Mem, come down here!" He ran back up the corridor, still shouting. Aven ignored him, closing his eyes. He felt a cool hand on his forehead, and heard Aria's voice.

"Aven? What's wrong?"

He swallowed and opened his eyes. "Not sure. Sick—"

"Oh, no," Aria murmured. She stroked his hair. "It's all right. We'll be all right. Memfis will make it right."

A few minutes later, Memfis came rushing in, followed by Owyn. The big man dropped to his knees next to Aven, pressing one hand to Aven's forehead. "Fever," he said. "Owyn, get some water."

"Right." Owyn started toward the privy door.

"Where are you going?" Memfis asked, turning slightly. His jaw dropped. "You gave them both *fresh* water?"

Owyn stopped and turned to look at Memfis. "Of course I— oh. Oh, shit. Salt water. You told me he had to have salt water."

"And what did you give him to eat?" Memfis asked. Owyn went pale. He swallowed, and seemed to hunch over on himself.

"Cheese. I gave him cheese. You told me... and I fucked it up."

"It's not broken, Owyn. We can mend it. He'll be fine. Go get the salt water," Memfis said. His voice was surprisingly gentle. "The bone broth, and add two extra measures of salt to it when you heat it. And tea."

"Right. Salt water. Broth with two extra measures of salt. Tea." Owyn repeated it over and over as he left the room.

"What is happening?" Aria demanded.

"Owyn got excited, and he forgot what I told him about the care and feeding of Waterborn," Memfis said. "Luckily, it was only the one meal. We'll get some proper salt into you, Aven, and you'll start feeling better." He sat down, took Aven's hand, and gently pinched a fold of skin on the back of his arm. "You're not too dehydrated yet. But it probably feels awful."

"Yes, sir," Aven said.

"Your mother never told you not to eat cheese, hm?" Memfis asked. "I can't imagine why she didn't. There's not a one of you Waterborn that can handle cheese or milk of any kind. You can't digest it."

"I've never seen it before," Aven said. "Hard to eat something you don't have."

Memfis snorted. "There is that. Smooth your feathers, Aria. He'll be fine. It was a mistake." He looked back. "Don't hold it against Owyn. He's got a good heart, and he's brilliant in the forge. It's just that when he gets excited, he forgets."

"Is he your son?" Aria asked.

"In everything but blood, yes." Memfis sighed. "And his story isn't mine to tell. He'll tell you, if he wants." He looked up. "That was fast."

"Figured we could start with the salt water, and by the time I get back, the broth and tea will be hot." Owyn came in with a jug and a cup. He set them on the floor next to Memfis. "Mem, can I help?"

"You are helping," Memfis said. "And yes, help me sit Aven up. And pour some of the water for him."

They both had to steady Aven to sit up, and Owyn handed him a cup. "Small sips," he warned. "It won't do you any good on the floor."

Aven grinned. "Sound like my mother." He sipped the water, the cool saltiness washing over his tongue. He closed his eyes and sighed. "Thank you."

"For what?" Owyn asked, sounding like he was going to cry. "For almost killing you?"

Aven turned. Owyn was close enough that their noses were almost touching, that Aven could see the deep gold flecks in his brown eyes. "For trying to take care of me. You made a mistake with the salt. Now you know better. We both know better." He smiled, looked down at his cup. "This isn't sea water, is it?"

"Sea salt, in water from the pump," Owyn said. "Is there not enough salt?"

"No, it's fine. It's good. It just tastes different." Aven drank more, feeling it rush all through him. "We had to keep a cask of sweet water for my father. And for Aria. I didn't even think about it when you served us sweet water last night."

"Mem told me you couldn't drink it, but I was so glad you were here—" Owyn broke off and got back to his feet. "I'm sorry. I'll go check the broth."

He left before Aven could say anything else. Memfis shook his head. "Tell me what happened?"

Aria came to sit down next to Aven. "Are you feeling better?" she asked.

Aven grimaced. "Not really." He drained the cup and went to refill it — Aria took it from him, filled it, and handed it back to him.

"You'll be better once you get some broth into you," Memfis said. "Tell me everything."

Aria nodded. "In a moment. Aven, lie down." She moved in close to him and peered into his face. "You didn't sleep, did you?"

"Not well," Aven admitted. "The bed didn't feel right."

"How do you usually sleep?" It was Owyn, coming back in with a tray. He set it on the table, and brought two mugs to Aven. "Left is tea, right is broth. My left, I mean."

"Thank you, Owyn. And how do I sleep ? Underwater, usually." Aven sipped the hot broth, sighing as the salty warmth chased itself down his throat. "Oh, that's good."

"Can't do anything about sleeping underwater," Owyn muttered. "How else?"

"When we were out in the deep, I'd sleep on the canoe—"

Owyn frowned, looking fierce and distant. Aven glanced at Memfis, who smiled.

"What's your thinking, Fire Mouse?" he called. Owyn nodded slowly.

"Underwater, he's not going to weigh anything. Can't do anything about that. It moves, don't it? The water? On the canoe, it's still going to move— I'll be back." He wheeled and ran out of the room.

"What's he doing?" Aven asked, sipping the broth, then the tea. He offered the tea to Aria, who took a sip, then made a face.

"He put salt in the tea!"

"Good. He thought of that on his own. That means he's paying attention. And as to what he's doing? He's creating," Memfis answered. "I told you. He's brilliant. But he doesn't think the way most people do. Most people, they think in lines, one thought following another. For Owyn, those lines are broken. Sometimes they overlap, and occasionally his corners have curves."

"Aven, finish those and lie down." Aria fussed at Aven until he'd drained both mugs and lay down, his head pillowed on her thigh. She started to idly stroke his hair as she told Memfis about her visions, about going to the Temple with her mother and being captured. About waking on the island with Jehan, Aleia and Aven, and knowing Aven as her own.

"We came to you, because Aleia and Jehan thought you would help us," Aria finished. "Aleia thought we could make it past all the ships if they thought it was just her and Aven. Jehan and I hid in the nets under the canoe until we were past." She paused. "Aven, how did they know?"

"Birds," Aven answered. "Mannon said there were messenger birds." He swallowed and sat up, taking another drink of broth. "Memfis, do you think they're dead? My parents?"

"No," Memfis answered. "No, because they're valuable. Mannon knows that. They're the coin he'll hold close to get what he wants." He met Aven's eyes. "Were the Diadem and the gems on the canoe?"

"No," Aven answered. "But Mannon doesn't know that. Aria didn't know that until I told her, after. I have them."

There was a metallic clatter, and Owyn reappeared, his arms loaded with a collection of things that made no sense to Aven's eyes. Memfis got to his feet.

"What do you have, Fire Mouse?"

"Need your help," Owyn answered by not answering. "I can't reach the rafters. You're tall enough."

"Reach the..." Memfis started. He stopped, then looked up. "Tell me what you need for me to do, Mouse."

Owyn handed Memfis a length of chain, then pointed. "This needs to go over that rafter."

Aven and Aria moved to sit on Aria's bed while Owyn bossed Memfis around, telling him what to do. Before too long, Aven knew what Owyn had brought.

"A hammock?" he laughed. "Owyn, that's perfect!"

"You've used one?" Owyn asked. He looked pleased at the praise, but also a little disappointed.

"Once or twice, when we visited the family canoes," Aven answered. "There wasn't a good place to put one on our island, and we only had one mast on our canoe."

Owyn nodded, looked at the half-finished work, then at Aven. "Can you sleep in one? Because I can't make you float, but I can help with the room not moving."

Aven smiled. "Yes, I'll be able to sleep in one. Thank you, Owyn."

CHAPTER ELEVEN

COCOONED IN THE HAMMOCK, Aven slept, and woke feeling more like himself. The lights in the little room were dimmed, but he could make out a figure sitting on the bed, reading by the light of one of the dimmed lamps. He frowned, then realized that whoever it was didn't have wings. Not Aria.

"Owyn?" he said, and scrubbed his hand over his face.

"Look who's awake," Owyn answered cheerfully. He closed his book and set it aside. "How are you feeling?"

"Better," Aven answered. He grabbed the sides of the hammock and swung out. "Where is Aria?"

"She woke up early, so she's up in the house. She had breakfast with Mem, and they're trying to figure out clothes for her." He reached over and turned up a lamp, then looked Aven up and down. "You could pass for Earth or Fire. The coloring is right. But there's no way we're going to be able to hide that Aria is Airborn."

Aven grinned. "The wings—"

"They do make it kind of obvious," Owyn said with a smile. "Now, you've slept the whole night around. It's past dawn. Lucky it's Respite today, so the forge is closed. No one going to come in and see we have guests. So you can come up." He got up, studied Aven again. "You might fit my clothes, at least until we get some for your measure. The shirts and the trousers will be short, though."

"I'd like to see the forge," Aven said as he followed Owyn up the stairs. "I've never seen one before."

"I'll show you." Owyn stopped at the top of the stairs. "Mind if I ask you a question?"

Aven looked at him, curious. "Not at all. What?"

"You and Aria. Are you paired?"

"Paired?" Aven repeated. "I... I'm not sure what that means."

To his surprise, Owyn turned slightly pink. "I mean... well... are you... you know." He took a deep breath, then lowered his voice. "Are you sleeping with her?"

"Oh. Oh, no." Aven looked down. "I... I'm her Companion. The Water gem is mine. That means that she might ask me. But she hasn't asked yet."

"And you haven't asked her?" Owyn asked. Aven coughed.

"That's rude, Owyn," he answered. "Women set the course."

Owyn gave an uneasy chuckle. "Oh. Oh, I see. Come on. We'll go get you some clothes first. I'll have to see about shoes for you."

"Shoes?" Aven looked down at his bare feet, then followed Owyn down the hall to another staircase and up. "I've never worn shoes."

"I didn't think so, but you can't go walking in a forge barefoot. It's not safe." Owyn opened a door and gestured for Aven to enter. It was a small room, with a narrow bed like the ones in the hidden room. There was a chest underneath the window, a desk and chair, and shelves full of books. Owyn brushed past Aven and went to the chest. "Right. This might be weird for you. Your folk don't wear trousers either, do they? On account of the change?"

"Right," Aven answered. He went to the shelves and looked at the books. "I can't change if something is keeping my legs separate."

"I understand that, but no one else wears kilts, and it's not like you're going to be doing a lot of swimming here."

Aven grimaced. He hadn't thought of that. The idea of not being able to swim was disturbing enough that he changed the subject, "I've never seen so many books, Owyn."

"You read?"

"My father taught me. But we only had three books, and all of them were on healing. And they didn't last past my fifteenth birthday. They don't last well on the water."

"Yeah, I guess they wouldn't. You're welcome to read them, so long as your hands are clean," Owyn said. "And if you think this is a lot, you should see Mem's library. It's downstairs." He laid clothes on the bed. "Now, if you need help, just ask."

Aven nodded. He took off his carry-bag and laid it on the bed, then picked up the shirt, a long sleeved thing made from soft cloth. He pulled it on over his head and smoothed it down. "Owyn, why did you ask about me and Aria?"

Owyn leaned against the wall. "Well, it's like this. She's pretty. You're pretty. And I... well, I like pretty. Pretty girls. Pretty boys. But I won't get in the way of two pretty people who are together. So if you're not together...." His voice trailed off, and he grinned. "You don't mind, do you? If I'm interested in Aria?"

Aven looked up from trying to figure out the trousers, realizing that Aria must not have said anything to Owyn. "I don't mind, Owyn. But... you're interested in me, too?"

"Yes, you," Owyn answered with a laugh. A laugh that cut off abruptly. "Unless you don't like boys looking? Maybe more than looking? Do you like boys?"

Aven smiled. "I don't mind you looking. And I like to look at girls and at boys. But I just don't have a lot of experience one way or the other. I've never had anyone who was willing to do more than look at the Mudborn before. Except Aria, and I think all she wants right now is to just look."

"Mudborn?"

"What my mother's folk call me," Aven said. "Because my father is Earthborn."

"That's mean. I don't like it." Owyn looked thoughtful. "And... what you said about Aria? I think you're wrong," he said slowly. "Water folks. You all answer to your women, right? Women set the course, you said."

"That's right." Aven frowned down at the trousers. "How do I wear these, Owyn?"

"Turn them around. The opening goes in the front." Owen scratched the back of his neck. "One leg in each tube, and mind the goods when you button them."

"Mind the— Owyn!" Aven laughed. "Right, why is it important that Waterborn follow their women?"

"Because Airborn follow their men," Owyn answered. "You should take the kilt off first. It'll get in the way. I'll turn my back, if you want."

"No, that's fine. I don't mind," Aven said. He unfastened his kilt and laid it aside, suddenly very aware that Owyn was looking. He studied the trousers once more, then sat down and pulled them on. "So, what you're saying is that you think I'm waiting for Aria to set the course—"

"And she's waiting for you," Owyn finished. "Yes, that's what I'm saying."

Aven considered it for a moment, then looked up. "I didn't know that. About the Airborn, I mean. Of course, the only person I ever met before Aria that wasn't Water was my father!"

"You really don't know anything about the other tribes?" Owyn asked. When Aven shook his head, Owyn whistled. Then he went to his shelves. "Right, then. The latest edition of Antiri's *History of the Tribes* for you. That will bring you up to speed." He took a book down.

"Who is Antiri?" Aven asked. He stood up, pulled the trousers all the way up, and buttoned them. Then he looked down at himself.

"They okay?" Owyn asked. "I know they're short, but anything else? They pinch, or anything?"

"I don't know?" Aven answered. "I'm not sure. I've never worn anything like this before. I'm not sure how it's supposed to feel." He took a few steps around the room. "Nothing hurts, if that helps?"

"It shouldn't hurt," Owyn said. He moved in front of Aven and studied him for a moment. Then he frowned. "Something's not right."

"What?"

"Hold on," Owyn looked around, then went to the chest and rummaged around in it, humming softly. He came out with a long length of cloth, which he held between his hands. He carried to over to Aven, flipped it over his hand, then wound it round Aven's throat twice. "That's better. Can't really see your gills now. You look like any Fire or Earthborn. You still need shoes." He went to the table and came back with a piece of paper. "Lift your foot, will you?"

Aven picked his foot up, and Owyn put the paper on the floor. "Step on that," he said. When Aven had done so, Owyn traced around his foot with a stump of something. "Right. You can move now." He left the page on the floor, putting his foot into Aven's footprint. Even with shoes on, his foot was smaller than Aven's. "Thought so. None of mine will fit you. Maybe Memfis will have something. Or I can take this to the cobbler and see if he's got anything ready made to fit you. All right. Breakfast for you." Aven grabbed his carry-bag and slung it over his shoulder as he followed Owyn, who stopped as they were heading toward the door. "Aven, can you eat oat porridge?"

"I don't even know what that is," Aven admitted.

"Right. We'll find you something to eat. And, to answer your question, Antiri was the fourth or fifth Firstborn, and he wrote the first accounts of the four tribes, of their customs and history. It's been updated every few Firstborn since, but not since Riga. Do you know who that is?"

Aven nodded. "If Mannon is right, that's my great-grandfather. Which reminds me. What's the *Book of Silver*?"

Owyn whistled again. "Well, aren't we fancy blood, then?" he laughed. "You don't know anything about the tribes, but you know the *Book of Silver*?"

"Mannon said that he and my father are listed there as having the same father."

Owyn nodded slowly. "Right. Let's start back a bit. Waterborn, they trace their families through the mother line, right? Earthborn do, too. Airborn, they follow the father line." He waited for Aven to nod to show that he understood. "Fireborn, though. We don't marry the way you lot do. We don't make long commitments. We pair off, and it's not permanent. And since it's not permanent, there had to be a way to keep track of who's who so you don't get kids with six heads and no ears—"

Aven burst out laughing. "Owyn, that's impossible!"

"Maybe, maybe not," Owyn continued. "So all the bloodlines are tracked in the *Book of Silver*. If you meet someone, and you want to pair up with them and have kids, you go to the Council Hall, and you ask for a pairing check. They research your bloodlines in the *Book of Silver*, see if you're related and how, and if it's safe to have children. If you're related too closely, or too recently, the pairing won't be approved. Everyone is in the *Book of Silver*." He paused, then sniffed. "Except me."

"Why not?" Aven asked. They stopped at the bottom of the stairs. Owyn looked distant for a moment.

"On account of no one knows my bloodline. I mean, I might be in there. But there's no way to know it's me, you know?" He looked at Aven. "No, you wouldn't know. After Mannon took over, there was a rebellion here in Forge. A lot of people fought back, and a lot of people died. And there were a lot of orphans left behind."

"Like you?"

"Like me," Owyn said with a nod. "I grew up on the streets, from when I was too little to know my own name, let alone my parents' names. One of the other boys, he named me Owyn. And... that's all there is to me, I guess." He shrugged. "Mem took me in a few years back. Taught me to read and how to be a person and not an animal living wild. He's teaching me to be a smith. And he's teaching me to be a Smoke Dancer, but that's in secret. It's outlawed."

"And he calls you Fire Mouse" Aven remembered. Owyn grinned.

"Yeah," he said. "He says that when I get going, I don't have the sense that the Mother gave one."

Aven stared at him. "That's as bad as Mudborn!"

"Not really," Owyn said. "He only calls me that when I'm too excited about something to think properly on anything else. Like last night." He turned slightly pink. "I am sorry about all that. I knew about the salt. I mean, Mem told me, and I took notes. But then you were here and... and you were *you*... and I wanted you to like me." He stopped, his mouth closing so fast his teeth clicked together. "Shutting up now."

Aven didn't say anything for a moment. Then he stepped closer to Owyn. Owyn was shorter than Aven, shorter than Aria, but it wasn't difficult for Aven to lean close and kiss Owyn gently on the lips. "I do like you, Owyn. And I'm not mad at you for making a mistake," he said as he straightened. Owyn, he noticed, had gone even more pink. Then he smiled.

"Right. It's a shame we need to be somewhere else right now. Come on. I'll show you the forge, and maybe dunk my head in the quench. And if we're lucky, maybe we'll see a fire mouse so you can see why it's not an insult." He held his hand out to Aven. His hand was warm, his fingers calloused. What his father would call a good hand, Aven thought as he let Owyn lead him down the hall to a door.

"This is the forge. Watch where you step," Owyn said as he opened the door and led Aven inside. "We sweep the cobbles when we close the shop every day, but sometimes a nail or a metal scrap gets past the broom. Oh, there they are!"

"There who are?" Aven asked. Then he saw the tiny shapes moving on the ground. For a moment, he thought they were balls of flame. Then he looked closer. He laughed and went to his knees for a closer look. One of the creatures came closer, clearly as curious about Aven as he was about it.

"This is a fire mouse?" Aven asked. The little thing moved even closer, and he could see its button-bright eyes, and the long tail. "It's not really on fire, is it?"

"No," Owyn said. He crouched next to Aven. "They just glow like that. There are six of them that live in the forge. We've got a few in the kitchen, in the firebox of the stove. They're in any place where there's a fire. They like the heat. And they're curious. They're into anything new. Best way to catch a fire mouse is to put a new box on the ground. They're in it in a minute. That's why Mem calls me Fire Mouse. I do the same thing."

Aven studied the little animal, then laid his hand flat on the ground. A moment later, he had a handful of flame-colored fur. He smiled as the mouse sniffed his skin, tiny claws scratching his palm. "She's lovely," he murmured, stroking the mouse's back with one gentle finger. "She's so delicate."

"How did you know it's a she? I mean, she is, but how did you know?" Owyn asked. "And you're good. I couldn't get them to come onto my hand the first time."

"Fa says I have the Earthborn way with animals," Aven answered absently. "What do they eat?"

"Insects, mostly. That's why we don't mind them in the kitchen." Owyn offered his finger to the mouse in Aven's hand. She sniffed him, then hopped onto his palm. "This is Trinket. She's the bold one. Also my favorite, and she knows it." Aven grinned, watching as the mouse climbed up Owyn's sleeve, then down into the pocket of his shirt. Owyn looked down at her. "Oh, you're coming with us?" he asked. Then he got to his feet and held his hand out to Aven. "Come on. You need to eat. And we need to see what they've decided."

Aven got up and looked around. "I'd like to see this when you're working," he said. "To see what you do."

"Not without shoes you don't," Owyn answered. "Maybe tomorrow. We'll see what the plans are. Mem and Aria were in the kitchen, last I looked."

CHAPTER TWELVE

THEY MADE THEIR WAY back through the house, and found Memfis and Aria sitting at a table in what must have been the kitchen. Aria visibly brightened when she saw Aven. "Oh, you're awake! And look at you! You look wonderful!"

Aven smiled slightly, feeling self-conscious. He looked down at himself. The fire mice had distracted him from his new clothes, but now he was very aware of the trousers. "I'm not really comfortable with them," he said. "I mean, how can I change like this?"

"There's not going to be much swimming where we're going," Memfis said, echoing Owyn's statement from earlier. "We've a plan. Owyn, I want you to poke holes in it."

"All right," Owyn said, sitting down at the table. "Aven needs to eat. Can he eat oat porridge, Mem?"

"He can. And there's more cold roast, and some eggs." Memfis got up and went across the room, came back with a heavily laden plate and a full bowl. "Here you go. Oh, before I forget–" He went back across the room, came back with a jar. "Keep that with you, Aven. It's full of sea salt. You'll need it."

Aven nodded, taking the jar and putting it into his bag. He picked up a spoon and started to eat the contents of the bowl. "This is the porridge?"

"Yes."

"It's good."

Owyn reached across the table and took a smaller bowl, pushed it in front of Aven. "More salt. You probably want it. Mem, is there tea?"

"The kettle is still hot. Now, the Council is going to meet tonight. We'll be presenting you to them as Heir, Aria." Memfis glanced over at Owyn, who had gone to the stove. "Pour for me, Mouse?"

"Already was." Owyn came back with three mugs, setting them all on the table. He passed one to Memfis, one to Aven, and took the third for himself. "Trinket likes Aven, Mem."

Memfis looked startled for a moment. Then he leaned back in his chair and looked beneath the table. "You took him to the forge?" he asked. "With bare feet?"

"He asked," Owyn answered. "I swept the cobbles clean before we closed it yesterday. And we didn't go in very far. And he thought you calling me Fire Mouse was an insult. I wanted him to know it wasn't."

Memfis nodded slowly. "Don't make a habit of it. Bare feet in the forge is a good way to lose toes."

"Yes, sir," Aven said. He finished his porridge and picked up one of the eggs.

"What's a Trinket?" Aria asked. Owyn grinned and took the fire mouse out of his shirt pocket, setting her on the table. Aria looked delighted.

"It's so small!" she gasped, leaning closer. Memfis smiled, then turned toward Aven.

"Aria's been telling me about herself. I'm going to start training her in smoke dancing—"

"She's a Dancer, too?" Owyn interrupted. Then he sank into his seat a little as Memfis looked at him.

"Untrained, yes. We'll need to focus that talent." He looked at Aven. "What of you? Are you a healer, like Jehan?"

"Not as strong as Fa," Aven answered. "He said I was a good basic healer, but he didn't think I had the strength of gift to go further than second level."

Memfis nodded. "He went back for more training, after... after everything. What level did he end up? He was third when he was with us."

"He told me that he was a Fifth level healer," Aven answered.

"Fifth?" Memfis looked stunned. "And they let him leave the healing center?"

Aven blinked, growing tired of being confused all the time. "How many levels are there?" he asked.

"Five," Memfis answered. "And from what I remember, Fifth level healers are rare. They usually stay in the Healing Centers to teach." He sniffed. "Fifth level. I never would have expected it from him. But then again... he had reason to apply himself." He looked at Aven. "You don't know any of this, do you? You're looking exceptionally confused."

"Because I am." Aven looked down at his empty bowl and plate. "My parents told me nothing. I didn't know who they were before until we found Aria. I didn't know my father was related to Mannon until yesterday. Yesterday? Aria?" He looked at Aria, who looked up from the fire mouse when Aven said her name. "Was it yesterday? No, the day before." When she nodded, he sighed. "I don't know anything about any of the other tribes. About living on land. I don't know what I can and can't eat here. I'm more a hindrance than a help."

"You'll learn," Owyn said. "And we'll help you."

Aven smiled and reached out to touch Owyn's hand. "Thank you." He looked at Memfis. "I'm going to have to learn, and quickly. So what's the plan?"

"The Council will meet tonight, and we'll be presenting Aria to them as Heir to the Firstborn. You'll be by her side, as her Water companion. Which means you should start wearing your gem." He looked down at the table. "Bring them out? It's been a long time."

"You don't have yours anymore?" Aven asked. He pulled his bag into his lap and reached inside, into the hidden pocket in the lining. "Ama and Fa have theirs. Fa wears his. Ama's was put away. She didn't wear it." He laid the Diadem on the table, and the four gems. Memfis picked up the Fire gem and looked at it.

"It's different from mine. Probably because it's not mine. Mine... mine is gone." He stopped, laid the gem back down on the table with an audible click. "I... had a dark time of it, about three years back. Just before I found my Mouse here. I found myself alone, and I couldn't see clearly." He paused. Frowned. Stared down at his hands. "I drank too much in those days. Far too much. To drown out the memories. That night... oh, fuck it. It was Milon's naming day. I was missing him, and I said things to the night and to the Mother that I probably should never have said. And in my darkness, I smashed my gem on my anvil."

"Memfis!" Aria gasped.

"I regretted it in the morning, once I could think clearly again. It was my last link to my Milon, and I'd destroyed it." Memfis shook his head. "That morning, I got rid of every drop of alcohol in the house. And I closed the shop, took my smoke blades, and I went into the mountain. I went into the vents, where we learn to dance the smoke. And I went looking for a reason to keep going." He looked up. "I danced the smoke, for the first time in years. I had... a handful of visions. Clearest ones I'd had in ages. The first one led me to you, Owyn."

"Mem," Owyn's voice was soft and solemn. "I never knew. I didn't know any of this."

"There was no reason to burden you with it," Memfis replied. "That was the first vision. Finding my Fire Mouse. Which led to other visions."

"Oh," Aria breathed. "And... you're going to teach me to do this? To control the visions?"

Memfis snorted. "No one controls visions, Aria. They come when they will, and they either make sense immediately, or you're smacking your head once you're finally past it and you understand what the vision meant in the first place." He smiled. "What I will teach you is the discipline that you need so that they don't sneak up on you." He frowned. "You have visions. I know you said that already, but have you always, or just recently?"

"Fifteen years. I was ten when they started."

Memfis nodded slowly. "That's about right. Later, when we're alone, I want to know what the first thing you saw was."

Aria frowned. "Why?"

"Because it's the curse of the Smoke Dancers. The first thing we ever see is how we're going to die." Memfis shook his head. "So later, I want to hear what you saw. Or, you can tell me to mind my own business."

"We're meeting the Council tonight," Aven said. "And then what?"

"Then? We'll be leaving Forge. It's past time I left here anyway. This city..." He looked around. "We're waiting for the mountain to explode. It'll be soon, I think."

"You mean, really?" Owyn interrupted. "You really think that's going to happen? It's not just the street preachers telling tales for coin?"

Memfis sighed. "We've gone over this, Owyn. The world is out of balance. Adavar isn't happy with what's happened to His children, and the Mother less so. The longer Mannon is in power, the more they're going to make that displeasure known."

"Fa said the same thing," Aven said. "He said the storms were like what an oyster does, to make a pearl. Mannon is the grit inside."

Memfis looked thoughtful. "Your father said that?" he asked. "That's something I'd have expected from Aleia." He shook his head. "Never mind. A good part of the city is empty. People have gotten themselves out of range. Those that are left either stay to help those who can't leave, or they follow Mannon and don't believe anything will happen."

"Then why was Mannon going to burn the city?" Aria asked.

"Because he thinks we're a hotbed of revolution," Memfis answered. "Which Forge is not. But the Council knows where the hotbed is located, and that's where we're going once we leave here. So, we'll spend the rest of the day preparing, and tonight, we'll go before the Council. Aria, you'll wear the Diadem. Aven, you should get used to wearing your gem, too."

Aven nodded, and saw Aria looking at him. She smiled, glancing at Owyn. Aven grinned in response and Aria turned to Memfis.

"Then should Owyn get used to wearing his as well?" she asked.

"Wearing *mine*?" Owyn asked. "Wearing my... wait. Wait, did you just... no. No, you're not serious?" He bolted out his chair, moving so fast that the chair clattered to the floor. By the time he stopped moving, he was halfway across the kitchen. "You... you're not serious?" he repeated. "Me? A... a Companion? Me? But..." He stopped, crumpled to the ground, and burst into tears.

Aven was out of his chair in a heartbeat, but Aria still beat him to Owyn's side. She went to her knees next to him, pulling him into her arms. "Owyn, it's all right," she said. "Yes, you."

"We both recognized you," Aven added, sitting down on Owyn's other side. "We both knew it was you, from the minute we saw you."

Owyn shook his head and hiccupped. "You... not me. Not *me*! No one wants me. 'Cept Mem." He hiccupped again, and scrubbed his hand over his face. "Nobody ever came for me, ever looked for me. Nobody ever wanted me."

"You're wanted now," Aria said, her voice firm. "Aven, will you get it?"

Aven got to his feet and went to the table, picking up the fire gem. He brought it back to Aria, then sat back down on the floor, his shoulder pressed against Owyn's.

Aria took Owyn's hand and pried his fingers open, then laid the gem in his palm. "This is yours," she said. "If you'll have it. If you'll have me." She looked up a nd met Aven's eyes. "Have us," she corrected. "Stand with us, Owyn. As Nerris stood with Abin and Axia."

Owyn sniffed, looked down at the stone in his hand. He gave a watery laugh. "Does... does this mean I need to learn to make roses?" he asked. "Nerris made roses of silver and gold. I've never learned to work in precious metals. I work in iron and bronze."

Aria giggled. "If you want to make a rose of iron and bronze, it would be perfect," she said. "Honestly, I'll be happy if you give me a flower that you picked from the side of the road." She touched Owyn's cheek, then turned his head and kissed him. Owyn made a muffled sound of surprise, then responded eagerly, turning and pulling Aria close. Aven shifted so that he was kneeling behind Owyn, putting his arms around them both. When Aria broke the kiss, she looked at Aven and giggled.

"I kissed him first," she teased.

"No, you didn't," Aven answered, laughing. "I kissed him upstairs."

Aria giggled again, then jumped as Memfis cleared his throat. He hadn't moved from the table, and had an amused look on his face.

"Owyn, two things."

Owyn blinked, shook his head, then looked at Memfis. "Yes, Mem?"

"First? Not on the kitchen floor." Memfis' voice was very matter-of-fact. "I'm sure you can find a better place. Second, you'll all want to wash up before we go to the Council, so take them to the baths."

Owyn looked at Aria, then back over his shoulder at Aven. He turned slightly pink and ducked his head. "I...."

"I remember how it was, Mouse," Memfis said. "I remember what it was like. So I'm changing the plans. I'll do the preparations. I've already done most of it — there are benefits to being a seer, after all. There will be clothes and weapons ready when it's time to go."

"And shoes," Owyn added. "Aven needs shoes."

"And shoes." Memfis smiled, scooped Trinket up in his hand, then got up and left the kitchen.

Owyn watched as Memfis left, but he didn't move. For a long moment, he sat with his head still bowed, looking down at the stone in his hand. Finally, he sighed and asked, "Aria, why me?"

Aria looked at Aven, then back at Owyn. "I don't know," she answered. "I don't know if anyone knows. All I know is that I knew you were my Fire from the moment I saw you."

"I knew you, too," Aven added. "And I knew Aria, even before I knew she was there. I knew there was something in that ship that I needed, and I had to find it. Find her."

Owyn looked back at Aven. "Really? Was that what it was?" he asked. "And here I thought it was just that you were pretty. I mean, you are, but I thought that was why I wanted you. You both, I mean. Not just Aven."

Aria reached up and touched Owyn's face again. "You're ours now. And we're yours."

"And I don't have a bed big enough for all of us," Owyn said softly. "I don't want to choose between you. Not for the first time. We should all be together."

"Considering that we haven't had a first time yet, either?" Aven asked. Owyn stared at him.

"You haven't? No, you said you hadn't. You said you weren't paired. But why not?"

"There's no privacy on a canoe," Aria answered. She sounded exceedingly grumpy about it, and Aven bit down a laugh.

"And there was no time before we left our island," he added. "So... no, we haven't."

"So out of the three of us, I'm the only one who's not a virgin?" Owyn asked slowly. He took a deep breath and nodded. "Right. Never thought that part of my life would be useful. Okay . We're not. Not yet. Not until we all know each other better. I don't want there to be any regrets."

Aven sat down, his shoulder against Owyn's back. "Fa said that they were together almost a year before he and Ama and the others shared beds. I didn't think that we'd wait that long. Why regrets?"

"I don't think I could regret anything to do with either of you," Aria murmured.

Owyn shook his head. "We're not taking the chance. I'm the expert, so I say we're going slow. We go slow, no one gets hurt." He twisted to look at Aven. "All right?"

Aven smiled. "You're the expert." He leaned in and kissed Owyn quickly. "What are the baths?"

"Oh, the bath house." Owyn answered. "It's across the back alley. Mem does their metal repair, so we get to use it whenever we want, even when it's closed for Respite. And we won't be seen going in that way. So it's safe to go have a bath and a soak in the springs."

"A soak... Owyn, are these *hot* springs?" Aria asked. When Owyn nodded, Aria jumped to her feet. "A hot bath! Yes, please! Can we go now?"

"A hot spring?" Aven got up slowly, then held his hand out to Owyn. "What makes them hot?"

"Being on the Smoking Mountain," Owyn answered as he got off the floor. "The heat from the volcano heats the water. It's a little warmer than blood temperature, Mem says."

"Is it salt?"

Owyn frowned. "You mean, like sea salt? No. There are minerals in it, from the mountain. Why?"

"Will it trigger the change?" Aria asked. Aven shook his head.

"I don't know. We'll find out, I guess." He held one hand out to Owyn, the other to Aria. "Which way?"

"Wait." Aria went to the table and picked up the Water gem. "You should be wearing this."

"In the bath?" Owyn said. "No, Aria. We'll put them on after. I don't want to damage mine, not when I just got it."

They put the gems and the Diadem back into the carry-bag, and Aven took it back down to the hidden room. Then Owyn picked up a lantern and led them out the back of the kitchen and across to another building. He took a key from his pocket and opened the door, letting them inside, where they waited in the dim light until Owyn lit the lamps. He led them down the hall to a pair of doors that faced each other.

"Changing rooms," he said. "Aria, the women's changing room is that way. Aven, this is the men's. There's a stair leading down on the far side of the room. That takes you down to the springs."

"And I'm to go here, while you go there?" Aria asked. "And where do I leave my clothes?"

"There are places to put them inside, and towels. Bring a few towels with you." Owyn frowned. "There are robes, too. But they won't fit you. You can wrap a towel around yourself, if you don't want to walk around naked. See you in the water."

Aven laughed as he followed Owyn into the changing room. "You just got these clothes on me."

"And now I'm getting those clothes off you," Owyn said. "And not in a happy fun way. We're going to get clean." He looked thoughtful. "How do you take a bath, out in the ocean?"

"On our island, we had a sweet water spring, and it spilled into a bathing pool. When we were out in the canoe, we were in the water a lot," Aven said. "I've never been in a hot bath before."

Owyn nodded. "Because how would you have heated the water, on a wooden canoe in the middle of the ocean. You'll either like this or hate it."

Aven blinked. "That's usually how it works, isn't it?" He took off the scarf and his shirt, then stripped off his trousers. "I'm supposed to wear a robe?"

"It's polite," Owyn answered. "There, that stack. Put it on and go on downstairs. Take a lamp. I'll be right with you."

Aven picked up a robe made from soft, thin cloth, slipping it on, then taking towels and a lamp and going down the stairs. This wasn't anything like any cave he'd ever seen, and he was glad of it. He could smell the water long before he saw it, and the air was humid and warm. And the spring, when he finally could see it, was a deep, tiled pool, gently steaming in the dim light from his lamp. He set the lamp down on a shelf, stripped off his robe, and knelt to test the water.

"How is it?"

"Hotter than I'm used to," Aven answered, looking up to see Aria had followed Owyn's advice, and wrapped herself in a towel. "You've done this before?"

"Oh, yes," Aria answered. She laid the towel aside and dipped one foot into the water. "Oh, that's lovely." She sat down, swung her legs into the water, then slipped in. The water came up over her breasts, and she dunked herself to her chin, then spread her wings wide. Aven followed her into the water, feeling a little silly at his trepidation. He was a creature of water — what did he have to fear from it?

The water was hotter than it had felt on his hand, and he gasped as he sank into it. But once he was used to it, it did feel good. He found there were benches on the far side of the pool, and he sat down there.

"What do you think?" Owyn called as he came down the last stairs.

"I like it," Aven answered. "Do you just soak?"

"Well, once we're all wrinkly, there's another room with soap and rinse water. Then we can come back here to soak some more." Owyn took off his robe and laid it with Aven's, then got into the pool. He dunked himself completely underneath, coming up shaking his head to that water sprayed everywhere. Aria splashed him in response, and he turned toward her.

His back was a mass of scars — thin, silvery stripes mingled with twisted, raised ridges turning fiercely red in the heat.

CHAPTER THIRTEEN

"OWYN!" AVEN GASPED. "What happened to you?"

Owyn turned to Aven, and Aria cried out in shock. Owyn's jaw dropped. He looked from one of them to the other, then sighed. "I... I'm sorry. I should have warned you. I just.. I got so comfortable with you both that I forgot you don't know." He swallowed. "You don't know me. Really. And if you knew... you might not want to."

"Owyn," Aven murmured. "May I look?"

Owyn just shrugged. "Yeah, sure. It doesn't bother me anymore. It doesn't hurt, if you're asking that, oh Water healer."

Aven nodded, trying not to be stung by the tone of Owyn's voice. He rested one hand on Owyn's shoulder, and ran the other hand down the length of Owyn's spine. The scars ran from his nape to his arse, wrapped around his sides, and varied in age. To Aven's surprise, it was the cleaner marks that showed signs of being newest — the badly healed scars were much older. And there was a brand, on Owyn's shoulder, just over the shoulder blade — four vertical lines crossed by a fifth.

"What happened here?" Aven asked. "Some of these are old. You couldn't have been more than a child—"

"Six or seven, I think," Owyn interrupted. "The first time I got caught. Do you know it's warm when you do that? It's all warm under my skin. It feels nice."

"Caught doing what?" Aria asked. She moved closer, standing in front of Owyn, and rested her hands on his chest. "What did you do?"

Owyn covered her hands with his. "Told Aven this. I didn't tell you. Did Mem tell you I was an orphan?" When Aria shook her head, he nodded. "Right. My parents died in the last big uprising, I think. I was little. Two or three, maybe. And no one claimed me, so I ended up on the streets. One of the older boys, he took care of me. Named me Owyn. Garci, that was his name. He taught me to beg, and he taught me to steal." Owyn gave a weak laugh. "And I'm a lousy thief. In Forge, when a thief gets caught, they're publicly whipped."

"They whipped a *child*?" Aria's voice spiraled up. "Did no one speak against it?"

"Not a damned one," Owyn said. "It's the law. There's no exceptions to the law."

"That's a horrible law," Aria said. She looked at Aven over Owyn's shoulder. "First thing we're changing."

"I'll remind you," Aven said. He moved closer, rested his hands on Owyn's waist. "There's more than one set."

"There's five, I think. Five old sets, and one new one. I'll explain the new one last. I was caught stealing five times. The last time, I decided that was it for being a thief. I was older, I could survive another way." He looked down at the water. "So I became a whore."

"Oh, Owyn," Aria breathed. Aven looked at her, at how pale she'd grown, and wondered what he was missing. What in the name of the deepest depths was a whore?

"I couldn't have been more than fourteen. Too young to get into a brothel, but there were taverns where the men weren't fussy. And it wasn't all that bad, really." Owyn shrugged. "My first one... when he found out he was my first, he paid me four times what I'd asked him. Told me to take care of myself, and asked if he could see me again.

Most of them were really nice about it. It was good. Until it wasn't."
He glanced back at Aven, then frowned. "You look confused."

"What's a whore?"

Owyn blinked. "You... you don't know? You don't have whores...
well, I suppose not. How could you? Out in the middle of the ocean."
He took a deep breath. "It means I sold myself to men for sex. They
paid me to have sex with me."

Aven nodded slowly. "That's... healers do that. My father told
me."

"That's Earth tribe. Fire tribe since Mannon took over? Being
a whore is illegal." He reached up and touched the brand on the
back of his shoulder. "That's what this is. You get caught whoring,
you get branded. And when they cross the stripes? You're deemed
incorrigible. You're arrested, and you're publicly beaten. Then you
become the property of the city, and your indentures are sold. Which
means you become a slave, because there's no way to buy your
indentures back." He looked around. "I want to sit."

Aven took his hand and led him to the bench, sitting on his
right. Aria sat on his left. "What happened?" she asked.

Owyn made a face. "I told you about my first one? Fandor, that's
his name. He turned me in that last time. He'd seen I had four stripes.
He figured he could buy my indentures, and I'd be his personal
slave—" He shook his head. "The chastiser beat the shit out of me,
then they put me on the block. Fandor was right there in front. He
told me not to worry. That he'd arranged everything. It would all be
over soon, and then I'd be his. That was when I knew he'd turned me
in." Owyn's hand in Aven's shook. "I screamed at him. Told him that
if he bought me, if he ever touched me again, that I'd kill him. So...
they gagged me, and they started the sale." He let out a long breath.
"And Memfis bought me. He hired a healer to see to me—"

"*Hired* a healer?" Aven gasped.

To his surprise, Owyn laughed. "All of this, and *that's* what gets you mad?"

"Healers aren't supposed to ask payment," Aven grumbled. "Fa said so. He said there was a healing center here."

"Not for years and years. Here, healers don't work for free. And they don't do what you do. They don't have the Earth touch. They have herbs and potions." Owyn shrugged. "That's why the last set of scars are the cleanest. They're the ones that were actually treated properly. So... that's me. Mem, he treats me like his son, but I'm not, and I know it. I'm his slave. Orphan, thief, whore, slave."

"Smith. Smoke Dancer," Aven said.

"Companion," Aria added, her voice firm. "In case you were thinking I'd change my mind about that last, once I knew."

"You're serious?" Owyn asked. "You really mean that? You still want me? After everything? I mean, I'm a marked criminal, and a slave."

Aven slid his arm around Owyn and pulled him tight to his side. "Owyn, do you know what the Water tribe says about our past?"

Owyn's brow furrowed. "No, I don't think I've seen that in any of my books."

"My mother says that the Mother has a ledger where she makes note of all of the deeds of all of her children. The good we do, the successes, the times we come out ahead, she writes in ink."

Owyn nodded. "And the failures? The fuck-ups?"

"She writes in water."

Aria blinked. Then she smiled. "I like that."

"I don't understand," Owyn protested. "If you write them in water, then when the paper dries, the marks... oh." He stopped. "Oh. Really?"

"Really." Aven turned, and found himself nose to nose with Owyn once more. "It's written in water, Owyn."

Owyn smiled slightly. "And all over the skin of my back."

"You're being obtuse," Aven protested. "What happened in your past is written in water. It happened, we know. It was written in the Mother's ledger. But knowing it doesn't mean we want you any less."

"Besides, doing what you had to do to survive made you the man we are probably going to have long arguments over," Aria added. When Owyn looked at her, she blushed slightly. "Over who is going to be in bed with you on a given night."

Owyn laughed. "Why argue? We could have one big bed."

Aria blinked. "We could?" She looked at Aven. "All of us in one bed?"

"There are only three of us right now, Aria," Aven reminded her.

"But still. There will be five. We could have all five? I wouldn't have to choose one—"

"Or two," Owyn interjected.

"And leave the others feeling like I don't want them?" Aria finished. For a moment, the only sound was water dripping.

"I suppose..." Owyn said slowly. "I mean, being as I am the expert. If you wanted to have five in one bed, you could do it. If you had a big enough bed. And if that's what you want, you might want to upholster the floor of a large room." He looked distant for a moment. "Do you know if the other two are boys or girls?"

Aria shook her head. "I don't know. I won't know until I see them. And apparently, you'll know them, too."

Owyn nodded. "I can't say that I've done that many at once, but I imagine it could be done. We'll be heading to the Earth tribal lands when we leave here, I think. They're the closest. Maybe we'll be able to stop in a healing center and find out."

"A healer would know?" Aven asked.

"That's what I've heard. That healing centers have great big books that cover all sorts of sex stuff. I don't know if it's true, though," Owyn said. He relaxed against Aven's side. "I like this. Aria, come closer." He held his arm out to her. "Come be with us."

She glided through the water, then stopped. "Where should I be? You look too comfortable for me to ask you to move. Should I be on your other side? Or on Aven's other side?"

"Go on his other side," Aven said. "He needs to have us both holding him right now."

"Why?" Owyn asked, looking at Aven. "I mean, I don't object, but why do you say I need it?"

"Because you need to be certain we're not letting you go," Aven answered, meeting Owyn's eyes. "That you're safe with us."

Owyn breathed out a long wordless sound that might have been a sigh. Or a moan. "Make me regret saying we're going to wait, why don't you?" he said. Then he laughed. "Come here, Aria."

Aria cuddled up to Owyn, resting her head on his shoulder. "I don't mind waiting. Even though I know you're mine. I can wait for you to be sure."

Aven shifted, turning slightly so that he could pull Owyn closer, and put his arms around both of them. He closed his eyes and took a long breath, trying to relax in silence broken only by dripping water. It was harder than he thought. The quiet left him with nothing to distract him, and his fears were all starting to surface and circle...

"Ven?"

Aven blinked at the sound of the diminutive his parents called him. "Since when do you call me that, Aria?"

"Since I wanted your attention," she answered. She reached across Owyn and touched Aven's chest. "We'll find them, Ven. You heard Memfis — they're alive."

"Probably," Aven said, and hated himself for the correction. "They're probably alive. Because they're valuable." He closed his eyes. "Aria—"

The water sloshed around him, and someone covered him, straddling his legs and pressing their body against his. He opened his eyes to see Owyn, who studied him a moment, then took Aven's face in his hands and kissed him. Aven gasped, then wrapped his arms around Owyn and clung to him, pulling him closer as the dam burst and the tears started. He heard Aria's soft words of comfort, felt her touch on his shoulders, on the back of his neck, in his hair. But it was Owyn's solid weight that helped, his strength providing Aven an anchor in a storm of grief and loss, bringing him into a safe harbor where he could finally think again. He rested his forehead on Owyn's shoulder, feeling himself shaking.

"Better?" Owyn asked, nuzzling Aven's ear. Aven nodded.

"I think so," he answered, feeling the tightness in his throat. "I'll be all right."

"Liar," Aria said gently. "You're hurting. You're trying to hide it. Don't hide it, Aven. Let us share it."

"But I'm supposed to take care of you," Aven protested.

"Tell you what, then," Owyn said. "How about we all take care of each other?" He smiled and kissed Aven's lips gently, then moved to get off Aven's lap. Aven tightened one arm around Owyn, pulled Aria closer with the other. He closed his eyes, holding them both as tightly as he dared.

"I'm terrified," Aven whispered. "How do we fight him? How can we stop him?"

"We'll find a way," Aria said. "We'll fight him. And we'll find them."

"I don't know what I'm doing. I've never been on land before. I don't know what I can eat, I don't know how to dress, or how to act." He opened his eyes. "I feel like I'm sinking. I can't breathe, and I'm drowning. It's..."

"You're panicking," Owyn said gently. "I understand. I know. I've been there. I *know*. You're not alone, Aven. Ven? That's what Aria called you. Ven, you're not alone. We've got you. I'm not going to let you drown." He rested his hands on Aven's shoulders. "Look, I didn't start off taking care of you very well, but I'll do better now. I'll take care of you, and you'll take care of me, and we'll both take care of Aria and whoever else joins us along the way. I'll teach you both what I know about living. And you both teach me what you know about caring. Deal?" He huffed softly. "I didn't let them break me when I was a kid. I didn't let them break me when I was older. I'm not going to let them break me now. And I'm not going to let them break you."

There was a hint of steel in Owyn's words that Aven found more than a little comforting. He nodded, closed his eyes again, focusing on the weight and warm against his body — Owyn on his legs and chest, Aria against his left side. He had them. He'd be all right. And he'd learn.

"I don't know about you two, but I don't want to turn into a wrinkly old man," Owyn said lightly. "Let's go scrub up. Then we can come back and soak if we want."

They splashed out of the pool, and Owyn led them both into another room, where there were more benches around raised vessels of water. There were large dippers, and jars of what Owyn told them was soap sand. He poured some into his hand and started to scrub it, and Aven was surprised to see that it foamed slightly.

"Sand doesn't do that on the island," he said, repeating what Owyn had done.

"That's because it's soap," Owyn answered. "Which you don't have, I guess?"

"Not like this." Aven poured a dipper of cooler water over his skin, watching as the foam washed away. "What is it made out of?"

"Soap?" Owyn looked thoughtful as he scrubbed his chest. "I... I have no idea. Mem might know."

"You need fat of some kind, and lye, and perfume if you want a scent," Aria answered. "It's a long process, and tedious. I do not know how they made it look like sand, though. This is not like the soap we make."

"Want me to wash your back?" Owyn offered. Aria shook her head.

"Soap is not good for my wings. It will strip the oils from my feathers, and make it harder to fly. I'll go back to the pool and clean them." She looked at Aven, looked thoughtful, then smiled. "You could wash Aven's back," she suggested. "He has lovely shoulders."

"I was noticing that," Owyn said.

"What?" Aven looked at the both of them. "What about my shoulders?"

"They go on for days," Owyn answered. Aria laughed and left, going back out to the pool. Owyn grinned and continued, "Probably because you swim a lot, but you've got muscles on muscles across your back and your shoulders. And you've got a reach — well, you don't even have to stretch to hold both of us."

"And you like that?" Aven asked.

"Ven, I could just look at you all day," Owyn answered. "I told you, you're pretty." He moved behind Aven, and Aven felt the rough soap sand scraping against his skin. Having someone else scrubbing his back was new, and he was surprised at how good it felt. He tipped his head forward, sighing in pleasure as Owyn's strong hands massaged soap into his shoulders and upper back, then his lower back. They strayed lower, over his arse, and Aven shivered. Owyn froze.

"I should stop," he said. "I said we were going to wait."

Aven turned to face Owyn. "No, you should definitely not stop."

"Not... you want me to keep going?" Owyn sounded breathless. "What about Aria?"

Aven smiled, resting his hands on Owyn's waist. "She left us in here for a reason."

Owyn's eyes widened. "Oh?" he breathed. "Oh. In that case...." He smiled. "I live to please my Firstborn. But I'm going to please you first."

AVEN WASN'T SURE HOW long they stayed in the bathing room, how long Owyn played with him. When they finally stumbled out, they were both laughing, leaning on each other for support and stumbling on legs that felt to Aven as if his bones had turned to sand. Aria was sitting on the bench in the hot pool, and smiled as they splashed into the water.

"Oh, good. You did take the hint," she said, moving to join them and putting her arms around both of them. "You both look ever so much better."

"I do feel better," Owyn admitted. "But... I thought you were a virgin? How did you know that was going to help anything?"

She giggled. "I didn't. But I thought that since Earthborn healers use sex as part of their healing practices, that it might help you both." She hugged them. "Now, come and sit and tell me!"

CHAPTER FOURTEEN

BY THE TIME THEY WERE back in the forge, it was midday. Memfis met them at the kitchen door, and Aven was certain that the older man knew that something had happened in the baths. He had studied them all for a moment, nodded once, then told them that he was going out to see what news was in the streets. They were to stay inside, lock all the doors, and not answer if anyone came to call.

"We'll have a late night," he said. "I recommend you all see if you can sleep. Alone, Owyn."

"That's no fun," Owyn grumbled. Memfis laughed. Then he'd left. Owyn barred the door behind him, then looked at Aven and Aria.

"Well, I can't sleep with you, but I can still sleep near you," he said. "Aven's sleeping in the hammock, so I'll take the other bed." He led them down the hall to the hidden stairs, and down into the hole.

"Owyn, you left something out of your story," Aria said as she sat on her bed. "What happened to him?"

"Which him? Garci?" Owyn frowned. "I'm not sure. You don't get attached, on the streets. He disappeared, and I never looked."

"The other him. The one who betrayed you." Aria suddenly looked fierce. "The one I intend to have words with."

"You'd best start thinking of those words, then. You'll see him tonight."

"He's on the Council?" Aven asked. He climbed into the hammock.

"Yeah," Owyn said as he stretched out on the other bed. "He's District Five's Loremaster. Which means nothing to you." He rolled onto his side to face them. "There are eight districts in Forge. Each of them has District leaders. There's a Loremaster, who keeps the records. There's the Master Smith, who trains the metalworkers and is in charge of the schools. And there used to be the Smoke Dancer. When Mannon outlawed smoke dancing, he replaced that position in each district with the Magistrate. They're in charge of the laws, and every single one of them reports to the Guard Captain, who reports to Mannon."

"Wait," Aven said. "We're going before the Council tonight. That means Mannon will know—"

"No, because we're not seeing that Council," Owyn interrupted. "That Council meets once every ten days or so, and does nothing. Tonight, we're seeing the Dark Council. The Dark Council meets in secret, they meet at night, and the Magistrates aren't invited. The Smoke Dancers, however, are. Mem is on both Councils, in different roles. In the regular Council, he's this District's Master Smith. In the Dark Council, he's this District's Smoke Dancer."

"That's confusing," Aria said. "How do they keep the secret council secret?"

Owyn grinned. "They don't. Mannon knows there's a Dark Council. He's got spies inside. Everyone on the Dark Council knows who the spies are, though."

Aven frowned, working it through. "So, they're a distraction?"

"Exactly. The Dark Council in Forge keeps Mannon looking here, and not looking closely at the Earth tribes, which is where the real rebellion is."

"Which is why Mannon was shipping inferno oil to Forge?" Aria asked. "Because he thinks there is rebellion here?"

"That's the scary part," Owyn admitted. "I don't think anyone realized that Mannon was at the point of taking steps against the Dark Council yet. I mean, all they do is talk! Bitch and moan, moan and bitch, complain about tariffs and new laws, what will we ever do, see you next month." Owyn flopped down on the bed. "I mean, how can he take all that seriously? There are never any real plans made."

"Tonight, there will be," Aven said. "And what will the spies do when they hear?"

There was no answer for a moment. "I don't know," Owyn said. "I don't know how they can stop the news from getting out. But, I mean, it's not like he doesn't know you all are in Forge, right?" Owyn looked up. "I mean, everything happened in Forge's harbor. He has to know you came here. Where else would you go?"

"That is not going to help us get any sleep, Owyn," Aria said. "You're right. He must know we came here. Is he in the city now, looking for us?"

"Nah," Owyn answered, sounding cheerful. "We'd know if he was here. The entire city would be in an uproar. He's tried it before, and we all knew he was here within an hour. You can't keep something like that secret. Not in a city full of Smoke Dancers." He shifted around on the bed. "Right. We need to sleep. I don't know what Mem is planning, but if he wants us rested, that might mean we're going to be up all night."

"How will Memfis get back inside?" Aria asked as she lay down. "You barred the door."

"He's got a key, and he'll ring the bell so we know it's him," Owyn answered. He gestured toward a tiny bell in the corner. "No one knows this is down here, and no one can find the stairs in that closet. We've used this hole before, to hide people that the Magistrates were looking for. House has been searched... twelve times? Yeah, that's about right. Anything goes wrong in this district, the Guard

Captain comes over, chats with Mem, looks around, and goes away frustrated."

"Because he knows Memfis is on the Dark Council?" Aven asked. The gentle swaying of the hammock was starting to relax him, and he yawned.

"Exactly. He knows that Mem has to be up to something, and it sticks in his craw that he can't find what it is." Owyn chuckled. "All right. Sleepy time."

Silence fell, broken only by the soft sounds of breathing, and the creaking of the hammock chains. Aven drifted off, not quite asleep, not quite awake, but in a half-aware state where he heard the bell as a distant chiming that didn't seem to be important enough to wake him fully. He heard soft voices without registering what was being said, drifting off into a deeper sleep that was broken by the touch of lips against his. He jerked awake, recognizing Aria's scent as he reached for her.

"Are you awake?" she asked, pulling back.

"If I say no, will you kiss me again?" Aven answered. She giggled, and he smiled and pulled himself out of the hammock. He stretched, then looked around. "Where's Owyn?"

"Upstairs with Memfis," Aria answered. "Memfis came back with clothes and shoes, and he says we're to come up and eat before we leave for this council meeting. But we have time, so we do not need to rush."

Aven nodded. He walked over to the bed and sat down, leaning back against the wall and closing his eyes. "I don't like waiting," he said. "It gives me too much time to think." The bed shifted as Aria came to sit down with him. He put his arm around her automatically, pulling her warmth to his side.

"What are you thinking about?" Aria asked. "Right now."

"Right now?" Aven tried to tease a single thought out of the swirling mass in his mind. "Why did you leave us alone?"

"You and Owyn?" Aria rested her head on his shoulder. "Should I not have? You seemed to enjoy it. When you told me, you were very enthusiastic."

"I just thought you would be my first," Aven admitted. "I thought that we—"

"I thought about that. And I decided that there were two good reasons to let Owyn have you first. First, you needed the release more than I needed to keep you to myself. You will be my first. And I will be your first woman." She ran her fingernails up and down his arm. "Does that make sense?"

Aven turned and kissed the top of her head. "It makes sense. Thank you. I did need that. I don't think I'd have slept otherwise." He rested his cheek against her hair. "Aria, you're setting our course. What do we do next? How do we stop this?"

"Memfis is setting the course," Aria corrected. "Or rather, Memfis is suggesting the course, and I am taking my guidance from him. Because I don't know what our next step should be. I don't know enough. We'll need people. Mannon has men. He has guards. He has power. We have pretty rocks and a diadem. The scales are stacked in his favor."

Aven huffed softly. "You think?"

"But we have the Mother behind us," Aria added. "That must count for something. We'll just have to take things one step at a time. Which means there will be waiting." She sighed. "And thinking."

"Or not thinking," Aven added. "We could spend the waiting time in bed."

Aria laughed. "We could. Aven, there are ways that healers know, for a woman to not get pregnant. Do you know them?"

"I know of them. Never had to prepare any of them, or use the gift for it." Aven realized something. "That's the other reason why you pushed me at Owyn?"

"Neither of you will be in my bed until I'm certain I won't come away with a child. I'm not ready for that. Not until we're safe." She paused, then amended, "Safer."

Aven nodded. "That makes even more sense. I don't have any supplies, but we're going to the Earth tribe lands. We'll be able to get them. Or speak to a healer who actually has experience with this. All I know is my reading and what my father taught me."

"Then we can wait. And perhaps the next time, I will watch you and Owyn." She rubbed her cheek against his shoulder. "Lessons for the future on how to please my men."

Aven hugged her more tightly, then let her go. "We should go up."

They went up the stairs to find the house quiet. There was no one in the kitchen, or in the upper rooms, and they searched until the only place left to look was the forge.

"We'll have to just go to the door and look," he said, looking down at his feet. He and Aria were both barefoot, and he wasn't going to violate what Memfis and Owyn both said was a safety rule in the forge. He took Aria down the hall toward the forge, and stopped when he heard a strange voice.

"There's someone there," Aria whispered. Aven nodded, gesturing for her to move against the wall. He crept down the hall, closer to the door, until he could hear the voices clearly.

"It's Respite," Memfis was saying. "I'm not firing my forge on Respite. You know me better than that."

"I know that this is a job that needs doing," a man answered. "And you're the Master Smith in this district—"

"Who is not violating the Respite to make... what *are* these, Fandor? What abomination is this?"

Aven went tense. Fandor. The man who'd betrayed Owyn. Another thought occurred to him – Owyn was in there, in the forge. He had to be.

"Those are for the Magistrates," Fandor answered.

"And since when are you the Magistrate's errand boy?" There was a crinkling of paper, and Memfis' voice suddenly was very loud. "Go home, Fandor. If this is indeed an order from the Magistrates, then the Magistrates can bring it to me. Tomorrow, when my forge is open."

"If that's your final word," Fandor sounded sulky. Then his voice became warmer, edging towards seductive. "Owyn. You're looking well." When Owyn didn't answer, Fandor continued, "You know, Fisher, my offer is still on the table."

"You can take your offer and shove it up your arse," Owyn snarled.

"Now, now. Fisher, your boy is putting on airs."

"My *son* is right," Memfis said. "You can take that order and you can shove it up your arse. You've been told no. And since telling you no doesn't seem to make it through your ears, Fandor, let me try it this way. Fuck your offer, and get out of my forge." There was a scraping of metal against metal. "And another thing — do not come back to my forge. You are banned from my forge and my anvil. Neither I nor any smith of my training in this District will take your custom." There was a loud, ringing crash of something metal and heavy against something else. "I've said it, and sealed it on my anvil. You're the Loremaster. Make note of it. Then get out."

Fandor laughed. "Because I want to take a whore off your hands? Really, Fisher?"

"Because I am through with you harassing my son," Memfis growled. "Now be off, or I'll bury this hammer in your skull."

They heard a door slam. For a moment, they heard nothing. Then the door to the house opened. Memfis didn't look surprised to see them. He pointed back toward the kitchen, and followed Aven and Aria down the hall. In the kitchen, Memfis looked around, then shook his head.

"Go down to the hole," he said. "I'll be along in a moment."

Aven nodded, and went to take Owyn's hand. Owyn looked very pale, and didn't say a word until they were all down in the hole. Aria took Owyn from Aven, taking him to the bed and sitting down with him. Aven paced, unable to sit. He wanted to hit, needed to rage, but there was no target for his anger.

"He called me his son," Owyn said softly. "He...Mem. He called me his son."

Aven turned to face them. Aria had put her arm around Owyn's shoulders. "He's never done that before?" she asked.

"No," Owyn answered. "No, he never has. I... I never realized he thought of me that way. I..."

"I've always thought of you that way. I've just never said it to you before. I've never said it out loud before yesterday," Memfis said as he came into the room. His arms were full of bundles, which he handed to Aven. "Put those down, will you? Then come join us. This needs to be said. It's well past time it was said."

Aven took the bundles and put them down on the second bed, coming back to find Memfis sitting on the floor. Aven looked at the space that Owyn and Aria had left for him on the bed, then shook his head and leaned against the wall next to them.

"Aven?"

"I'm too... too something to sit. Angry. I'm too angry," Aven answered. He folded his arms over his chest. "I want to smash his face in, and I don't even know what he looks like!"

"Trust me. It would be an improvement," Owyn said, his voice dry. He reached out and took Aven's elbow. "Come on. Sit. I want you to sit with me. You can protect me just as well from here."

"Let him be, Owyn," Memfis said gently. "He's all stirred up, and he needs a minute to settle. Yes, I should have said that a long time ago. I don't know why I didn't. I really don't. You've been everything a son could be these three years, and I should have filed the papers with the Loremasters the day you came to me." He rubbed his palms on his thighs. "I was afraid, I think. If I admitted to myself how important you are to me, then I'd run the risk of losing you. Everyone else I've ever loved, I've lost. If I didn't say it, didn't admit it, then you'd never go. The Mother knew. I thought that was enough." He sighed and shook his head. "I should have known better. Milon would have kicked my arse for stupid thinking."

"Why?" Owyn demanded. "Why now?"

"Because you are leaving," Memfis answered. "I have to let you go. I have to let you be the man you were born to be. And I realized that I would never forgive myself if I didn't acknowledge you for what you really are before you left." He sighed. "And because if I didn't cancel those damned indentures, you couldn't legally leave Forge. Which means they could have hunted you down and taken you from me. Possibly even executed you."

Aven blinked, looked at Owyn and Aria, then back at Memfis. "Why didn't you cancel the indentures before?" he asked.

Memfis looked down. "I honestly can't answer that. I've had the paperwork locked in my desk for three years. I don't know why I never took the last step and took it to the Senior Loremaster." He took a deep breath, then looked up at Owyn. "But it's done. That's where I was. The papers are filed. Your name will be written in the *Book of Silver* as Owyn, son of Memfis, son of Trezi, of the line of Nerris."

Owyn went white. "Son of... but you said no one could know your real name! You said if anyone knew who you really were, that they'd turn you over to Mannon!"

"I won't be here for it," Memfis said. "I'm coming with you. We'll leave tonight, after the Dark Council meets." He rubbed his hands on his thighs again. "Since it's Respite, the papers won't be official until tomorrow. We'll be gone by the time it's announced in the District squares. But Loremaster Danis owes me a favor. He's known me since before I was Fisher. Truth be told, he helped me create Fisher. I trusted him with that, I can trust him to do what's necessary here."

"What about Fandor?" Aven asked.

"What about him?" Memfis asked in response. "There's nothing he can do." He shook his head. "Coming here, though. That didn't make sense. Why come here with something for the Magistrates? Especially since the Magistrates keep their own smith?"

"What was it that he wanted?" Owyn asked. "You didn't show me the design."

"Never seen the like of it before," Memfis said. "Some kind of restraint. A collar, attached to a rod, and with manacles at the bottom of the rod — Owyn!"

Owyn had gone white, and for a moment, Aven thought the other man might faint.

"That wasn't for the magistrates," Owyn said softly, his voice harsh. "That was for me."

"What?" Memfis sounded shocked. "What do you mean?"

"I mean, that was something he liked to do. He liked to tie me. And since he'd pay me well when he did it, I went along with it. He had something like that, in leather." Owyn rubbed his face. "I hadn't thought of that in a while. But yeah, collar, stiff strap down the back, and then your hands cuffed behind you. And a gag. You can't stop him, and you can't scream. Well, you can, but it doesn't sound like anything." He shook his head. "Mem, he wanted you to make that to use on me. I'm sure of it."

Memfis nodded slowly. "And having it made by me, with you knowing that I'd made it? With you possibly having helped me make it, as my apprentice? Owyn, that's all kinds of fucked up."

"I know," Owyn agreed. "I know. And it's just the kind of thing he'd get off on." He looked around and sighed. "Mem, we can't stay here. He wouldn't be doing that if he didn't have something on you.

Something that would force you to hand me over. We need to go. Now. Right now."

CHAPTER FIFTEEN

IT WAS STILL DAYLIGHT outside. Aven could see the sun shining through the cracks in the stable door. There was something of a late afternoon glow to the light. He carried bundles and helped Owyn stow them in the back of the cart, then watched as Owyn harnessed the gray, furry animal.

"Is this a horse?" Aven asked.

"No," Owyn answered. "This is Stubborn, and he's a mule." Owyn looked up from pulling a strap tight. "You'll be seeing a horse before tomorrow, if I don't miss my guess. Probably riding one, too."

"Riding? A horse?" Aven shook his head. "I don't know how to do that."

"You're going to learn really damned fast, then." Owyn went back to his work. "We're going to need to make a lot of ground quickly. That means horses." He shook his head. "Aven, I've been trying to make sense of this. What could Fandor have that would make him so sure that Mem would just hand me over?"

"Could he know that Memfis is really Memfis?"

Owyn shrugged. "Maybe?" he said. "I mean, it's possible." He dug in his pocket and pulled out something that he offered to Stubborn on the flat of his hand. "Anything is possible."

Aven nodded, leaning against the cart. His carry-bag bumped against his hip, and he looked down at it. Then he looked over his shoulder. No signs of Memfis or Aria. He reached into the bag and fumbled around until he found the pearl. "Owyn, you remember you were saying that you'd have to learn how to make roses out of iron and bronze?"

"Yeah. What about it?"

"Could you set this into one?" Aven held out the pearl. Owyn's eyes widened, and he came closer. He picked up the pearl, studied it for a moment, then whistled low.

"That's... you could buy the whole damned district with that!" he said softly. "Where did you get it?"

"Harvested it myself," Aven answered. "It's for Aria. I was going to give it to her after our first night together. But I think it will mean more if it's from the both of us. So can you make the rose?"

Owyn licked his lips. He frowned, then cocked his head to the side and looked distant. "Yeah, I can make it," he said slowly. "But I don't know how to set pearls. I'm a blacksmith. I don't work with jewels." He nodded. "We could take the finished rose to a jeweler, though. Have them do it right. Oh, but... I won't have a forge for a while. Maybe not a long while."

"Then it will wait," Aven said as he tucked the pearl away. "Aria wants to wait, in any case. She doesn't mind us having our fun together, but she won't have either of us until she can be sure that she won't come away pregnant."

Owyn nodded. "Nice that someone is thinking about that," he said. "Right. Stubborn is ready. Let's go get them."

"Do you know where we're going?" Aven asked as they headed back into the house.

"Not a single idea, nope."

They found Memfis and Aria in the kitchen, packing food into baskets.

"All the bundles are packed," Owyn reported. "Your smoke blades are packed, and the cases that you told me to grab. The lock-box. What else?"

"There's one more thing," Memfis answered. "Aria, I think we're done here. Come with me to the forge." He led the way down the hall back to the forge. He closed the door behind them, and lit a lamp. "Stand over there on the mat. I know the floor is clean there. Owyn, help me move this." He rested his hand on the anvil.

"Move... the anvil?" Owyn repeated. "We'll need Stubborn, and he's already hitched to the cart."

"No, we won't. We just need two strong men." Memfis ran his hand over the anvil's surface. "I never knew what these visions meant," he said absently. "I just knew I had to do what they said. Now I understand." He set both hands on the heavy wooden base of the anvil. "Come on, Owyn."

Owyn joined him, and the two strained to push the anvil. To Aven's surprise, the entire base slid, far more easily than he would have expected, and the stone floor shifted before it, sliding into the wall.

"Is... Mem, is this thing on tracks?" Owyn gasped.

"Push now, look at the handiwork later." Memfis grunted in response.

The anvil moved two feet to the right, revealing a door set into the floor between the now visible tracks. Memfis rose and rolled his shoulders, while Owyn dropped to his knees.

"When did you do this?" he demanded, examining the tracks on the ground. "I wouldn't ever have known this was here! And the floor moving into the wall — I can see the seams, now that I know to look for them."

"I did it... about twenty years ago," Memfis said. "Yeah, that's about right. When I started the shop, and before I crawled into a bottle. And why? When you have the same vision fifteen times without stopping, you listen."

"Fifteen?" Owyn gaped. "That's... you've never told me that was possible."

"Including twice in one night," Memfis added. "And usually, it isn't possible. Visions are usually one and done. Twice, maybe, if the seer is very sensitive. I only know of two cases where the same vision was repeated multiple times, and this is one of them." He knelt and opened the door. "I didn't understand then. Now, I do. Should I go in order, or as I pick things up?"

"Considering that we don't know what's down there?" Aven answered. "You decide."

"You really are like Aleia. She was a smartass, too." Memfis grinned and took out a long case. "This is yours." He handed it to Aven. The minute it was in Aven's hands, he knew what it was. But he didn't believe it, not until he laid the case down and opened it.

Hook swords. He picked up one, and marveled at its perfect balance. They were beautifully made, the blades etched with patterns that looked like waves.

"Those look very dangerous," Owyn murmured, coming closer. "Are you good with them?"

"My mother said I was," Aven answered. "Memfis, these are beautiful. I've been trying not to think about Ama's blades... they're gone."

"These won't replace your mother's blades," Memfis said gently. "But those were made for you and you alone. Bear them well." He took another case out. "Mouse, these are yours. You're ready for them."

"Oh," Owyn breathed. "Oh, I know what you did." He took the case and set it on the ground, opening it and sighing in wonder. "Really? You really made these for me? Oh, Mem. Oh..." He stopped in the act of reaching into the case. "Should... should I start calling you Fa now? Since I'm your son and all."

"Do you think I didn't know that's what Mem meant all these years?" Memfis asked gently. Owyn grinned.

"I guess it does, doesn't it?" He reached into the case and drew out a pair of S -shaped staves.

"Memfis had a pair of those when you met us," Aria said. "What are they?"

"Smoke blades," Memfis answered. "The mark of the Smoke Dancer. Also, the weapon of the Smoke Dancer. Owyn has been using a wooden training set. A metal set—"

"Means you're telling me I'm a full Smoke Dancer," Owyn interjected. He'd taken both blades out, and was cradling them in his arms like a baby.

"Yes, that is what I'm saying," Memfis agreed. He reached into the space and took out one last thing — a box that was about half the size of the cases. "Aria, this is for you."

Aria took the box and set it on a workbench, opening it up. She took out something that looked like nothing Aven had ever seen before. Apparently, it was new to Aria as well. "Memfis, what is this?"

Memfis got up and held his hand out. "Let me have it, and give me your hand. Are you right or left handed?"

"Right handed," Aria answered.

"Then give me your left. This is cumbersome once it's on, but you'll get used to it." He took the thing, and slid it onto Aria's hand like a gauntlet, strapping it around her wrist. He turned her palm up so that she could see the strap that ran across it. "See this? Once this is armed, don't squeeze your hand until you're ready to shoot something."

"Shoot — Memfis, is this a crossbow?" She leaned over her hand and studied it. "It's so small!"

"This one took me the longest. Getting the mechanism right took almost a year. Now watch." He shifted two filigree curves on the back of Aria's hand, and they popped free of the gauntlet and sprang out to reveal the arms of the bow. "The catch is here," he said, and demonstrated how to arm the bow. "Quarrels will fit into the armpiece. The active range is about nine feet."

Aria nodded. "It's beautiful."

"And your box isn't empty," Memfis pointed out. Aria blinked, then looked again and took out a tube of barbed spears as long as her arm.

"Javelins," she said. "I can use these."

"You've had these all hidden for twenty years," Aven murmured. "Twenty years ago, I was still learning to walk on land. I was practically a baby! We all were." He took a practice swing with his right-hand blade. "And this is perfectly balanced for my hand. You knew the man I was going to be before I did."

Memfis chuckled softly. "Benefits of being a seer," he said. "Now, we need to leave, before whatever Owyn says is coming becomes now."

"Should we put the anvil back?" Owyn asked.

"No reason to," Memfis answered. "I don't think we'll be coming back any time soon."

Owyn frowned. "Not... not back? Then... give me a minute." He went over to the forge and knelt down. "Hey. Hey, it's me." At the sound of his voice, the fire mice appeared. One of them scurried forward and clambered onto Owyn's knee. He laughed, scooping Trinket up in his hand. "So, I suppose you're wondering why I called you out?" he asked the mice. "It's because we're leaving. Mem and I. We're going away, and I don't know when we'll be back. If we'll be back. So you all... you need to find another place. Another fire. This one... we're not firing it again. It's going to stay cold." He looked up. "Aven, how do I know if they understand me?"

The answer came from Trinket, who chittered at Owyn, sounding as if she was scolding him. Then she ran up his sleeve, and climbed down his chest into the pocket of his shirt.

"Trinket!" he gasped. "You can't come with us! It won't be safe!"

"I think she made her decision, Owyn," Aven said. "She wants to stay with you."

"What about the others?" Owyn asked. "They... oh. They went." Aven looked down to see that the other mice had already vanished.

"They understand more than you give them credit for," Memfis said. "More than any of us gave them credit for."

"They're like Melody, then," Aria said. She took Aven's arm. "What do you think Melody will think when she meets Trinket?"

"I don't know," Aven said. "Trinket isn't anything like any animal Melody has ever seen. She might not know what to do with Trinket. I doubt she'd think a fire mouse was food, though. She doesn't eat land animals."

"Who's Melody?" Owyn asked.

"A water-cat," Aven answered. "My water-cat, I suppose you'd say. But I think she tells her pod that I'm her boy, so it's open to interpretation."

"You have a water-cat?" Memfis said. "That's... that's interesting. Very interesting."

Aven looked down at Aria. "Why?" he asked. Aria smiled.

"You'll find out tonight," she said, and hugged him. "Memfis, shouldn't we go?" She let Aven go and turned to go back into the house. Memfis followed her, leaving Owyn and Aven standing in the forge.

Aven watched them go. He considered going after them, then dismissed the thought. He was confused enough. Instead, he picked up the case with his swords in it, then draped one arm over Owyn's shoulders. "Owyn, you'll tell me if I cross any lines I shouldn't, won't you?"

Owyn looked confused, then grinned. "That's a sweet question to ask. Yes, I'll tell you." He looked through the door leading into the house as he idly spun one of his smoke blades. "Come on. They're up to something."

They went through the house, finding Memfis and Aria in the stable. Memfis nodded as they came in. "Stow the weapons in the back. We don't want them visible."

"I've got it," Owyn said as he clambered into the bed. He nestled his blades in the bottom of the hollow, then took the case from Aven and set it down. He covered them both with canvas, then made a face. "It'll be lumpy."

"It's the best we can do at the moment," Memfis said. He looked toward the door, and his eyes widened. "Horses." He looked around. "Shit. I wouldn't have thought he'd be able to move that quickly, or we'd have left immediately. Ah... Aven. Change clothes. Now."

"What?" Aven gasped. "Do we have time for that?"

"We're going to have to brazen our way out, and if they're here to take Owyn, he can't be seen. Mouse, take the coal cart into the corridor and close the door. Aria, those bundles there. Those are Aven's clothes."

Aven stepped out of the way and stripped quickly, changing into the clothes that Aria handed him. They fit him better than Owyn's clothes — the trousers came to his feet, and the sleeves of the shirt covered his wrists. He was putting the new boots on when Owyn came back inside and closed the door that led into the house.

"Owyn, you get into the back with Aria. Aven, you're my nephew Este, understand?"

"Este, yes."

"Your father is my brother. Your mother is Waterblood. You're here to visit family," Memfis continued. "And right now, I'm taking you to visit your grandmother for the first time."

Aven nodded, picked up his carry-bag, and slung it over his shoulder. "Anything else?"

"Just let me talk," Memfis said. "Go on. Aven... Este, you're up with me. Owyn, go with Aria."

A few minutes later, the cart looked as if it was laden with bundles and baskets, and Memfis was opening the stable doors. Aven sat on the bench, feeling uncomfortable, holding on as the cart lurched forward when Memfis led Stubborn out into the yard. He went back and closed the stable, then came forward; the cart shifted like a storm-tossed canoe as Memfis climbed up onto the bench next to Aven.

"Nervous?" Memfis asked, pitching his voice so that it would be overheard by anyone outside the wall surrounding the courtyard. "She won't bite you."

"I've no idea what to expect," Aven said. "She doesn't even know about me, does she?"

"She'll love you. Never you worry about that." Memfis smiled. "Go open the gates."

Aven jumped down from the cart and went to the gate, pulling it open. As he came around the gate, he saw the crowd out in the street — a dozen men on tall animals that had to be horses.

"Uncle?" he called.

"It's all right, Este," Memfis called back. "Come on. They won't keep us long. Karse, what can I do for you?"

Aven returned to the cart and climbed back to his seat as one of the mounted men urged his beast forward. "We're here about your boy, Fisher."

"Owyn?" Memfis frowned. "What's he done?"

"There's been a complaint filed—"

Memfis sighed. "Let me guess. Fandor?"

"Says that your boy owes him fifty casts."

"Fifty... Karse, if my boy had fifty casts, he'd have bought out his indentures, and those of six other boys for good measure. And had casts left over to live on!"

Karse shook his head. "I know, Fisher. It doesn't make sense. But we have to investigate–"

"Karse, let me tell you something you don't know," Memfis said. "You know what my boy was, right?"

"Yeah, I know." He glanced back at one of the men with him, a younger man with sandy blond hair. He nodded, and Karse turned back to Memfis. "I know," he repeated. "Why?"

"Because if you know that, then you know that Fandor is the one that put him there." Memfis leaned forward. "And Fandor wants him back. He was here this morning, harassing my boy until I banned him from my forge, and from this district."

"Fisher, you didn't!" Karse gasped, and his horse danced underneath him.

"Sealed it on my anvil," Memfis said. "So ask yourself why this complaint is sworn now, hm?" He frowned. "When was this debt incurred?"

Karse frowned. He took a paper from inside his coat, looking down at it. "It... doesn't say."

"If it happened before Owyn was sold, then the debt is considered a loss, right?" Memfis asked. "And if it happened after, well, then, it's my responsibility. Wait a moment." He handed the reins to Aven, who yelped.

"Uncle!"

"Stubborn won't run away with you, Este," Memfis said. "I need to go back inside." He climbed down from the cart and went back to the house. Aven swallowed, looking down at the floor of the cart.

"Este?"

Aven looked up to see that Karse had come closer. "Yes, sir."

"Can't say I've seen you before."

"New here, sir," Aven answered. He looked around and gave a nervous grin. "Never seen a place like it. I'm from up north. Came to visit my uncle."

"You definitely do have a bit of bumpkin about you," Karse said. "No offense meant, but you've clearly never been in a city before." He peered closer. "Waterblood?"

"Yes, sir," Aven answered. "Half. I take after my mother."

"Be careful, then. You'll dry out faster here," Karse said gently. He looked past Aven, who turned to see Memfis coming out of the house. He walked past the cart and up to Karse, handing the man a large pouch.

"Fifty casts. Tell him he can choke on it." Memfis took hold of Stubborn's harness. "Now, are we done?"

Karse stared at the pouch. "Fisher, if there's no truth to this complaint, why pay?"

"Because my boy — and between you, me, and the rest of your men, once the paperwork is official tomorrow, I'll be calling him my son—"

Karse burst out laughing. "I wondered when you'd finally do it!"

Memfis smiled. "Because he's told me what Fandor did to him. Because I know, and you know, what happens if you take someone indentured in on a debt complaint." Karse nodded slowly, and Memfis continued. "And because fifty casts is a small price to pay to keep my son safe."

Karse nodded again. "I'll see the complaint vacated, then. Since the debt is paid. Where is Owyn, anyway?"

"We've a big job coming up, so I sent him off to the coal fields. He'll be back tomorrow."

"You sent him on Respite?"

"Actually, I sent him yesterday, and told him not to rush, because it was Respite. He's having a holiday." Memfis smiled. "Now, can we be going? My mother is expecting me."

Karse nodded. "Met your nephew here. Didn't know you had a brother."

"Jhansri was adopted, same as me. You know I've got no bloodline to speak of. He settled up north a ways, built a canoe with a Water girl."

Karse grinned. "Sounds good. Nice to meet you, Este."

"Nice to meet you, sir," Aven said. He relaxed slightly as the men rode away. Memfis led the cart out into the street, closed the gate, then climbed back up next to Aven and took the reins.

"You handled yourself well," Memfis murmured. "Let's get going. It's got to be hot back there."

"What was that all about? What would have happened if you hadn't paid?" Aven asked.

Memfis looked around, then pitched his voice low. "If an indentured slave goes into debt, they become the property of their creditor until the debt is paid. Even if their indentures are owned by someone else."

Aven coughed. "So if you hadn't paid—"

"They'd have marched Owyn off in chains, and handed him over to Fandor."

"And, let me guess. There's no way to pay off the debt?"

Memfis shook his head. "Nope. A quarter of whatever pittance the law decides the slave is getting paid goes to the debt. The rest goes to the owner of the indentures. And there's interest on the debt, which is always more than what that quarter applied will cover. So the poor sot ends up being a slave to two masters."

"That's barbaric," Aven muttered. "And Mannon made these laws?"

"Mannon made these laws," Memfis confirmed.

"Mannon makes bad laws," Aven grumbled.

"The word you want is shitty," Memfis said. "Mannon makes shitty laws. Mannon makes laws that are good for people who have money, or power, or connections to money and power. If you don't? Well, too bad."

Aven considered the words, then shook his head. "I don't like it."

"I'd be surprised if you did," Memfis said, sounding amused.

"Not the laws. The word. Shitty seems too mild a word." Aven shrugged. "I don't know any stronger, though. Me— Fisher, where are we going?"

"You heard me. My mother is expecting me."

CHAPTER SIXTEEN

"MEMFIS," AVEN ASKED as Memfis drove the cart through a wide gate. "Is this a palace?" He glanced behind them, and saw that two men were closing the gate.

Memfis chuckled. "No, but I can see why you'd think so. You're about to meet the scion of one of the first families of Forge, a straight line descendant of Nerris and Axia."

Aven shrugged. "That doesn't impress me nearly as much as you seem to think it should," he said. "I'm a straight line descendant of Abin and Axia. So this person is technically related to me."

"What about this, then?" Memfis offered. "Her bloodline is the first page of the *Book of Silver*."

Aven looked at him. "Shouldn't the entire Fire tribe's bloodlines start on page one of the *Book of Silver*?"

Memfis burst out laughing. "True. Very true."

"You told Karse you were taking me to meet your mother. My grandmother, if we go with the story. Is she really your mother?"

Memfis looked around. "It's safe inside these walls. She's Fisher's adoptive mother," he answered. "She knows who I really am. She's known me since I was a boy. She's not my mother, but she's the closest I have to one." He drew back on the reins, and the cart slowed and stopped. "You can go let them out," he added, nodding toward the back of the cart.

Aven jumped down and went to the rear, moving bundles so that he could flip back the canvas cover. "Owyn, Aria, we're here."

Owyn sat up, blinking sweat out of his eyes. "And we're needing another bath after that," he grumbled.

"And something to drink," Aria added. She wiped her face. "Where are we?"

"Big house, belongs to someone important. That's all I know," Aven answered. Owyn looked up.

"Lady Meris," he said. "She's the Senior Smoke Dancer for the city. Sits on the Council. Both Councils. She's been part of ruling Forge for fifty years at least."

Aven frowned. "I thought you said smoke dancing was illegal."

"Now it is, sure," Owyn said. "Except for her. Lady Meris... she's honorary grandmother to most of Forge. If Mannon tried to have her removed from the Council, there'd be blood in the streets. So she's the last official Smoke Dancer, and the oldest. And the best. And there's a Magistrate chomping at the bit, waiting for her to stand down so he can finally take her place. But she just keeps on going."

"Out of pure, unadorned spite," Memfis said as he joined them. "She says she's keeping her seat until the Firstborn once more wears Axia's Crown. Come along. We shouldn't keep her waiting." He turned and headed toward the house. Aven glanced at the others. Owyn just nodded, then turned and followed Memfis.

"Are you all right?" Aven asked Aria. She nodded.

"I wish I knew more of what is going on. What Memfis is planning," she said as they started walking after Owyn. "I feel as if I'm in the middle of *The Lay of Axia's Choice*, and I'm missing half the notes of the song."

Owyn turned around, walking backwards. "You sing?" he asked. "Why haven't I heard you sing?"

"Because there hasn't been much time for music for a long time," she answered, and took his arm. "I haven't sung a note since before I left my flock. Do you sing?"

"Yeah, some. I like music. How about you, Aven?"

"A little," Aven admitted. "Not as good as some, but I can carry a tune. I drum. But most of the Water tribe knows how to drum. It carries well underwater." He looked ahead. "There's someone there."

At the door of the house, they saw a woman, stooped with age and leaning on a cane. Her crepe-like skin was dark, but not as dark as Memfis', and her hair had gone completely white. She was the oldest person Aven had ever seen. Older than his grandmother, he was certain. Possibly old enough to be his grandmother's grandmother. Memfis leaned down to hug her. Then he turned to look for them.

"Come here," he called. "You need to meet our benefactor." He turned back to the old woman. "Meris, this is—"

"I think I know who she is," Meris said, her voice stronger than her appearance would have indicated. "Memfis, you've brought me a great gift."

"I couldn't not bring her, Meris." He held his hand out to Aria. "Aria, daughter of Milon, this is Meris. Your great-grandmother."

Aria stopped, her nails digging into Aven's arm. "My... my what?" she gasped.

"You didn't warn her, Memfis?" Meris said. "Oh, that's cruel. She had no idea I even existed."

"You didn't know about me, either," Aria said.

"I did. I knew. Milon told me that his Liara was expecting, the last time he came to visit me." Meris held her hands out. "Come and let me look at you. My eyes aren't what they used to be."

Aria let go of Aven's arm, and moved to stand in front of the old woman. Meris straightened slightly, one hand on her cane for support. She smiled.

"You're his, and no mistake about it," she said. "I can see him smiling in your eyes." She held her hand out. "Come inside. I want to know you. I've waited a long time for you, my dear."

Aria took Meris' hand, and Meris led her into the house. Memfis gestured for Aven to follow. Owyn waited until Aven was next to him before he started walking.

"She's a legend, Lady Meris is," he said, his voice low. "She's possibly one of the strongest Smoke Dancers ever. She wore the Fire gem for Firstborn Riga. Her oldest daughter was Firstborn Tirine, and her younger was Milon's mother."

"Does that mean I'm related to Milon? And to Aria?" Aven asked.

"No, Riga didn't sire either girl," Memfis answered, falling back to walk with them. "They were full sisters, and their father was another Smoke Dancer."

"His name was Versin," Meris called back, and laughed. "My eyes are failing me. My ears are not. Memfis, once we're settled, introduce me to the young Water man."

"What about me?" Owyn protested. Meris looked back and smiled.

"I already know you. My darling reprobate. My bonus grandson. My Owyn."

Owyn grinned. "I know. I just wanted to hear you say it."

"And you're a brat," Meris finished.

Aven snickered. "She really does know you," he teased. Owyn elbowed him gently. "How's Trinket? How'd she do on the trip?"

"Burrowed into the straw and went to sleep," Owyn answered. He patted his pocket. "She's here now, and she's fine. I wish she'd have stayed. We're not going to be safe."

"Maybe she'll stay here?" Aven suggested. Owyn looked up at him.

"I'll have a talk with her. And with Lady Meris. But Meris keeps cats, so maybe not."

They walked through the halls, and Aven knew that if he'd been left to his own devices, he'd have been hopelessly lost in a matter of minutes. Finally, they stopped in a large room lined with bookcases. There were cushioned chairs here and there, and a long, high wooden table along one wall that bore bottles of various colors.

"Come in and sit," Meris said. "Aria, sit here by me. Memfis, introduce me." She sat down in a tall chair and smiled. "It's all right, my dear. I don't bite."

Memfis turned to Aven, who came to stand in front of Meris. He bowed, the way he would have to his own grandmother.

"Meris, may I present Aven, son of Aleia and Jehan?" Memfis said formally.

"Of what canoe?" Meris asked. Aven blinked.

"Arana's canoe, Mother," he answered, giving her the formal title he'd have offered to any older woman of the Water tribe. She smiled.

"You're surprised I know to ask that?," she asked. "I spent years with a Waterborn as one of my closest friends. Hara, of Listell's canoe. She was our Water. Arana's canoe, that's a very exalted bloodline. And Aleia and Jehan? My Milon's Aleia and Jehan?"

"Yes, Mother," Aven said.

"Then you're Riga's blood! His... let me think. His great-grandson." She leaned back in her chair. "Well."

"I only just learned that," Aven admitted. "Ah... yesterday? The day before? I've lost track of the days."

Meris nodded. "I see." She looked thoughtful, then up at Memfis. "We shouldn't keep them, Memfis. We'll only bore them with our talk."

Memfis arched a brow, then nodded. "Owyn, why don't you show Aven and Aria down to the kitchens, and get something to eat?"

"Do we have to go?" Aria asked. She blushed when everyone looked at her. "I... I've only just found you. I don't want to leave yet."

Meris smiled gently. "I'm not throwing you out into the streets , my dear," she said. "Just sending you off for a bit. We've time before the Council meeting to get to know each other." She made a graceful shooing gesture. "Now go along. We'll walk in the garden later, just you and I."

"Come on," Owyn said. He led them out of the room, and into the hall. Once the door was closed, he looked up and down the hall. Then he turned to them, a serious expression on his face. "Come on," he repeated, this time in a whisper. "Follow me. Don't argue."

Shocked, Aven looked at Aria, who shrugged. They followed Owyn down the hall to another door, and into another room.

"Owyn, what are we doing?" Aven asked.

"Listening," Owyn answered. "Look, you don't have to. Not if it makes you uncomfortable. But I need to. I... you need to know why. I don't like it when people talk about me behind my back. On the streets, that shit gets you killed. I learned that lesson a long time ago, and I learned it well. So, I listen." He looked at Aven, then Aria. "If I don't know, I get nervous. Scared. And... yeah, it's not good. Mem understands. He usually is pretty good about making sure that I know what's being said. But this? He usually doesn't shut me out. He knows I don't deal well with it. And he only ever does it with Meris, so... I listen." He pointed to another door. "That closet backs up to Lady Meris' library. We'll be able to hear them if we're quiet."

Aven looked at the door. "Memfis won't like this, will he?"

"Probably not. But this is about us. And what we don't know might hurt us," Owyn looked at the door. "Are you coming, or not?"

"I am," Aria said. "I don't like being sent from the room like a child."

Aven nodded. "I've spent the past few weeks feeling as if I've been swimming my entire life through muddy waters, and just never knew it. I'm not going back to ignorance now."

Owyn smiled. "Right. Once I open that door, not a word, not a sneeze, not a fart. Got it? If we can hear them, they can hear us." He opened the door and they crowded inside. The closet was small, and cramped, and they couldn't close the door because of Aria's wings. They ended up with Owyn kneeling, and Aven standing over him, with Aria pressed against his back. And, as Owyn said, they could hear every word.

"— drink, Meris?"

"Just tea. Which you should have as well. I don't want you crawling back into a bottle, Memfis."

Memfis' voice grew louder, and Aven realized that this wall was the same as the one that ran behind the long table of bottles. "As if I would," Memfis said. "No, I need my head on straight for this."

"Tell me your thoughts, then."

"I'm still getting my thoughts in order," Memfis said eventually. "She's the dove. I'm certain of it."

"Memfis, really. We were all of us certain about Yana." There was a long pause. "No. No, I'm wrong. You were the only one who said you weren't certain. I was always impressed that you didn't tell the rest of us 'I told you so' when she vanished. So convince me. Why are you so sure of Aria, when you weren't about Yana?"

"Yana didn't have any of her Companions. She wasn't interested in finding them, either. Aria has two of the four. Aven is the water-cat. Owyn is the flame," he chuckled. "My Owyn. My Fire Mouse."

"Are you surprised?" Meris asked. "He's been through the heart of the furnace to become the man he is. And then you took him and put an edge on him. He still has his flaws, but he's a masterwork all the same. Memfis, you should be proud of him."

"I am," Memfis said.

Aven looked down and smiled, resting his hand on Owyn's shoulder. Owyn tipped his head back.

"You're that sure of them," Meris said. "And what? What are you hoping to accomplish tonight?"

"Tonight? I'm getting them the fuck out of Forge—"

"Memfis! Language!"

"Sorry. But not much. You know as well as I do that this place is Mannon's back pocket. And he knows they're here."

"They're connected to the fire in the harbor?"

Memfis sighed. "I don't have the whole of it, I don't think. Aven was ill. Aria told me some of it, but I think Aven will need to tell you the rest."

"Memfis, if you can't convince me, you can't convince the others," Meris said. "So convince me."

"It's not my place to convince you, Meris. That's for Aria and her Companions. She does have the Diadem. I've seen it. And... Meris, she's a Smoke Dancer. Untrained, but she's had her waking vision. And she's had the vision of the dove."

"She inherited the gift?" Meris sounded shocked. "And she's had visions without being in the vents? Mother of us all, Memfis, how can she possibly dance in the vents with wings? There isn't room!"

"Apparently, she dances on air," Memfis said. "From what she's told me, all of her visions were had on the wing."

"Oh," Meris gasped. "Oh! How are you going to teach her?"

"I have no idea," Memfis said. "Now, tonight? All I want is the supplies we'll need on the road. I'm not looking to start the war tonight, Meris. We need to find her other two first. That was the mistake the last time."

Aria tapped Aven on the shoulder. He turned to see her gesture out of the closet. She stepped out, and Aven tapped Owyn. They slipped out of the closet and closed the door.

"More questions than answers," Aria said. "Do either of you know who Yana is?"

"You know I don't," Aven answered. "What's the vision of the dove?"

"That I will tell you later," Aria said. "Owyn?"

"I know it. I've had it. But I've never heard the name Yana before," Owyn added. "Let's go to the kitchen. We'll get something to eat, and go out into the gardens and talk. The gardens are private, and I don't know about you two, but I'm hungry."

Aven nodded. "I could eat. All right." He looked back at the closet. "That didn't make much sense."

Owyn nodded, and led them out of the room and down the hall. There were people in the kitchen who seemed to know Owyn, and who were more than happy to put together a meal for them to share in the garden.

"And no cheese," Owyn said. "And could we have extra salt, please?"

An older woman chuckled. "I know how to feed a child of water, Master Owyn. Go along with you, and I'll bring the basket to the garden."

Owyn turned slightly pink, and led Aven and Aria through the kitchen and out into a large garden surrounded by a high wall. Owyn led them to a wooden structure covered with plants, and where there was a stone table and several benches.

"You spend a lot of time here?" Aria asked.

"We come every Respite," Owyn said. He tucked his hands under his arms. "Huh. I just realized something."

"What?" Aven asked.

"Mem is a lousy liar." Owyn snorted. "He told Karse that he'd sent me out to the coal field yesterday, didn't he? That's what I thought I heard."

"He did," Aven agreed. Then he groaned. "But Fandor saw you at the forge today!"

"Right." Owyn sighed. "Good thing we're out of here tonight." He looked up and shook his head. "He scares me."

"Fandor?" Aven asked.

Owyn nodded, starting to shift gently from foot to foot. He tucked his chin down to his chest. "If he gets his hands on me again, I don't think I'm surviving it." Owyn's voice was quiet.

"We're not letting him get his hands on you," Aria said. She moved to stand behind Owyn, putting her arms around him and resting her cheek on his shoulder. "You're mine now. No one is taking you away from me."

"Ours," Aven corrected. "He's ours. You have to share."

Owyn smiled and covered Aria's hands with his own. "Keep telling me that, will you?"

"Mine," Aria repeated. "Mine, mine, mine." She paused, glanced over at Aven, then sighed. "All right. Ours."

"Yes, ours," Aven agreed, coming to stand in front of Owyn. He rested his hands on Owyn's shoulders, then stepped closer, wrapping his arms around Owyn and Aria. "Ours."

He felt Owyn sigh against his chest, and rubbed his cheek against Owyn's short hair. Behind him, he heard a door opening. Their meal, he assumed, and let go so he could turn. There was a man there, a stranger.

"No," Owyn's moan sounded like it came from a wounded animal. "No, no, no..."

Aven knew immediately who this was. Fandor. How had he gotten into the garden? No time to think of that now — he stepped in front of Owyn, hiding him from view. "Go inside," he whispered.

"He is between us and the inside," Aria said. She joined him. "And I think he came from inside. Try to get past him." she said softly.

"I can't leave you!"

"I am armed. You are not." She raised her left arm, and armed her crossbow. "You will come no further," she ordered.

"I heard you, you know," Fandor said. "He's not yours. He never was. He's mine. My little slut, and I'm not leaving without him." He gestured, and men in the same uniform that Karse had worn came filing into the garden. "You don't have enough arrows to take all of us, girl."

Aven stepped back, drawing Owyn with him, back into the shelter of Aria's wings. He looked around, hunting for a weapon, something he could use... Owyn whimpered, and Aven turned to see another group of men behind them. They were surrounded.

CHAPTER SEVENTEEN

"ARIA," AVEN CALLED, his voice low. She glanced over her shoulder, saw the other men. Her eyes narrowed.

Fandor looked thoughtful. "Aria," he repeated. "An Air girl named Aria. A Water boy... I assume you're Aven? Oh, Mannon will pay very well for you two."

Aven swore softly and looked around once more. There had to be something— oh, of course! There were metal hooks, as long as his leg, holding hanging pots of flowers all around the outside of the structure. He stretched, jerked two out of the ground, and let the pots fall with a crash.

"Owyn, duck under the table," he whispered. "Stay there."

Owyn dropped to the ground, and Aven stepped outside of the structure, his back to Aria. The hooks were heavy, although lighter than his swords, and Aven hoped they were strong enough to take some punishment. He hoped he remembered everything he'd learned from his mother. He hoped someone heard the pots breaking. One of the men facing him moved, and Aven growled at him. The man jumped backwards, clearly startled. Behind him, Aven heard a snap, and someone yelled in pain. That seemed to be the signal — the rest of the guards rushed toward them, and there was no longer time to think, only to react. Aven blocked, dodged, and left guards howling in pain as he used the hooks as bludgeons, hearing the hollow sound of cracked skulls and the snap of broken bones.

Turning as he used his right hand hook to sweep the legs out of a guard trying to get past him showed him that Aria had taken wing, and was picking off Fandor's men from the air. Aven wasn't sure where Fandor had gone. Hopefully, not for reinforcements.

A moment to breathe, and Aven looked around. His hooks were bent, and he took a moment to replace them with short swords taken from the broken men that now littered the garden. He picked his careful way around to where Aria came to rest, then looked back toward the table. Owyn was still there, curled into a ball beneath the stone.

"Where is he?" Aria demanded. "Fandor. Where did he go?"

"I lost track of him," Aven admitted. He whirled as a door opened, only to relax when he saw Memfis. Memfis stepped out, and his jaw dropped.

"What happened here?" he demanded, looking as if he'd been slapped. Then he turned and roared, "Meris!"

"What in the Mother's own name?" Meris asked. "Memfis, what are you shouting for–?" Her voice trailed off as she came out into the garden. "Mother of us all," she breathed. "What happened here?"

"Fandor happened here," Aria snapped. "He came from inside the house. He knew Owyn was here. And now he knows who we are. He is going to Mannon."

"Came from—" Meris repeated. "Come inside. Come inside now. Where's Owyn? Where's my Owyn?"

Aven turned and went to the table, crouching and setting the short swords down. "Come out," he said gently. "I'm not letting anyone take you."

Owyn had curled in around himself, his forehead pressed to his knees, and he'd wrapped his arms around his head. Shaking his head made his entire body shake. "Can't," he said, his voice shaky and muffled. "Can't come out."

"Owyn," Aven said.

"No!" Owyn moaned. "Can't. Can't."

"He's caught," Memfis said as he came to join Aven. "He's spiraling. It's going to take him a while to come out of it."

"Can we get him inside?" Aven asked. Memfis shook his head.

"You try and pull him out of there, you'll just make it worse. I haven't seen him this bad in a long time."

Aven nodded. Then he shoved benches out of the way and crawled under the table with Owyn.

"What are you doing?" Memfis asked.

"He's not coming out, so I'm going in," Aven answered. "That all right?" he asked Owyn. "I can come in and be with you?"

There was a long pause, then a low, harsh whisper, "Yes."

"Touching or not touching?"

Another pause. "Touching."

Aven rested his hand on Owyn's back. "I'm not letting him take you. I'm not letting you get hurt. If he tries to kill you, he'll have to go through me first." He looked over at Aria, who was talking with Meris. Or maybe talking at Meris, who didn't seem to be saying anything in response. "He'll have to go through both me and Aria. You're ours now." He kept on talking in low gentle tones, shifting until he had maneuvered himself fully under the table, with Owyn between his legs. Only then did he put his arms around the smaller man. "I've got you. I'm not letting you go." He felt Owyn shudder, and tightened his arms, repeating himself over and over, "I've got you."

When he finally looked up, it was darker in the garden. Someone was lighting lanterns, while someone else was taking care of the injured men that Aven and Aria had left lying around. He couldn't see Memfis, Meris and Aria anymore.

"Memfis?" he called.

"Above you," Memfis answered. "Sitting on the table."

"Ah," Aven said. He shifted slightly, feeling Owyn move with him, and pressed a kiss to the back of Owyn's neck. "Where are Meris and Aria?"

"They went inside. Meris is furious. She's got the Guard Captain for the City inside, and is filing formal charges against Fandor for trying to kidnap her grandson. Karse is there, too."

"Is Aria in there with them?"

"Aria is, I think, in the closet of the room next to the library, listening. We're not risking her."

Aven looked up at the underside of the tabletop. "You knew about that?"

Memfis snorted. "It's why we have conversations about Owyn in the library in the first place. I know how he reacts. Meris knows, too." He chuckled. "Besides, he likes it better if he thinks he's getting away with something."

"I *can* hear you," Owyn muttered from inside the circle of Aven's arms. "Just in case you were wondering."

Memfis peered down over the edge of the table. "And you can respond? Aven, you do good work."

Aven smiled and kissed Owyn's neck again. "Feeling up to coming out of here and into the house?"

"Not yet."

"How about a blanket, then? It's getting damp." Memfis climbed down off the table.

"Blanket is good," Owyn answered. He didn't move at all as Memfis walked away.

"Food might be good, too," Aven suggested.

"Not... not yet," Owyn answered. "Not... no."

"All right. When you're ready." Aven shifted, resting his forehead on the back of Owyn's neck. "I'm not going anywhere."

"This... this is nice," Owyn murmured. "I... it's nice."

"You did this for me, before. In the baths. You said you understood." Aven smiled. "You didn't have to show me you understood, you know."

To his surprise, Owyn giggled. "Not my idea."

"I know. Do you mind if I kill him?"

To Aven's shock, Owyn sat upright and twisted in his arms, his eyes wide. "No!" he gasped. "No, you can't kill him!"

"Why not?" Aven asked. "Owyn, I doubt I'd actually have the chance. But why can't I, if I did have the chance? Remember, I don't know much about land."

"Because he's a Loremaster," Owyn answered. "He's a city official. If you kill him, they'll take you and throw you into the Smoking Mountain."

"What?" Aven gasped. "You're not joking?"

"Not even half. City officials are sacred." Owyn snorted, then intoned, "They are chosen by the Mother to serve her children." It sounded as if he was quoting something, but Aven didn't know what. "They're not. Not anymore. They might have been, once, but most of them... they buy their positions."

"If the positions are supposed to be sacred, how can they be bought?" Aven asked.

Owyn shook his head. He leaned back into Aven's chest, resting his head against Aven's shoulder. "Because since Mannon, the whole city is corrupt. From the very top to the very bottom. There are a few good ones left. Meris, and Mem. Karse. He' s a good one. Most guards would have pocketed those casts. Karse almost certainly gave them to Fandor. But most of the others? They'd stab their own mothers if it would make them a clipped cast. You saw it. There were guards here with Fandor. There were guards here to take me away."

"I'm starting to think I prefer it out on the waves," Aven grumbled. Owyn nodded.

"Tell me about it," he said. His voice sounded sleepy, and his tense body slowly uncurled as he relaxed in Aven's arms. "Tell me about living on the water. And... you can breathe underwater, can't you? That's what the gills are for."

"That's what the gills are for," Aven agreed. "I change when I'm in salt water. That's why trousers are really weird for me."

"And shoes. I can't imagine you've ever worn anything on your feet before." Owyn yawned and closed his eyes.

"Are you all right?" Aven asked.

"Better than I was," Owyn answered. "Keep telling me. Tell me about Melody."

Aven laughed. "Melody is a water-cat," he said. "I told you that. She's big. A lot bigger than Trinket."

"Cats are bigger than mice," Owyn mumbled. His entire body seemed to be limp, heavier than Aven would have expected.

"Water-cats are bigger than me," Aven said. "She's almost two of me, laid end to end. Long, like an eel. Mostly tail, really. She's gray, all over. And soft, smooth."

"No scales?"

"No. More like leather." Aven smiled. "Mouth full of sharp teeth, like a shark. But smarter than a shark. Fa found her when I was a baby. She was hurt, and he put her to rights. We raised her, until she joined a pod. But she stays close to us. She's been with me since before I could walk." He looked down and stopped talking — Owyn was asleep. He shifted gently, putting his back against the central pillar of the table, and watched the shadows creeping across the grass. A door opened, light spilling out of the house as Memfis came back outside. He looked surprised as he reached the table and knelt down.

"He's asleep?" he murmured. "Aven, I don't think I've ever seen him come out of that state so quickly."

"This is normal?" Aven asked. "He always sleeps?"

"Always. Panic uses a lot of energy. He goes so completely into a panic that it usually takes him hours before he stops, and he usually only stops because he passes out from exhaustion. Lean forward." Aven did, and Memfis wrapped a blanket around him and Owyn. "You look like you could use a nap yourself."

"I don't kn—." Aven yawned, then grinned. "All right. I do know. Yes. What's going on in the house?"

"The Guard Captain is gone, and promised Meris that he'd present Fandor's head to her on a platter, with the guards who were here with him as garnish. Word has gone out to the rest of the Council that the adoption papers were filed earlier today for Owyn, and that Fandor has disgraced his position as Loremaster by attempting to kidnap the son of another Councilor. The Council will meet to formally to recognize the adoption and remove Fandor from his position."

Aven nodded. "What happened to the men? I saw someone taking them out, but I wasn't paying much attention."

"They were all turned over to the Guard Captain. Some were guards. The rest of them were gutter trash, in it for a quick cast." Memfis shifted around. "The dead—"

"How many?"

"Killed? Seven, I think. Five darts, and two heads bashed in." Memfis chuckled. "I never thought those ornamental hooks were good for anything other than looking pretty."

"They were solid enough. And the same basic shape as my swords." Aven took a deep breath and closed his eyes. "I thought I was supposed to be sick or something. Isn't that what happens when you kill your first man? That's what all the stories say."

"If you're sick now, it'll be into Owyn's hair, and he'll thrash you for it," Memfis said. "And no. It doesn't take everyone like that."

"Does Aria know? That she killed five men?"

Memfis gave a low laugh. "I told her. And she said she wished it had been more. She's furious that someone dared to try and lay a hand on her Owyn." He nodded toward the house. "She hasn't come out because she's still too angry. She's afraid that she'd frighten Owyn even more."

Aven smiled. "Tell her she should come out. He'll appreciate having her here when he wakes up." He blinked. "When do we go to the Dark Council?"

"We're not," Memfis said. "They're coming here. Meris put her foot down. I'm not sure how I'm going to talk her into letting us leave afterward. She's convinced that if we step foot outside her gates, that Owyn will vanish like smoke."

Aven nodded. He abruptly went from sleepy to tired in his bones, and sleeping with Owyn in his arms sounded like the best idea he'd ever had. "She might not be wrong. Until they find Fandor, we'll have to walk carefully."

"I think he's learned his lesson," Memfis said. "He won't risk his precious hide again. Not now that he knows that Owyn is protected."

Aven thought about pointing out that Owyn had been protected before. He'd been protected by Memfis, and by Meris. By high walls that should have been enough of a barrier to stop an attempted kidnapping. But Fandor had gotten through anyway. How? How had he gotten into the garden? Who had let him into the house? He thought about it, but surely those same thoughts had also occurred to Memfis? Aven shook his head. "The walls and the house and you and Meris weren't protection enough?" he pointed out. "We should still be careful."

Memfis chuckled. "You're as bad as she is." He patted Aven's leg. "We've set guards to keep watch on the gardens. They're patrolling, so you might hear them. Don't worry. You're safe to sleep out here, if you want." He looked up. "I'll wake you in an hour. That will give you both time to wash up and eat before the Dark Council arrives."

He got up and walked back to the house, and Aven sighed and closed his eyes. The blanket was warm, and Owyn's gentle, deep breathing was soothing, summoning Aven into sleep. He could get used to this, he mused. He heard, as if at a great distance, the sound of footsteps crunching on gravel. The guards, Aven thought, letting himself float into darkness, into sleep.

Only to be dragged abruptly back to awake by something wet and stinking pressed over his mouth and nose, by a hand hard around his throat, by the icy-shock of Owyn's warmth being pulled away. He gasped, breathing in the stench, opening his eyes to see a man crouched over him— Fandor! Aven grabbed at the hands at his throat, over his mouth, but his arms felt leaden, and his fingers didn't want to work. He saw Owyn, struggling in the arms of another man, a cloth pressed over his face. Then the world swirled and swayed and faded from night to a dull gray to a dead black.

CHAPTER
EIGHTEEN

"ARIA, MY DEAR, SIT down!" Meris repeated. "You're making me tired."

Aria glanced at the older woman. She was having trouble thinking of Meris as a relative and as her great-grandmother. Liara had been with her family when the Firstborn had fallen, and had remained with her flock to raise her daughter, but she'd never married, had refused all offers of marriage. Aria's bloodline as the daughter of Milon, the last Heir, made her something of a prize among the marriageable daughters of the flock. But in the Air tribes, a mixed blood daughter had little status, and a fatherless daughter had no status at all. Which meant that while her flock was headed by her grandfather, and while she had aunts and uncles and cousins, none of them had ever really known how to treat Aria in terms of family hierarchy. She'd never been close to any of them. It had always just been her and her mother, and her mother's rather grandiose views on who Aria was and how she should behave. She'd learned better since, but having this tiny, old woman welcome her so warmly was strange, and Aria wasn't sure if she believed Meris when she said how much she wanted to know Aria.

"Grandmother," Aria said. "I'm not sure I understand how Fandor got in. He came out through the house. I'm certain of that."

"He had to have," Memfis said as he came back into the library. "There's no access to the street from that garden. That's why it's supposed to be safe."

"How did he get into the house," Aria asked. "Has anyone found out?"

Meris frowned. "Memfis, I haven't spoken to Elanthe yet. Would you ring for her?"

Memfis nodded and went to the corner, pulling a golden rope that dangled there.

"How are they?" Aria asked.

"Aven says you should come out. He thinks Owyn will appreciate having you there when he wakes up," Memfis answered. "But we'll give them an hour. He was falling asleep when I left him. And Owyn is asleep, which means that Aven is a better healer than he thinks he is." He went to the table of bottles and filled a glass with a clear, amber-colored liquid.

"Memfis—" There was a definite warning tone in Meris' voice that left Aria wondering what was in the bottle.

"It's one drink, Meris," Memfis protested. "One. To settle myself. Walking out there—" He shook his head. Then he looked down at the glass he was holding and put it down. "And you're right. One leads to two leads to Memfis not being able to see straight."

"And we need you fully functional," Meris said, her voice firm. She turned in her chair. "Where is Elanthe?"

"Who is Elanthe?" Aria asked.

"My housekeeper," Meris answered. "You probably met her in the kitchen."

Aria thought about the people in the kitchen. "There was a woman there. She told Owyn that she knew how to feed a child of water. She told us to wait in the garden, and she'd bring us something to eat. But she never came out."

"That was probably Elanthe. She's very fond of Owyn," Meris said. "Memfis, be a dear and go see where she is?"

"May I come?" Aria asked. "I want to see to my men."

That drew an amused chuckle from Meris. "Of course, my dear. We'll all go." She rose from her chair, steadying herself on her cane. "As we go, we should talk. If you'd been raised as you ought to have been as Milon's daughter, in the Palace, you'd have been trained to know what to expect should you be chosen Heir. You've had none of that training. You probably have no idea what to expect as Heir."

Aria tucked her wings in close to her back and fell in next to the older woman. "I hardly think that there's any training that would have prepared me properly for what's happened over the past month."

"Oh, of course there isn't," Meris agreed. "But if you'd been born as you ought to have been, in the Palace of the Firstborn, you and Aven and any other children born to the Companions would have been taught from birth what to expect, and what was expected of you. Now, I'll do my best to fill in the gaps in that training. But what I was thinking of here was more along the lines of what to expect from your Companions. You have two of the four, and I think you may have already found your Heart —"

"My heart?"

"Meris means Aven," Memfis said.

"I do think that he is the one, yes," Meris said. "But I also think that Aria doesn't know what I mean, so do hush, Memfis." Memfis laughed and continued walking; Meris took Aria's arm.

"Now, what I mean by Heart," she said as they continued down the corridor. "The Heir is the center of the Companion's world, and it's not an easy task to be a Companion. So, in every group of Heir and Companions, there is one who is the Heart of that group. The Heart is the one to whom the Companions turn for guidance, for comfort, for support in their most important role. Sometimes, the

Heart is the Heir themselves, and they care for their Companions as much as the Companions care for them. But in times of great need, the Mother sees fit to divide the burden of rule. In those cases, the Heart helps the Heir to bear the load. The Heir rules and cares for all of the people. The Heart sees to the Heir, and to the other Companions."

Aria smiled. "Then yes, that is Aven," she agreed. "Grandmother, will we all recognize each other every time? Aven said that he knew I was in the hold of that ship, as soon as he stepped onto the deck. We both recognized Owyn when we saw him. Will we all know our Earth, our Air?"

Meris looked startled. "You *both* recognized Owyn?"

"Of course," Aria answered. Then she considered how surprised Meris had seemed. "Is that odd?"

"It's unusual," Meris said slowly. "It's unusual for the bond to be so strong that anyone other than the Heir recognizes the other Companions. Did Owyn know you as well?"

"I think so," Aria said. "He told us that he thought it was simple attraction. You would have to ask him for more." She looked down the corridor to see Memfis turn into an open door, and recognized it as where Owyn had brought them earlier. She fought the urge to walk faster, but it was hard. She felt incredibly alone. She wanted Aven and Owyn at her sides, where they belonged. "What do I do when I find my others, Grandmother?" she asked.

"That, I can't answer," Meris answered. "I don't know the next step. None of us do."

"Who is "us"?"

"The Smoke Dancers," Meris said. "We've tried to look, but there are too many variables. Any time a Smoke Dancer has sought an answer of what to do about Mannon, and how to restore the Firstborn, all we've seen has been the vision of the dove. For over twenty years, there's been nothing else."

"That's the vision I had that sent me to the Temple," Aria said. "Did Memfis tell you? I saw them — the dove, the water-cat, the flame, the flower, and the broken feather." She sighed. "The broken feather — that disturbs me."

"I'd be surprised if it did not," Meris said. She stopped, and Aria looked up to see Memfis had come back into the corridor. He looked shaken, and he carried Aven's carry-bag in one hand. The strap was torn.

"They're gone," he said, his voice sounding harsh. "The garden is empty. The kitchens are empty. They're gone."

For a moment, nothing he'd said made sense. Gone? Empty? What? Then she realized what he meant, what Memfis having Aven's carry-bag had to mean. She pulled away from Meris and ran, pushing past Memfis and into the kitchen. She didn't stop, racing out into the dark gardens. Hadn't there been lights before? She didn't stop to think about it, heading for the wooden structure — the gazebo, Meris had called it. That had been where she'd last seen Aven and Owyn.

"Aven!" she called. "Owyn!" No answer, and she turned to see Memfis behind her. "What did you see?" she demanded.

"I came out and saw the lanterns were out," Memfis said. He sounded puzzled. "Owyn doesn't like the dark, so I went to the gazebo to check on them first. I found the bag, and the blanket. Nothing else."

"Lights," Aria said, turning around. It was dark enough that she couldn't make out anything. "We need lights. We need to see what happened here." She turned back to the house, saw Meris in the doorway. "Grandmother, someone in your house betrayed you. Betrayed us."

"Memfis, light the lanterns," Meris said, her voice steely cold. "I am going to find Elanthe and find out just what happened here." She disappeared into the kitchen, and Memfis followed. He came back a moment later carrying a lamp and a long slip that he used to light the lanterns around the garden. Then he joined Aria at the gazebo. The benches had been overturned, and the ground around the stone table was churned up. Aria stooped and picked up the blanket — it was torn. No, no, it was *cut*.

"Is there blood?" she asked softly. "Can you see?"

"No," Memfis answered. He bent, and picked up a rag that had fallen out of the bundled blanket. He sniffed it, and made a face.

"What is that?"

He held it out. "Sniff, but don't breathe too deeply."

Aria sniffed, smelling a bittersweet something. "What is it?"

"Dreamflower elixir," Memfis answered. "It's what healers use to knock patients out when they're in pain. It's powerful stuff."

Meris came out of the kitchen. "Memfis." Memfis and Aria both turned. "Elanthe—"

"Please tell me she's not dead?" Memfis asked.

"No, but I don't know if she'll wake," Meris said. "I'll have to send for a healer."

"And the other servants?" Memfis asked. "Turin, and Elise, and what's his name, that new—" He stopped. "Well, shit."

"The new groom," Meris said softly. "How long has he been planning this, do you think?"

"Does it matter?" Aria asked. "Fandor has my men. Where would he take them?"

"I don't know," Memfis said. "Karse. We need Karse. He might know."

"We need better than might, Memfis," Aria snapped. "Owyn says that if he is under Fandor's power again, he will not walk away. He believes that Fandor will kill him."

"He *said* that?" Memfis gasped. "No." He turned around. "Meris—"

"We'll find them," Meris said firmly. Then she sighed. "I should have listened to you earlier, Aria."

Aria turned, going to Memfis and taking the ruins of Aven's bag. The strap had been cut, and she wondered if she could repair it for him.

If she'd have the chance to give it to him.

"Yes," she said softly. "You should have."

AVEN CLOSED HIS EYES and tried to breathe, tried to think. His head was pounding, and waves of nausea kept washing over him, worse than when he'd eaten the cheese. He struggled to control his sickness — they'd left him gagged, and he didn't dare vomit, or he'd suffocate. He drew another long breath through his nose and started tugging against ropes once more. He'd woken up here, bound to a high-backed chair in what appeared to be an ornately furnished room. He couldn't see much of the room — the gag was fastened to the back of the chair, so he couldn't turn his head. He could feel tight ropes crossing his upper arms and his waist, and his legs were bound together, then tied to the chair. His wrists were tied to the arms of the chair, and whoever had done it knew what they were doing — he had pulled and fought until his wrists were raw and he was dripping in sweat, but he hadn't managed to shift an inch. And, the worst of it all, he was fairly certain that he was alone.

Where was Owyn? He growled into the gag. Sacred or not, once he was free of this blasted chair, he was going to use Fandor's guts to make fishing nets. He tugged hard, and felt warmth trickling over the back of his wrist. The pain did only a little to clear his head and drive the nausea back. What had been on that cloth?

Unbidden, he heard his father's voice, a half-forgotten lecture. *Dreamflower elixir,* Jehan said. *There's a pretty blue flower that grows up in the mountains. It's called Maiden's Tears. If you cold press the flowers, you get a perfume oil. If you heat distill it, you get dreamflower elixir. It's a powerful tool in a healer's kit — puts the patient to sleep, and keeps them under for about an hour. That's usually long enough to do whatever you need to do, and you don't have to use power to keep them asleep. You can focus on the healing.*

We've done this one, Fa, Aven remembered saying.

Fine, then, Jehan said. *Tell me the side effects.*

When used in excess, the patient may suffer headaches, nausea and vomiting, Aven recited. *There's also the chance of delirium, and in too large a dose, death.*

And how much is too much? Jehan asked.

That was the puzzle. No one really knew how much was too much, and the smart healer used dreamflower drop by drop on a breathing cone until the patient was asleep. Fandor hadn't used a breathing cone. He'd soaked rags in the stuff. No wonder Aven felt the way he did.

Owyn was smaller than Aven. Had the amount of dreamflower that was necessary to put Aven to sleep been too much for him?

Was that why Aven was alone? Was Owyn dead?

Aven wanted to scream, and he tugged hard against the ropes again, feeling more blood flowing over the back of his hand. After a few minutes of thrashing , he fell still, panting. He was caught, and Fandor would probably hand him over to Mannon. There was nothing he could do to save himself.

He'd failed them.

What happened, he wondered, when a Companion died? Would the Heir find someone to take their place? He hoped so. He hoped Aria wouldn't mourn them too much. He hoped Memfis would get her to safety. He hoped she'd find the pearl, and know that it was supposed to be for her.

Behind him, he heard a click, and a draft cooled the sweat on the back of his neck. He stiffened, hearing soft footsteps, and another click. He could hear movement behind him, but nothing was said. Then someone moved into his line of sight — a young man. He was barely dressed, wearing an open vest, and low-slung trousers that were open from waist to ankle, showing off the entire length of his legs from his bare feet to his hips. There was a silver collar around his neck, half hidden by long, white-blonde hair. He held one finger to his mouth, then raised his brows. Aven nodded, as much as he could, and the young man smiled. He moved out of sight, and Aven felt something tugging at his head. The gag fell away, and Aven swallowed, coughed, then swallowed again. The ropes around his chest and arms loosened next, and the young man reappeared. He repeated the gesture, holding his finger to his lips. Aven nodded, and watched as the young man knelt and started untying ropes. While he worked, Aven turned and looked around the room.

"Where are we?" he whispered. The young man looked up, and Aven saw that his eyes were as golden as Aria's. He was, Aven realized, incredibly beautiful. And he was... something. Something Aven knew that he needed, the same way he needed Aria, or Owyn.

Mother of all... was this one of their Companions?

The young man shook his head, tapped his throat, then shook his head again. He finished untying Aven's legs, and reached for the ropes at his left wrist.

"You don't speak?" Aven whispered. "You can't speak?"

He nodded, untying Aven's right wrist. He wrinkled his nose at the sight of the abrasions.

"I'll see to it later," Aven whispered. He looked over his shoulder. "How do I get out of here?"

His rescuer nodded, and finished freeing him from the chair. He rose to his feet as Aven got up, and pointed to the door. He held his finger to his lips again, then frowned and started moving his hands in gestures that Aven knew, but would never have expected from someone who wasn't Water.

"You know Water signs? How do you know Water signs?" Aven whispered. He shook his head. "No time. Four guards, you said?"

A brilliant smile, and a nod.

"All right. How do we get past them?"

The young man went to the door. He opened it a crack and peered outside, then gestured for Aven to follow him. Silently, they crept through the corridors, down stairs, and into a kitchen. There, the young man pointed urgently at a door.

"That's the way out?" Aven asked. An emphatic nod, and Aven looked at the door. Then he looked back at his rescuer. "Come with me."

Gold eyes went wide, and the young man shook his head.

"They're going to know you let me go," Aven insisted. "You're in danger."

The young man laughed, silently. He went to a corner by the large fireplace, where Aven could see a chain attached to a ring in the wall. The young man picked the chain up, attached it to his collar, then went to his knees on a small pallet. He smiled up at Aven, unfastened the chain, then refastened it. He smiled again.

Aven frowned, then realization dawned. "Whoever put you here doesn't know you can undo that," he murmured. "They think you're secure. So they won't know how I got away." The young man nodded, then pointed at the door. Aven looked at it, then went to one knee in front of the young man. "You saved my life, and I don't even know your name."

The young man smiled, his face turning ever so slightly pink. He raised his hands and signed, *"My name is Del."*

"Del," Aven said. "Thank you. If I can, I'm coming back for you."

Del's eyes widened. He shook his head, then turned and looked at the door from the kitchen into the house. He pointed at the other door. Aven took the hint. He got to his feet and ran, out the door and into the night.

ARIA HEARD MEMFIS BEFORE he entered the room. He'd gone for help, and had been gone long enough that she was starting to wonder if he was coming back. She set another stitch into the strap of Aven's bag, examined her work, then got up from her chair as the door opened. Meris entered first, looking tired and frail. Memfis came behind her, followed by two more men. The uniforms they wore were similar to the ones Aria had seen on men in the garden, and she touched the gauntlet on her left wrist.

Memfis saw the movement. "Aria, this is District Captain Karse, and his second, Trey. They can be trusted." He turned, and saw what was on the table next to where Aria had been sitting. "You emptied the bag?"

"I needed to fix it. It was too heavy when it was full." She looked down at the jar of salt, the Diadem, the gems, and the single pearl that she hadn't known Aven had been carrying. She reached out and touched the Diadem.

"Is that..." Karse started. He came closer, looking at the table. "Is that what I think it is?"

Aria met his eyes. "If you think it is the Heir's Diadem, you are correct."

"Karse," Memfis said. "Allow me to present Aria, daughter of Milon."

Karse's eyes went wide. "Milon? The real Heir?" He turned to Memfis. "Fisher, you son of a bitch. Why didn't you tell me?"

Memfis snorted. "There's a lot I don't tell you, Karse."

"Sure, I know that. Like your real damned name, Memfis." Karse turned from a shocked-looking Memfis back to Aria, then went to one knee. "My Heir."

Aria swallowed, stunned. Out of everything that could have happened in this moment, this was not something she'd foreseen. "Karse, please stand. We don't have time for pleasantries."

Karse got to his feet. "What's happened? What's wrong?"

"Fandor," Memfis said. "He's taken Owyn. And he took Aven—"

"Who?" Karse frowned. "Would that be the one you called Este?" He blinked. "Well, shit. You said his father's name was Jhansri. I wondered why that sounded familiar. He never went by that name, did he? He was Jehan. Healer Jehan, the Earthborn." He rubbed his forehead. "That's what was bothering me about him. He looked so familiar! He looks like his father!"

"You knew Jehan?" Memfis asked. "How?"

Karse laughed. "You never knew, did you? My father served in the palace. He was an assistant to the major-domo. Died there, with the Firstborn and the Heir. I was born there. And when I was four, I broke my arm there."

Memfis looked startled. "I remember that!"

"But who remembers the face of a four-year old, especially twenty-five years later?" Karse asked. "But I knew you. I remembered you. And I knew you'd be dead as last winter's leaves if anyone knew who you really were. So I kept the secret." He turned. "Aven is your Water?"

"And Owyn is my Fire," Aria added. "Fandor is going to kill my Owyn, and give my Aven to Mannon if we don't find them."

Karse dragged his fingers through his hair. "Shit. That's not going to be easy to do. Unless..." He scowled. "Your Owyn wasn't the first, you know. Fandor's had other boys. And yeah, we think he did for some of them, but we couldn't ever prove it. But there are survivors, and one of them will know where he might be."

"How long will it take to find one?" Aria asked.

Karse grinned. "Not long," he answered, and turned to Trey, who'd been standing silent by the door. "So? Where would he take them?"

Trey scowled. "If he was stupid? He'd take them home. But as much as I'd like this to be simple, he isn't stupid. And he knows we'll be looking for him. So he wouldn't take them home." His scowl deepened. "He keeps a warehouse, backs up on Tannery Row. And there's a brothel, off Weavers Court. You said he wants to sell one to Mannon?"

Aria stared at him, her eyes wide. "Yes."

"Then my guess is he's at the warehouse. Tannery Row is right on the walls, and it's near the northern gate. Gate guard there is in his pocket, too. It'd be easy to get in and out of the city without anyone noticing from there. And if he's planning on doing for Owyn, the lime pits are close by there, too."

"Lime?" Memfis' voice sounded strangled.

Trey just looked at him. "I thought you knew. S'what he did to my brother. Would have done to me if I hadn't got away from him." He turned back to Karse. "That's my best guess. But we should cover all three. I wouldn't put it past him to separate them, especially if he wants Owyn for himself."

Karse nodded, looking thoughtful. "Do you think Owyn would be at his house?"

Trey shrugged. "Fuck if I know. If we could out-think the bastard, we'd have pitched his arse into the mountain by now."

Karse nodded. "Fine. Pick your team. You know who's loyal to me. You take the house, and if Owyn isn't there, I want any evidence you can find. You've a good eye, you know what to look for. Send Leist to the place off Weavers, tell him to bring healers, and I want everyone out of there and into a safe house, right down to the fire mice in the stove. I'm going to the warehouse."

"I'm coming with you," Aria said. Karse looked as if he wanted to object.

"She's armed, Karse," Memfis said. "She killed most of the men in the garden tonight."

"Is that so?" Karse murmured. Then he bowed. "As you wish, my Heir."

CHAPTER NINETEEN

AVEN RAN OUT THROUGH the empty, dark courtyard and into the streets, trying to put some distance between himself and the building where he'd been captive. He turned blindly, knowing that if someone came after him, if someone caught him, that he was dead. He needed to find a place to hide, someplace safe. He stumbled, nearly fell, and slowed to a stop, his thoughts finally catching up with him.

He had no idea where he was. How was he supposed to know where to find someplace safe?

Memfis' forge was safe, but there was no one there.

Meris' house? He already knew it wasn't safe there, but where else could he go? It would at least give him a place to start. And Aria might still be there. He wouldn't be alone. But first he needed to find the house. He thought back to riding in the cart with Memfis. The sun had been setting, and it had been directly behind the house when they'd driven up to the gate. That meant the house was on the west side of the city. He looked up at the skies. He might not be able to see the horizon from here, but he'd known the names of these stars as long as he'd known his own name. He studied them for a moment, and knew his direction. West was that way — thankfully, it was also the same direction he'd been going, the same direction as *away*.

He started walking, this time paying attention to the houses around him. They were easily as nice as the one that Meris lived in, but not as large. The gates were smaller, and the houses were closer to them. He wasn't sure what that meant, other than the interior courtyards must not be as large. And how big was this city, anyway? He stopped at an intersection, and wiped his face. He was hungry, thirsty, and now that the rush of energy from his escape was fading, he was exhausted. He looked up, got his bearings, and started walking again.

Del. Silent Del, who wasn't Water, but somehow knew the secret language of the Water tribe. The collar meant he was a slave, but that didn't matter. He was one of theirs, Aven was sure of it. A Companion. Which one? That didn't matter either. What mattered was going back for him. He turned, realizing that he had no idea how to find the house where he'd been imprisoned again. How was he going to go back for Del if he couldn't find where he'd been? For a moment, he thought about retracing his steps. But no — if he was caught, he'd never get away. Not a second time. Best to keep moving. He frowned as the street he was on ended, then turned and backtracked, trying to find a way around. It did no good — every west-bound street stopped at a wall. The wall, Aven realized. He was as far west as he could be in Forge, and still be inside the walls. And he had no idea where to go from here.

Where now? He looked up, trying to remember if he'd looked at the sky while he'd been in Meris' garden. He didn't think he had. Then he looked up and down the street. Most of the windows were dark, the houses silent. There was no one out that he could ask for help.

North, or south? They'd entered the city from the south, Aven remembered. And... and Meris' house had been in the west, but they'd gone north out of the forge to reach it. He turned to the left and started walking again.

The road curved, following the curve of the wall, and the buildings grew more and more shabby, the streets more uneven. It didn't smell right, and Aven was about to turn back and go south when he saw lights. He hesitated, then headed toward them. Maybe someone would be able to tell him where he was, and how to get to Meris' house from here.

As he got closer, he heard voices, and music. A door opened, and the noise grew louder as a pair of figures stumbled out into the street. They came toward Aven, and didn't seem to notice him at first.

"Hey," one of them grunted. "Hey, it's someone."

"I'm someone," the other man replied. He looked up, saw Aven, and blinked. "Oh. Someone else someone. You looking for someone, boy?" He frowned. "You found someone."

"I was looking for directions," Aven answered, realizing that the men were both drunk. But he didn't have much of a choice. He needed help. "I'm lost. I'm trying to find my way back to my grandmother's house."

The first man snorted. "Who's that, then?"

"Lady Meris," Aven answered. "Do you know her? Am I going the right way?"

"Meris? Nah, you're heading the wrong way," the first man said. He waved in Aven's general direction. "Back that way. District Two. Firze, how far?"

"Huh?"

"How far to District Two from here?"

"Oh. Um... nine intersections? I think? Where are we?" He looked around, frowned, then nodded. "Yeah. Nine. You new here, boy?"

"Just came today," Aven answered. "My uncle brought me to meet my grandmother. I went out for some air, but I got lost, and it got dark, and now I don't know where I am."

"You walked a good bit," the first man said. "C'mon. We'll walk with you a bit. We're going that way. He's Firze. I'm Tolly."

"My name is Aven." The words were out of his mouth before Aven realized he shouldn't be using his real name.

"Nice to meet you, Aven," Tolly said as they started walking. "Where are you from, that you're just here today?"

"North," Aven answered. "I've never been in a city like this before."

"There are no other cities like this," Firze said. "Probably why you got lost."

Aven nodded, relaxing a little. They seemed like friendly enough people. They walked on, and Tolly pointed out different places and streets to him.

"Now, this here is Tannery Row," he said. "Goes all the way to the north gate, back that way. When we hit the west gate, it turns into Temple Way."

"Tannery," Aven repeated. "Is that why it smells bad?"

"Smells bad?" Tolly said. "Firze, does it smell bad around here?"

"Dipshit," Firze said fondly. "You know tanning smells bad. You just don't smell it no more."

"True," Tolly said. "I'm used to it." He stopped. "Hey, is that a patrol?"

"Patrol? In Tannery? Who the shit patrols Tannery?" Firze stopped. "That's no patrol."

"They're on their way somewhere," Tolly murmured. "Come this way, Aven. Let them pass."

"Who is it?" Aven asked, stepping out of the road and moving up against a building.

"The Guard. We don't mess with them, and they leave us alone." Tolly stood next to Aven. "Tannery Row... things aren't always on the right side of the Guard here, you know? Now, they know it. And we know it, so we make sure they get their cut of whatever it is, and they leave us alone. But this... someone's in for a lot of hurting, if they're coming through like this."

Aven could see the group more clearly now. A lot of mounted men, armored and armed. A cart at the center of the group, driven by a man that looked almost familiar. And next to him—

"Aria!"

He blurted out her name, and saw her head whip around to face him. The look of shock on her face had to be mirrored in his own, and he was out into the street before she could jump down from the cart. So when she jumped down, it was into his arms. She clung to him, and he buried his face in her hair and just held on to her. It took him a minute to realize that she was crying. It took him another minute to realize that he was, too.

"I'm all right," he whispered to her. "I'll be fine."

She nodded and pulled back, sniffling. She wiped her face, then laughed and wiped his. "I didn't think I'd ever see you again," she whispered.

"You're not getting rid of me that easily," Aven answered. "Mother of us all, it's good to see you."

"It's good to see you again," the familiar man said. "Do you remember me? We met this afternoon."

Aven blinked and raised his head. He studied the man for a moment, then remembered his name. "Karse, isn't it?"

"Yes. Now, you got yourself away. Where were you?"

Aven shook his head. "I don't know. A house. Small courtyard. But I don't know where. And I didn't get away without help."

Karse nodded and looked past them. "What are you two doing here?"

"Nothing, sir!" Tolly called back. He sounded both nervous and stone-cold sober.

"They were helping me, Karse," Aven said. "They were showing me the way to Meris' house."

"Were they now?" Karse said, his eyebrows raised. "Well then, there's a blessing for you. Thank you both, for your help."

Aven turned. "Yes. Thank you."

Tolly's eyes were wide. "You're welcome... what the fu—" he stopped, turning red. "I'm sorry. Please, excuse my language, my Heir."

My Heir? Aven turned back to Aria, and realized that she was wearing the Diadem. "You're wearing it," he breathed. "I've never seen you wear it."

"Memfis thought it a good idea. Karse and Meris agreed." Aria answered. She turned back to Tolly and Firze, and smiled. "Apology accepted, my friends. Thank you, for your help. Now, please don't say anything about seeing us, will you?"

"Not a word!" Tolly swore. "Not even to my own mother!" He grabbed Firze's arm and dragged him down the street.

Before they disappeared, Firze stopped, turned, and shouted, "Here's to the Heir! May she never fall!"

Karse groaned. "He was drunker than I thought. Let's get moving before people realize what he said. Aven, up in the cart. Tell us everything."

Aven climbed up into the cart, with Aria between him and Karse. He rubbed his forehead and tried to get his thoughts in order. Before he could say anything, Karse asked, "Was Owyn with you?"

Aven stared at him. "Do you think I'd be here alone if he was?"

"Had to ask. There were three places Owyn might be," Karse answered. "You were in a house, you said?"

"Yes."

"Then Owyn's either in the warehouse or the brothel." Karse nodded. "We're heading to the warehouse. I sent men to the house, and to the brothel. We'll find him."

"I was in Fandor's house?" Aven asked. "There was someone else there. A slave. I'm pretty sure he was a slave. He was supposed to be chained in the kitchen. He helped me escape."

"Supposed to be?"

"Apparently, they don't know he can undo the locks," Aven said. "He wouldn't come with me — he chained himself up again before I left. His name is Del, and he doesn't talk—"

"Del?" Karse interrupted. "Oh, shit. That's just wonderful." He looked around, then waved. A man rode up next to him, and he gave rapid instructions. "Go back to the house. Tell Memfis that whatever he's planning, he needs to do it now. We're out of time."

"Why?" Aria asked.

"Because Del *is* a slave," Karse answered, picking up the reins and snapping them, urging the horses on faster. "But he's not Fandor's slave. He's Mannon's. Mannon's personal slave, and Mannon never lets him out of his sight. If he's here, so is Mannon."

THE WAREHOUSE WAS LARGE, dark, and completely empty. Karse's men searched it from top to bottom twice, and several of them remained behind as Karse turned the cart back down Tannery Row.

"He's at the brothel. He has to be there," Karse muttered. "I just hate going back to the house without having him. If anything happens to him, Memfis is going to crawl back into a bottle and not come out."

"You're calling him by his real name," Aven said, his voice low. "Did he tell you?"

"Nah, I knew. He didn't know that, but I knew," Karse looked at him and smiled. "I knew your father, by the by."

"You did?"

"I was born in the palace. Your father put my arm to rights when I fell out of a tree." With one hand, he pushed his sleeve up, revealing a white scar. "Bone poked right through, it was that bad." He shook his head. "You're looking peaky, Aven."

"I'm thirsty. And hungry. And my head aches from the dreamflower." Aven closed his eyes. "Now what?"

"Now, we hope that Leist has beat us back to the house, and Owyn is there and safe," Karse answered without looking at him. "And maybe Trey found something at the house. Or someone."

Aven nodded. He glanced at Aria. "I promised Del I'd go back for him if I could. Aria, I think he's one of us. One of yours."

She gaped at him. "A Companion?"

"He felt like it." Aven leaned forward and rubbed his face. "I don't know if he's Air or Earth. But his eyes are like yours."

"Aria has ember eyes," Karse said. "It's a Fire trait."

Aria nodded. "And I have my Fire— oh. Oh, no."

Aven frowned, wondering why Aria suddenly looked so upset. Then he realized, and gasped, "Mother of us all! No. No, he's not dead. Aria, he's not!" His stomach turned, and he shook his head. "He can't be dead."

The cart lurched as Karse snapped the reins again. "From your mouth to the ears of the Mother," he muttered. No one responded. No one said anything else, until they drove through the gate at Meris' house. Karse stopped the cart at the door, then looked around as a man came toward them.

"Leist, tell me you have him," he said. There was an almost pleading tone to his voice.

"The place was empty, Karse," Leist answered. "Dust an inch thick on everything. There's been no one there for a month or more. Trey's here, and he says it looks like Fandor's gone, too. The house was empty, looked like it had been ransacked."

"That happened after I got out," Aven murmured.

"He wasn't there?" Aria asked, her voice very quiet. Very calm. "He wasn't at the house with Aven. He wasn't at the warehouse. He was not at this other place, this brothel. Where is my Owyn? Where else would Fandor have taken him?"

Aven climbed down from the cart and stopped, steadying himself with both hands as the world wobbled. He heard footsteps behind him, and jumped when a hand closed over his shoulder.

"It's me," Memfis said. "How are you?"

"A little battered," Aven answered. "Hungry, thirsty, and I have a dreamflower headache."

"I figured on the thirsty and hungry part," Memfis said and handed Aven a cup. "Owyn wasn't with you?"

"No. I'll tell you the rest later." Aven sipped the salted water and sighed. "Thank you. Where's Meris?"

"I made her go lay down." Memfis glanced at the house. "She's old, Aven. Old enough that I'm worried about her, with all this insanity."

Aven frowned. "I'll sit with her, see if there's anything I can do. Later. What do we do now?"

"That's for Karse to say. Mannon is in the city, and we still have to face the Council. We have to get out of Forge, but I can't leave without knowing—" Memfis raised his voice. "Karse, what now?"

"Working on that!" Karse turned to another man. "All right, Trey. Where else? He's running now. Where else would he go?"

Aven closed his eyes, drinking his water, trying to think. There was something... he'd heard something, or maybe he'd seen it. Something that he knew would help them. He was certain of it... if he could remember...

"Aven?" Memfis said, his voice quiet. "What is it?"

"I..." He shook his head. Then he remembered Owyn laughing. *And it's just the kind of thing he'd get off on.*

"The forge," Aven murmured. "I... has anyone checked the forge?"

"What? The forge?" Memfis gasped. "*My* forge? My house?"

"Yes," Aven said. He straightened, drained the last of his water, and turned to look at Memfis. "Remember this morning? Fandor wanted you to make that restraint? Owyn said he thought it was for him. And you both agreed that Fandor wanted you to make it because if *you* made it, with Owyn helping you make it, then Owyn would know that you had a hand in what was happening to him." Aven blinked, his mind racing. "It has to be. Fandor knows we're not at the forge anymore. It's safe for him to hide there. No one is going to look there. Why would they? So he's taken Owyn there, and he's going to hurt him, and kill him, in the one place where Owyn was always safe from him. Because that will make it that much worse for Owyn."

Aven stopped, and realized the silence that surrounded him. He turned, and saw that everyone was staring at him. He felt his face growing warm.

"I don't think Aleia could have done that better, Aven," Memfis said. "You're right."

"She'd have done it faster," Aven answered. "How long have they been there?"

"Too long. Trey, I want horses," Karse called. "No carts now. We're going in, and we're going fast."

"I'm coming with you," Aria said. "I do not need a horse."

"Me, too," Aven added. "I'm coming, too. Memfis, I want my swords."

Memfis nodded. "I'll get them."

Karse came closer. "Ever ridden a horse, Aven?"

"No."

"Then you'll ride with Trey." Karse turned and raised his voice. "Where are those horses? We need to move!"

CHAPTER TWENTY

AVEN HAD BEEN ON CANOES in the middle of raging storms before, but that experience had done nothing to prepare him for being on the back of a galloping horse. Aven clung to Trey's belt as the horse thundered through the streets.

"Are you all right back there?" Trey shouted.

"I'm never doing this again!" Aven shouted back.

Trey's laughter rolled over his shoulder. "It'll only get easier after this." Then he did something, and the horse slowed to a stop. There were other horses — Karse and Memfis, and other men from Karse's squadron. Trey helped Aven slide to the ground, and they joined the group. For the first time in his life, Aven felt seasick, and he finally understood his father a little better. A moment after they stopped, Aria landed lightly a little way down the street, and came to join them.

"I circled over the forge," she said. "I saw nothing outside, but there are lights in the second floor windows that overlook the street."

"Shit," Memfis breathed. "Aven, what now?"

Aven frowned, pacing, more to try and stop his legs from shaking than to help himself think. "How many ways are there into the house?" he asked. "There was the forge door, the kitchen door, and the stable. Anything else?"

"The main door to the house," Memfis said.

Aven nodded slowly. He lowered his head and kept pacing. Five steps forward. Five steps back. Step, step, step, step, step... he stopped and looked at Memfis.

"Can you pretend to be drunk?" he asked. Memfis' eyes widened. "I can, but why?"

"Because you're going in alone," Aven said. "You're going to distract Fandor so we can get around him and get to Owyn. If we rush the house, he'll kill Owyn right off."

Karse nodded. "Right. So Memfis goes in the main door?"

"Right. Making as much noise as he can, acting completely drunk," Aven said. "The other doors will be guarded, and someone will go in after Owyn."

"I'll go," Trey said. "I know what to expect. And Owyn knows me." He frowned. "Aven, you come with me. He might need a healer."

Aven coughed. He hadn't considered that. "All right." He reached up and touched the hilt of one of the swords strapped to his back. "These aren't going to be any good in close quarters. I'll need a knife, or a club." Several knives were offered, and Aven took one that was as long as his forearm. He strapped it to his thigh, then nodded.

"What about the rest of us?" Karse asked. "Where should we be?"

Aven looked down the street at the house. "Trey and I will go in the kitchen door, Memfis will go in the front. You should spread out, be at all the other doors."

"And me?" Aria asked.

"On the roof," Aven answered. "If Fandor gets past us, he's yours, my Heir."

She looked at him, curiously. "And I'm also out of the way and safe?" she asked.

Aven felt his face warm. "I wasn't going to say it," he admitted. "But yes. You're far too important to risk i n the attack."

She nodded, then stepped in and kissed him on the cheek. "I understand. Go and get him."

AVEN DISCUSSED THE layout of the upper rooms with Memfis, then he and Trey headed for the alley behind the forge, stopping outside the door that led into the kitchen. Trey reached for the latch, but Aven stopped him.

"Wait," he whispered, leaning closer to Trey's ear. "Listen. We go in after Memfis starts raising a fuss." He looked down. "Take your boots off. We'll move more quietly barefoot."

They set their boots next to the door and waited. A few minutes later, they heard a crash, and Memfis' raised voice. Aven blinked as the most prolific stream of profanity he'd ever heard came pouring from inside the house.

"Damn," Trey murmured. "I should be taking notes!"

Aven bit his lip to keep from laughing, and moved closer to the door. He closed his eyes, listening intently until he heard what he had been waiting for — Fandor's voice, and Memfis responding. He waited a moment longer, then opened the door and peered into the kitchen. It was empty, and he and Trey quickly crossed the room and passed in to the corridor. Aven led Trey up the stairs, and stopped to look in through the open door of Owyn's room. The room was empty, so they kept walking, heading toward the front of the house and Memfis' bedroom. It was the room that overlooked the street, the room where Aria had seen light in the windows. It was also directly over the room where Aven could hear Memfis shouting at Fandor. They stopped outside the door, and Aven looked at Trey.

"Once we're in," he whispered. "We need to bar the door. Whatever you can find."

Trey nodded, and Aven opened the door. The wood creaked slightly, and Aven heard a low moan from inside. Followed by an explosion of profanity from Trey that nearly matched the one they'd heard earlier from Memfis. Aven peered past Trey, and froze in horror.

Owyn was on his back on the bed, naked, bound, blindfolded and gagged. His upper body was wrapped in ropes, tight enough to dig into his skin, and his arms were tucked under his back. His legs were in the air — thick rope tied around one knee, then wrapped around his throat before being tied to the other knee. If he struggled, he'd strangle himself. And despite the ropes and what Aven knew had to be complete terror, his cock was almost painfully erect.

Trey pulled Aven into the room and closed the door, then looked around. "Help me move this," he said, moving to a large chest. It took both of them to move the heavy piece of furniture to rest in front of the door. Then Trey nodded. "Come on. Let's get him free."

Aven drew his knife and went to the bed. "Owyn, it's me. It's Aven," he said, sawing at the thick rope. Trey was doing the same on Owyn's other leg, and the ropes parted at roughly the same moment. "Trey is with me. Owyn, it's over. You're safe."

Another low moan, and Trey started to work on the blindfold. "Close your eyes, Owyn," he said. The cloth fell loose , and Owyn tossed his head, blinking furiously.

"We're going to sit you up, Owyn," Aven said, keeping his voice low. Now that he could see Owyn's eyes, he could tell that something wasn't right. His eyes were glassy, unfocused. Shock? Terror? As soon as Owyn was sitting, Aven rested his hand on Owyn's arm, starting a gentle healing probe. Owyn's heart was racing. That was only to be expected. But there was something else. Something strange. "Trey, he's been drugged. There's something in his blood."

Trey looked up. "Drugged? Oh... oh, shit. Oh, fuck." He fumbled at the gag, pulling it free, tossing it away. "Owyn, Wyn, can you talk to me? It's Trey. You know me, don't you? You better know me."

Owyn's voice was harsh, and his words slurred. "Trey. I... I know you, Trey."

"What did he give you?" Trey's voice was suddenly urgent. "He told you. I know he told you. He always tells them. What did he give you?"

Owyn scowled. Then he twisted, craning his neck to look behind him at Aven. "Aven. Pretty, pretty Aven." He smiled. "Love you, Fishie."

Aven snorted. "Fishie?"

"Stay with me, Owyn," Trey snapped. "What did he give you?"

Owyn looked back at Trey. "Told me... gave me Rut."

"Oh, shit," Trey breathed. Then, with more emphasis, "Oh, *fuck*!"

Owyn smiled. "Yeah. Fuck. Now." He strained against the ropes. "Fuck me. Now. Please."

"No," Trey looked at Aven. "You're a healer, you have to do something. This is going to kill him."

"What is it?" Aven demanded. "I've never heard of it."

"It... d'ye know what I mean by aphrodisiac?" Trey asked. "This is like that, but worse. It turns him on. Really on. He can't stop, he can't control it. He'll beg for it, from anyone. For hours. Until his heart bursts. That's how it ends. That's how it always ends. Whatever it is, it breaks down into a poison."

"Fuck," Aven breathed.

"Leave his hands tied," Trey continued. "He'll tear his shaft off at the root if we let him."

Aven nodded, trying to think. He knew this. He could do this. Toxins. How to remove toxins. Filter them from the blood. He heard shouting from downstairs, but ignored it. "Right. I'll need water. A lot of it. I'll have to filter his blood. Make him piss it out."

"What?" Trey gasped. "On the bed?"

"Do we have a choice?" Aven demanded.

"Ah... no."

"Then we do it. It'll be messy, but we don't have a choice. Throw something over him, if you're worried about being splashed. And keep him hydrated."

"Right," Trey looked around, then got up and checked the room's only other door. Aven heard water splashing, and Trey came back with a pitcher and a cup. "Right," he repeated. "Owyn, drink this."

Owyn tossed his head. "Don't want to drink. I want you. Want you both."

"Pour it down his throat," Aven said, his voice low. "Make him drink it. He's already dehydrated. If I try to start now, I'll kill him."

Trey nodded. He frowned, then grabbed Owyn by the hair and tipped his head back, pouring the water into his mouth. Owyn sputtered and coughed, and swallowed about half of it.

"Drink the next one, or Trey will do that again," Aven ordered.

"I'll drink!" Owyn spat. "I'll... I'll drink." He drained the next cup obediently, and Aven closed his eyes and started to work. He knew how — there were enough poisonous things that lived in the deep that his father had made certain that he knew how to deal with poisons. But this wasn't a localized thing. He had to filter all of the blood, forcing the poison out.

"Ah... Aven?"

"Busy," Aven growled.

"Aven, he can't piss!"

Aven blinked. "What?"

Trey gestured vaguely. "He's hard. He's not going to be able to piss. Not easily, anyway. Hey, can you trigger an orgasm like this? Using healing power?"

"I... what?" Aven frowned. "I... I suppose yes. Why?"

"Because if he shoots, he'll go limp. And he'll be able to piss."

Aven nodded. "Owyn, did you hear that? May I try it?"

Owyn laughed, weakly. "It'll feel better if it's your hand, Fishie."

"Not with you out of your head, Mouse." Aven let out a long breath. "I'll try. Let me work. And get more water in to him." He dove back into the trance, splitting his focus, filtering the blood, and trying to control the muscles keeping Owyn's cock erect.

It didn't work. He did something wrong. Owyn howled and tried to squirm away from Aven. Trey pinned him down, which only made Owyn scream louder.

"Let him go!" Aven said. He frowned, then touched Owyn's forehead. "Owyn, talk to me."

"Hurts," Owyn whimpered. "It hurts. I... Aven, help me!"

"I'm trying, Owyn," Aven said softly. "I... I'm going to put you out. It won't hurt anymore. Understand?"

Owyn blinked, then nodded. "I understand."

"How am I supposed to get him to drink if he's out?" Trey asked.

"Dribble it into his mouth, and I'll make him swallow," Aven said. He closed his eyes and took a deep breath. "Now."

A moment later, Owyn was asleep, and Aven went back to work. He figured out what he'd done wrong and triggered an ejaculation — Owyn nearly flooded the bed, first with semen, then with urine. Trey, to his credit, didn't even flinch, pouring water into Owyn's mouth in a slow stream, waiting for him to swallow, then doing it again. The process seemed to take hours, filtering and refiltering, until Aven could find no trace of the poison anywhere in Owyn's body. He did one final check, looking for damage to the kidneys and liver from the poison, until he was satisfied that Owyn took no lasting harm. Then he sighed, and sat up.

"It's done," he croaked. "Do we know what happened downstairs?"

"Already?" Trey answered. He looked almost as tired as Aven felt. "It hasn't been that long. I've got no idea what's happening downstairs. The shouting stopped. Let's get him out of the bed. That mattress is ruined."

"Small price to pay," Aven muttered. They moved Owyn's limp body from the bed to the floor, and Trey went hunting for something to keep him warm while Aven finally cut the ropes that bound Owyn's arms and wrists. Trey came back with blankets, but stopped Aven from moving Owyn.

"Let's wash him off, first. He smells like a back alley in high summer." He took the pitcher back to the other room to refill it, coming back with a cloth. Gently, he rinsed Owyn off, then dried him.

"He'll need a bath," Aven said as they moved him into the nest of blankets.

"He's lucky to be alive to need one," Trey replied. "That shit... it's not an easy death. Owyn would have known it, too. All the street boys know about Rut."

"I was wondering how you knew," Aven said. "You... is that what happened to your brother?"

Trey nodded, looking distant. "We were both of us some of Fandor's boys, from the brothel in Weavers. Thing is, with Fandor, once you get too old, he doesn't want you anymore. But he doesn't want anyone else to have you either."

Aven brushed sweat-soaked hair off Owyn's forehead. "Did Owyn know that? He told us that he thought that if Fandor ever got hold of him again, that he was dead."

"I thought he knew," Trey answered. "He wasn't ever part of the brothel, though. So I'm not sure. But he's lucky Memfis took him off the block — he was just old enough then to be too old."

Aven closed his eyes. "You know, things aren't this complicated in the deep."

Trey chuckled. "Maybe not. Welcome to dry land, Fishie."

"Don't you start," Aven warned. Trey just laughed.

⸻ ◦⟆⟆◦ ⸻

THE SILENCE FROM THE lower floors was nerve-wracking. Surely someone would have come up to tell them that it was over? That Fandor had been taken away? That they were safe? But no one came, and Trey moved from the floor to the barricaded door to the window, then back to the floor.

"I want to go out and look, but that would be stupid," he said finally.

"We didn't think this through, did we?" Aven asked. He sat next to Owyn, his hand on Owyn's forehead. His swords rested on the ground on his other side. "We're trapped in here." He frowned, as a thought occurred to him. "Trinket."

"What?"

"Owyn has a fire mouse. Her name is Trinket, and she was in his shirt pocket when he was taken. Did you see his clothes?"

"I know about Trinket." Trey frowned and got back up. "Let me look around again. I didn't see them, but I wasn't looking for them, either." He stopped. "What good will a fire mouse do us?"

Aven shrugged. "Other than being a comfort to him when he wakes up? Not much." He tipped his head back, looking up at the ceiling. The ceiling... the *roof*! "Aria! She's on the roof!"

Trey immediately went to the window and opened it. He leaned out and looked up. "Aria?" he called. "Can you hear me?"

Aven heard the sound of flapping wings. "Trey? Tell me you found him?"

"We found him, and he'll be fine," Trey said. "But we don't know what's happening."

"I do not know," she admitted. "The others went in. No one has come back out or come back around, and I can't see in."

"Circle," Aven suggested. He turned, and saw her peering in the window. "See if you can see Karse."

"I will do that," she said. Then she frowned. "He's really all right?"

"He will be," Aven assured her. "Now go on."

She flew off, and Trey closed the window. As he started back across the room, someone tried the door. It slammed into the back of the chest with a loud thump. They tried again, then must have leaned on the door, because the chest shifted slightly. Aven got to his feet and picked up his swords. Trey stepped in front of him, his short sword bare and ready.

"Trey!" It was Karse, and Aven relaxed. "It's over. Open this door."

Aven stepped forward, only to be stopped by Trey. Trey was frowning. "What's the password?" he called.

Now it was Aven's turn to frown. Password? Had they set a password? He didn't remember doing it. Maybe it was a guard thing. Trey glanced at him, then shook his head.

"Password?" Karse sounded incredulous. "What the fuck are you talking about? We don't have a password. We've never had a password!"

Trey grinned. "Just making sure," he called back, and sheathed his sword. "Put those down, Aven, and help me move this thing. We're done."

"You're sure?" Aven asked.

Memfis' voice joined Karse's. "Aven, it's done. Fandor's gone. It's over."

That was enough to satisfy Aven, who set his swords back down and went to help Trey move the chest. Memfis was first into the room, and his eyes widened when he saw Owyn bundled up in blankets on the floor.

"Is he all right?" he demanded. "Aven?"

"He's still in healing sleep," Aven said. "I thought it might be best to keep him asleep until he was someplace where he'd wake and know he was safe."

"That fuck Fandor gave him Rut, Karse," Trey growled.

Karse's eyebrows shot up. "And he's not dead?" He turned to Aven. "What the fuck level of healer are you?"

Aven backed up a step. "I've... never been formally evaluated at a healing center," he stammered. "My father trained me. He said maybe second level."

"Not if you beat Rut, you're not," Karse said.

"I had incentive to get it right," Aven added. The scrutiny was odd, off-putting. He'd done what he was supposed to do. He'd saved a life. What matter what level healer he was? "I want to get him some place safe. I don't know where his clothes are, Memfis. Trinket was in his shirt pocket. He'll want to know she's safe, too."

"We'll find her. And you look like you're about to tip over. When did you drink last? Or eat something?"

"Drink?" Aven frowned. "Before we came here. You gave it to me. Eat? I don't even know any more."

"Mother of us all," Memfis breathed. "You're going to hit the wall any second now."

"I've sent men for a carriage. We'll get you both back to Meris' house. It'll be fully guarded by my men. It'll be safe. You'll have time for a nap and a meal before the Council—"

"We're still doing that?" Aven gasped. "After all this?" He glanced at Owyn. "I'm not sure he'll be up to it. I'm not sure I'll be up to it."

"Your Heir needs to stand before them," Karse said softly. "You need to stand with her."

"I've got something you can take, if you want. A stimulant," Trey added. "It's harmless, but it will wake you up." He rested his hand on Aven's shoulder. "Go on. I'll find Owyn's clothes and his mouse."

Memfis walked over to where Owyn lay on the floor. He knelt, picked Owyn up, then slowly got back to his feet cradling Owyn in his arms like a child.

"Let's go."

CHAPTER TWENTY-ONE

ARIA PACED IN THE FRONT room, both aware of and amused by the guards hugging the walls to keep out of the way of her wings. She wondered if they thought she would hit one of them if they moved too close. It was a silly notion — she was completely aware of the space that she inhabited, and how much room she needed around her. She hadn't knocked something or someone over with her wings since she was a toddler, still learning to walk and fly.

"What will happen to him now?" she asked, stopping and turning to face one of the men. He had more braid on his uniform than the others, although not as much as Karse or Trey wore.

"You're meaning Fandor, Lady?" he asked. He frowned and looked thoughtful. "Well, we'll hold him in chains until the Council meets. Seeing as he's on the Council until they say otherwise, that'll be soon. And interesting."

"Interesting how? And what's your name?"

"Leesam, Lady," he answered. "And interesting in that I don't think a Council member has ever been expelled before. There are rules for it, sure. But it's never happened before. But kidnapping? Assault? And whatever else he was up to here? Those are capital crimes, and the penalties are clear. Council members don't get a pass, just because they're Council."

Before Aria could ask any more questions, she heard footsteps coming from the corridor, and Karse's voice.

"We've got him," he called. "Everyone can stand down. He's alive."

He came into the room, followed by Memfis and Aven. But Aria only had eyes for Owyn. Her Owyn, looking as small as a child, bundled in blankets in Memfis' arms. She moved in close, touched his cheek.

"What happened to him?" she asked. "How badly was he hurt?"

"He'll be fine," Aven said. She looked up at him, and blinked.

"Will you be fine?" she gasped. "Aven—"

"I'm tired, Aria. Hungry, thirsty, and tired to my bones," he answered. He smiled slightly. "The drug that Fandor gave him must have taken a while to take effect, because... well, Fandor hadn't done anything to him yet."

"Except poison him," Trey said from behind Aven. "The drug... actually, Aven, Rut hits hard and fast. Fandor... he left him like that as part of the torture."

Aven turned and frowned. "Fandor had him for at least a couple of hours. Trey, you never told me how long that this drug takes to kill."

Trey shook his head. "Let's just say that we're lucky that we got here when we did. And that you're a better healer than you thought."

Aria stared at them in shock, then went back to Owyn. He looked pale, and small. It wasn't right. He shouldn't be pale and small. "Why isn't he awake?"

"Because I want him to wake someplace safe," Aven said. "It'll help, I think, if he's safe, and if we're with him when he wakes up."

Aria nodded. She looked up at Memfis. "And you? How are you?"

"Better," Memfis answered. He looked down. "Better now."

"I'm going to go find Owyn's clothes, and see if I can find Trinket," Trey said. "Did he leave clothes here? Should I bring them? And you're going back to Meris' house?"

"That's the plan," Memfis said. "And yes, clothes would be good."

"Trey, our boots," Aven said. "They're still outside."

"I'll fetch them. Then I'll meet you there." Trey patted Aven on the shoulder. "See you later, Fishie."

Aven rolled his eyes. "You don't get to call me that!" he called after Trey, who laughed.

"Fishie?" Aria asked. Aven sighed.

"I'll tell you later," he said.

KARSE HAD ARRANGED for a carriage, which turned out to be similar to Memfis' cart, except instead of being an open box, it was closed. Aria looked at it and balked.

"I'm not getting into a cage. Not again."

"It's not a cage," Karse said. "It's a carriage."

"I will not," she repeated. "I will fly. I will meet you at Meris' house."

Karse looked as if he wanted to argue, then shook his head. "Yes, My Heir. Now, if we could get moving?"

Aria scowled at his back and went to stand with Aven, who was leaning against a wall, putting on his boots. "Are you riding in this cage?" she asked.

"I'm not seeing much of a choice. Not for me," he said with a tired smile. "I can't fly. I'm not getting back onto a horse if I can help it, and the last time I tried to walk, I got lost. And I need to stay with Owyn."

Aria nodded. "I don't like you being in a cage, though. I can't see you. If anything happens, I can't help you." He reached out and tugged her close, pulling her into his arms. She melted against him, resting her head on his shoulder, slipping her arms around his waist. She didn't want to ever let him go. "Aven, I can't lose you. I already almost lost you both."

"We're on guard now," Aven murmured, rubbing his cheek on her hair. "It won't happen again. Mother of us all, you smell good."

"Aven!"

"Like the wind," he added. Then he chuckled. "I'm tired. I need to sleep. But I can't until we get to Meris' house." He straightened and rubbed his hand over his face. "I'll need to bathe again."

"Explain 'Fishie'?"

Aven grinned. "Owyn called me Fishie when he was out of his head from the drug. Trey thinks it's funny."

Aria smiled. "It's adorable. Will you let him keep calling you Fishie?"

"I don't know," Aven answered. "I don't even know if he'll remember doing it." He paused for a moment. "Aria, he told me he loves me."

He said it slowly, hesitantly. Almost as if he was confessing to something wrong. And the look on his face...

She reached up and touched his cheek. "Did you think it would bother me? That he said it first?" she asked. "I'm not surprised. You're very easy to love."

Aven's eyes widened. "First?" he repeated, and his voice cracked. She smiled.

"You sound as if you're right out of the sea and your voice isn't back yet," she told him, and he laughed. She leaned against him, and his arms around her tightened. "And yes, first. I should have said it sooner. I didn't understand, though." She stretched, and kissed him gently. "Yes, Aven. I do love you. I knew you were mine, from the moment I saw you. And I know you love me, even though you haven't said it. Aven, I found the pearl."

"The... the pearl." He blinked. "My bag! I didn't even think of it. But you have the Diadem, so Fandor didn't take it—"

"The strap was cut," Aria said. "I fixed it, but to do it, I had to take everything out of the bag. And I found the pearl."

He nodded, his face turning red. "I meant it for you. For... for the morning after. And... I asked Owyn if he'd set it into a rose. I thought it would mean more if it came from both of us."

Aria stared at him for a moment. "Oh," she breathed. "Oh, Aven—"

He smiled. "Maybe you could act surprised when we give it to you? So he doesn't know? I think he'll be disappointed if he knows the surprise is spoiled."

"It isn't," Aria protested. "Because it's not finished yet. So no matter what, I'll be surprised."

Aven nodded. "Good. That's good. Karse is waving, and I think Memfis and Owyn are in the carriage. I should go and join them."

"I'll see you at Meris' house," Aria said. She kissed him again, then stepped back, pulling gently out of his arms. He straightened, met her eyes, and smiled.

"I love you, Aria," he said. And even knowing it already, the sound of the words made her heart soar.

"I love you, too," she replied. Then she grinned. "Fishie."

He rolled his eyes and laughed. She giggled and took to the skies, circling overhead until she saw him get into the carriage, until it started moving, trundling off toward Meris' house.

AVEN SETTLED ONTO THE bench seat across from Memfis and leaned his head back against the carriage wall.

"You can nap, if you want," Memfis said. "Until we get there."

"If I sleep, I won't be able to keep Owyn asleep," Aven said without opening his eyes. "Which means he'll wake up and panic. I don't want him to hurt himself, or you, if he wakes up flailing."

Memfis hummed. "How did you know that he might do that? He hasn't in years, but he used to."

Aven opened one eye. "I guessed?" He smiled and sighed. "I need to eat. Mother of us all, I'm hungry."

"I'm surprised you're still going," Memfis said. "But then again, you are your father's son."

Aven raised his head. "What?"

"Saw him go almost three days without sleep once, and almost without food," Memfis said. "Has he taught you about mountain fever yet?"

"I've read about it," Aven answered. "He never told me that he treated it."

"He didn't?" Memfis' raised his brows. "That's Jehan for you. Always hiding his light under a basket. It went through the Palace like flame through dry tinder. And he went to work with the Palace healers." Memfis paused, looking distant. "I don't think any of us had really seen him working before — I think we'd only been together a few months at that point. We didn't know each other, not the way Aria says you all do. Our bond wasn't the same. So we were all a little wary then. Until we understood where we all stood. Jehan was still a bit awkward. I don't think it had really sunk in for him yet that he was a Companion. But then he went to work, and he went from awkward to scary confident. He knew what he was doing, and the rest of us saw what Milon saw in him." Memfis went silent, and all Aven could hear was Owyn's soft breathing, the sound of the wheels, and the rhythm of the horse's hooves. "You're the Heart, you know."

"The what?"

"Meris told Aria. I'm telling you. It's a role that no one really talks about. There's the Heir. And there's the Heart. Most of the time, the Heir is the Heart. They're the one who holds the group together, who soothes the little jealousies and makes the... well, the group marriage work."

"Is it really a group marriage?" Aven asked. "Fa said that was a thing that happened in the Earth tribes."

"It is, and it is," Memfis said. "And really, what else would you call it? The Heir chooses their Companions, and they all spend the rest of their lives together. Isn't that a marriage?"

Aven nodded, leaning forward a little. "So if the Heir is the Heart, how am I the Heart?"

"Sometimes, the Heart and the Heir are two different people. Sometimes, there's too much for one." Memfis shrugged a little, the movement bouncing Owyn in his arms. "In times of strife, the Heir needs to focus on ruling and guiding the people. So the Mother gives the role of the Heart to another. This time, that appears to be you."

Aven considered it, and nodded. "So, I take care of the Companions, so Aria can take care of everyone else?"

"That's a good way of putting it."

Aven nodded again, leaning back. "I can do that. Is that why I know who they are, too?"

"I have no idea why your bond is so strong that you all know each other," Memfis said. "But I have a theory. You're not going to like it."

Aven arched a brow. "I'm listening."

"Your bond is stronger because you need to be fully one immediately. You don't have the time to figure out where you stand with each other. You need to know each other, and be certain of each other, from the first day. Because this isn't going to be an easy road for her, for any of you," Memfis said slowly. "You're looking at war. Civil war."

Aven coughed. "You really think so?"

"He's not going to stand down without a fight, Aven," Memfis answered. "You have to know that."

Aven nodded. "I know. I just don't like it. How do we fight him, Memfis?"

"They'll come. The ones who are waiting for her, for the true Heir. They'll come, and we'll take Adavar back."

"That doesn't answer how," Aven grumbled.

"And we can't answer how until we know who. And we won't know who until we get to the Earth tribe lands. Which means going before the Council to get what we need."

"Which we're not doing until we all have a chance to eat and sleep," Aven said, his voice firm. "And if I don't think Owyn is ready for it, it's not happening."

"We need to leave tonight, Aven," Memfis insisted. "With Mannon in the city, it isn't safe—"

Aven snorted. "I think I know that, Memfis," he said. He glanced down at his wrists, at the abrasions left behind by the ropes. "Owyn and I aren't going to forget that any time soon."

Memfis' answering snort was even more rude than Aven's had been. "You're alive to remember it," he pointed out. "If we don't get out of the city, that's going to change. I can guarantee that, by dawn, we'll all have prices on our heads. And there are people in this city who will sell their own mothers." He scowled, looked down at Owyn. "We can't wait, Aven."

BY THE TIME THE CARRIAGE stopped inside Meris' gates, Aria had already landed, and was waiting with Meris as Aven stepped down to the ground. He nodded to them, then looked around. He knew the faces of all the men, and relaxed slightly.

"They're all mine," Karse called from above. "If that's what you're looking for."

"It is, and I noticed," Aven said. He turned and looked up. "I didn't know you were up there."

"Best place to keep an eye on you," Karse answered. "Lady Meris, feed this Water boy before he falls down?"

Aven grinned and turned, only to find Meris had come up behind him. She looked up at him, then smiled and took his hands. "Aria told me. You saved his life. And you brought him back. Thank you." Aven smiled back at her, and on impulse, leaned down and kissed her cheek. She giggled like a girl and took his arm. "Come inside. There's a bedroom for the three of you, and I've had food brought. You can rest before the Council meets."

"I want to be sure that Owyn is up to meeting them," Aven said. "So we need to wait for him to wake."

"Oh, of course!" Meris agreed. "Aria, my dear, come along. Memfis, bring Owyn." She took Aven's arm, then took Aria's, leading them both into the house. Aven looked over her head at Aria, who met his eyes and smiled.

"Owyn's going to need a bath once he wakes—"

"There's a bath off the room I've given you," Meris assured them. "And I've overseen the food that's waiting for you. Which is guarded."

"By who?" Aria asked.

"One of Karse's men who stayed behind. Leist, I think his name is. He also acted as a taster, to make certain that there was nothing untoward added under my nose."

Aven nodded. "And is there extra salt?"

"There's a bowl especially for you," Meris said. She led them to a door, let go of their arms, and opened it. "Leist, it's me. It's us. They're here."

Aven followed her into the room, seeing Leist standing by the window, next to a table laden with covered bowls. The room was dominated by an enormous bed. Aven blinked and stepped out of the way so that Aria could come in. Behind her was Memfis, who stopped just inside the door.

"You could have warned me that you were giving them this room, Meris," he said. He came the rest of the way in and laid Owyn down on the bed.

"Nonsense," Meris sniffed. "Where else would I have a bed that would hold all of them? Now, Aria, the bag you were working on is in the chest there. I've got fresh clothes for all of you, and the bath is through that door there. Oh, and the food is here." She looked around. "The door will be guarded, and there are guards outside the windows as well. Is there anything I've missed?"

"What's wrong with this room?" Aria asked, coming up next to Aven and resting her hand on the small of his back. "Memfis, why did you want to be warned?"

Memfis looked up from Owyn, then sighed. "Because this was Milon's room, back before he became Heir."

"And after he became Heir, and left for the Palace, I had the room redone so that if he came to visit with his Companions, that there would be room for all of them," Meris added. "But that never happened."

"Oh," Aria said, looking around. "This was my father's room." Her voice was quiet, and almost expressionless.

Almost.

"Does that bother you?" Meris asked, her eyes wide. "I hadn't thought of that. We could move you to different rooms—"

"No," Aria interrupted. "No, if this is how we can be in the same room, then this is where I want to be."

Aven put his arm around her shoulders and pulled her to his side. "We need to rest," he said.

"The Council is going to meet with you in an hour," Meris said. Aven coughed, glanced at Aria. She looked up at him, frowned, then drew herself up.

"The Council is going to meet with us when I am ready to meet with them," she said, her voice firm. "And I will be ready to meet with them once I'm certain that my Companions are ready to accompany me. I will not be rushed, not for anyone." She looked at the bed, then back at Aven. Then she turned back to her great-grandmother. "If they want to know a time, tell them that you think I may be ready in two hours. But perhaps three. My Companions were assaulted. I want to be certain that they've come to no lasting harm."

Meris looked stunned, but it was Memfis' chuckle that drew Aven's attention. He was shaking his head.

"Come on, Meris," he said. "We'll let them rest. Let her see to her men. And we can debate who she just sounded like — Milon or Liara."

"It would probably be a combination," Meris said slowly. "I'll tell them. Three hours won't give you much time to get out of the city before dawn."

"We'll manage," Aven said. "If necessary, we'll find a place to hide until tomorrow."

Meris looked at him, then shook her head. "I don't want to see you hurt. Any of you."

"We'll be careful," Aria said. "Grandmother, we need to sleep."

Meris took Memfis' arm and let him lead her out of the room, with Leist following them. The door closed behind them, and Aria sagged against Aven's side. He turned to face her, holding her tightly, finally giving in to his need to hold her.

"Come to bed, Aven," she murmured against his chest. "We need to sleep. And you need to eat."

"Which first?" Aven asked. She chuckled and led him to the table. They faced each other and ate, leaving bowls covered for Owyn for when he woke. They didn't talk, but every so often, one of them would reach across the table to touch the other's hand. The lightest touch, almost a reassurance. They were together. They were safe.

When they were done, Aria went into the bath while Aven took off his swords and his shirt. He took off his boots, lining them up next to each other against the wall. When Aria came out of the bath, they went to the bed, gently shifting Owyn to the center of the wide bed. Aria lay down against his back, and Aven stretched out on his side, facing the two of them. On impulse, he reached across Owyn for Aria's hand, lacing his fingers with hers, resting their hands on Owyn's side.

They were together. They were safe.

CHAPTER TWENTY-TWO

AVEN WOKE UP FEELING as if he was being watched. He blinked, and saw Owyn's eyes were open.

"Hey," Aven whispered. He looked over Owyn, seeing Aria was still asleep. "How do you feel?"

"I feel..." Owyn frowned. "Not dead. Why am I not dead? I'm supposed to be dead."

Aven grinned. "Not if I have anything to say about it," he answered. He reached out and cupped Owyn's cheek, then leaned closer and kissed him. "You're not dying if I can stop it."

Owyn worked one hand free from the cocoon of blankets and grabbed Aven's hand. "But I'm *supposed* to be dead," he insisted. "He told me. He poured Rut down my throat and he told me—"

"And I forced it out of you," Aven said. "Do you want the specifics? I can explain."

Owyn blinked twice. "Yes. Please."

"Technical, or plain speaking?" Aven asked.

"I probably wouldn't understand the technical, so plain," Owyn said. "What did you do?"

"Do you know how your body works?" Aven asked. "How your blood carries things through your body?"

"A bit, yeah. Carries food and stuff, right?"

"Right. Well, one of the other things it carries is waste."

"Like a sewer?" Owyn asked. He nodded. "All right. Where does the waste go? I mean, before it goes out. I know what it turns into. But how?"

"Your body filters it. That's what your kidneys do. When blood passes through the kidneys, the kidneys filter out the waste. With me so far?"

"And... that's what you did?" Owyn's eyes went wide. "You... you forced it out of me? Out through the kidneys and..." He paused, tugged on the blanket that was wrapped around him and looked inside. "I don't smell all that good right now, do I?"

"You're going to want to bathe," Aven said, trying not to smile. "Trey said you smelled like a back alley in summer."

Owyn nodded slowly. He frowned. "I... I think I remember. Bits and pieces and..." He coughed. "I didn't... did I call you—"

"Fishie?" Aven asked. "Yes."

Owyn turned red. "Oh. Oh, no. Oh, I didn't... I wasn't going to... it was just in my head... I wasn't ever going to call you that to your face..."

"I don't mind, Owyn," Aven said. "If you want to call me Fishie, I really don't mind. If I can call you Mouse?"

Owyn nodded. "I... I remember you calling me Mouse. I like it." He frowned again. "What happened to you?" he asked. "They took both of us. What happened to you?"

"Apparently, they took me to Fandor's house, and left me there for Mannon," Aven answered. "But I got away. I got lost in the city, but Aria found me. And we found you."

"And where are we?" Owyn asked. He looked around the dimly-lit room. "We're safe?"

"We're at Meris' house, with Karse's guards everywhere." Aven shifted a little closer to Owyn. "If you're feeling steady enough, we're to go before the Council, and get out of the city before dawn. If you need more time, we're hiding until tomorrow night."

"No, I'm all right." Owyn closed his eyes. "I... what happened to him?"

"Fandor was taken away," Aria said. She propped herself up on her elbow and wrapped her arm around Owyn from behind. "Leesam said that they would hold him in chains until the Council meeting."

Owyn twisted and smiled up at her. "Good. That's good. I wish I could be here to see him get thrown in the volcano. But..." his face went blank. "Wait. Where are my clothes? The ones I was wearing. Where are they?"

"Trey went back to look for Trinket," Aven said. "He'll find her."

Owyn looked back at him. "You think she's all right? He didn't hurt her?"

"He would have had to catch her first," Aria said. "And she would never have allowed that."

"And if he was going to hurt her, he'd have done it in front of you," Aven added. Owyn's jaw dropped. Then he nodded, slowly.

"He would have," he agreed. "All right. We'll see what Trey finds. I... maybe we can go back there, if he doesn't? Before we leave?"

"We'll do that," Aria said. "We'll find her." She hugged Owyn tightly. "Do you want to eat?"

"No," Owyn said. "Not... not yet. I want to be here. With you both. Like this. Except... Aven, you're too far away."

Aven looked down at the bare hand-span that separated them, and shifted closer, until there was nothing between them but the blankets. He put his arm over Owyn, then rubbed his nose against the tip of Owyn's nose. "Better?"

"Almost," Owyn said. "But it'll do." He sighed and relaxed slightly. "I'm sorry I smell bad," he mumbled.

"Considering that I did it to you?" Aven said. "You're forgiven." He closed his eyes, feeling Aria's fingers tracing the veins on his arm.

"You did it— you don't like that sort of thing, do you?" Owyn asked.

Aven opened one eye. "What sort of thing?" he asked slowly. "Do I want to know?"

Owyn looked thoughtful. "You hadn't had anyone, until me. So you wouldn't know if that was your sort of thing, since we haven't done it. So I'm not telling you. Because I don't like it."

"You're talking in circles," Aria said. "What sort of thing?"

Owyn scowled. "Well... are you familiar with dogs? And what I mean by marking territory?"

"Oh, no," Aria breathed. "Really?"

"Really what?" Aven asked. "I know marking territory, but what do dogs do that seals don't?"

Aria and Owyn both looked at him, and it was Aria who asked, "What do seals do?"

"They have glands in their faces that give off a scent. They mark rocks with it." Aven frowned, trying to connect what they'd been talking about with the change in conversation. "Marking territory... with piss?"

Owyn nodded. "That's it. That's how dogs do it. Cats, too. And... some people."

Aria made a strangled sound. "That's awful!"

Owyn laughed. "Some people like that sort of thing. Not me. I told you, I don't like it."

"I don't find anything at all arousing about it myself," Aven agreed. "Besides, Aria's already marked us both." He rolled onto his back. "Meris said that my carry-bag was in the chest–"

"I didn't say you could move, you know," Owyn grumbled. He reached out and grabbed Aven's wrist. "Come back here."

Aven grinned and rolled back, moving closer than he had been before. "Better?"

Owyn smiled. "Much better. Except..." He paused, turned to look over his shoulder. "Aria, how much time before they come bang on the door?"

"If they come and bang on the door, I'm going to have words with them," Aria answered, her voice cold. "We have as long as I say we have." She smiled. "And I say you should take as much time as you want. If that's what you're asking?"

Owyn looked back at Aven, and his smile faded slightly. "I... Aven, this is me wanting this, right? And not the drug?"

"I thought I got it all," Aven answered. He rested his hand on Owyn's chest and closed his eyes, slowly checking Owyn's blood for any traces of the poison that would have killed him. "I don't see anything," he said slowly. He opened his eyes, looking into Owyn's. "If you're not completely sure, though, the answer is no."

"Will you at least kiss me?" Owyn asked.

"Absolutely," Aven answered. He wasn't expecting Owyn to surge out of his blanket cocoon and push him back onto the bed, turning them into a heated tangle of arms and legs and blankets. Owyn ended up stretched out over Aven, his fingers splayed over Aven's collarbone, kissing him hungrily. Aven slid his hands up over Owyn's ribs, fingertips tracing the edges of old scars. He heard Aria giggle, felt the bed shift. Then Owyn shuddered, his mouth falling away from Aven's as he moaned.

"Oh," Aria breathed. "Oh, I didn't—"

"No, you keep right on doing that," Owyn gasped. "Just... just touch. Let me know you're there. Let me know you..."

Aven wrapped his arms around Owyn and held him tightly. "We're here. We're both here. And we both want you. But we have to be sure you're really wanting it."

Owyn sighed and rested his head on Aven's shoulder. "And I'm not sure. I know you said it's gone, but I'm not sure. So... so, no. Not yet. Just be with me."

"Always," Aria said. She curled up next to Aven, who shifted to put his arm around her. She rested her head on Aven's other shoulder, and put her arm over Owyn's back. "Can you breathe, Aven?"

"I'm fine," Aven said. "He's not heavy. This is nice."

"It is, but we'll need to get up and bathe soon," Aria said. She sighed. "I don't want to. I want to stay here with you both."

"But we can't, can we?" Owyn said. "If we stay, we're at risk, and we put Meris at risk. We have to go." He sniffed, then grumbled. "Let me up. I'll go bathe. Do I have clothes?"

"Meris said there were clothes for all of us," Aven said. "Are you sure you want to get up?"

"If I don't get up, I'm going to do something I might regret later," Owyn answered. He kissed Aven, turned and kissed Aria, then shifted off of Aven and got to his feet. The blankets wrapped around him made him look smaller than he was. "Let me go bathe, and I'll eat while you two get ready. Then we can go save the world. Or conquer it. Which is it again? I forget."

"I think that depends on who you ask," Aria answered. "Go on."

Owyn laughed and disappeared into the bath. Aven hugged Aria to his side and closed his eyes.

"We should get up, too," she said. But she didn't move. Instead, she started trailing her nails over Aven's skin.

"You're thinking deep," he murmured.

"Just worried about meeting this Council," Aria said. "And why. What do we need from them?"

"Supplies," Aven answered. "That's what Memfis said, isn't it? When we were listening in the closet?"

"We can't get supplies anywhere else?" Aria asked. "It bothers me that we have to speak to so many. Any of them could sell us to Mannon easily."

Aven shook his head. "I don't know. But I trust Memfis. There has to be a reason he's doing it this way."

"He should tell us that reason," Aria grumbled, and pulled gently from Aven's arms. She got off the bed and went to the chest, taking out Aven's carry-bag. She brought it back to the bed and opened it, taking out the water and fire gems.

"You and Owyn will wear these," she said. "As he said, I've marked you both as mine. I want this entire Council to see that."

Aven smiled and sat up, folding his legs and watching as Aria laid out the clothes that Meris had left for them. "Don't mix them up," he warned as she shook out a shirt. "Owyn's clothes won't fit me."

"His are that pile," Aria said. "Yours are here. And this is mine — where did she *find* them?" She held up a long-sleeved wrapped coat, then turned it so that Aven could see the slits in the back for her wings, and the t- shaped panel that was meant to come up and between them. There were buttons, Aven saw, across the tops of the shoulders. "This was made in the mountains, by someone who knew what they were doing. How could she have known?"

"She's a Smoke Dancer," Aven offered. "She knew the same way that Memfis knew."

"I'm growing tired of that answer," Aria said. "If they know so much, if they can see so much, then why did they let you and Owyn get hurt? And if this gift of visions that they have — that we have — is only useful for inconsequentials, then what good is it?"

"You at least have something," Aven said. "Most of my gifts are only good in salt water." He swung his legs over the side of the bed and got up, coming around to stand with Aria. "There's an explanation. We'll find it. We'll get Memfis to tell us."

"That simple?" Aria asked. She looked down at the coat in her hands. "I don't think anything will ever be that simple ever again."

"Nothing is ever that simple," Owyn said, coming out of the bath. He had a towel wrapped around his waist, and was scrubbing at his hair with another. "Anybody who thinks it is doesn't know any better."

"I used to think things were simple," Aven said. Owyn's words stung, and he wasn't sure why.

"Sure," Owyn agreed. "But that was before you knew anything about anything, right? You were out on the water, and you didn't know the rest of this." He made a sweeping gesture. "You said it yourself. You were swimming in muddy water. You didn't know." He shrugged. "Who's next? There's plenty of hot water."

"You go, Aria," Aven said. Aria nodded and disappeared into the bath. Aven returned to the bed and sat down, watching as Owyn took a seat at the table. "If you want it hot—"

"Nah, cold food is fine," Owyn said, starting to uncover bowls. He picked one up and started eating, then frowned at Aven. "It's bothering you. What I said, it's bothering you."

"A little." Aven shrugged and leaned forward onto his elbows. "I don't understand why I was kept ignorant. My parents said it was for my own safety But now I'm really not safe, and I'm still ignorant—"

"Which makes you even less safe," Owyn finished. "Because you don't know what's coming. Aven, I don't know what to tell you." He took another mouthful, chewed slowly, then swallowed. "No. No, I do know what to tell you. It's not you that's the problem. You were kept in the dark — in the muddy water — and now you know the difference. Now you're learning, right?" Aven nodded, and Owyn continued, "You're not the problem. It's the people who know the difference, who know that things aren't simple, but insist that they are, because nothing that's going wrong hurts them. They're the problem. Because if they keep saying things are simple, then they're not going to change anything. Because simple is good, and changing things might hurt them. So, since it's easier on them, they insist that there's nothing wrong. Simple, see?"

Aven frowned, thinking it over. "You mean, there are people in this city who know about Fandor, about what he's done? And they don't do anything?"

"Because doing something means they'd have to admit that there are things they don't want to see." Owyn finished the contents of the bowl, picked up another. "Those people, they see what they want to see, and ignore the rest. But you, you saw only what you were allowed to see. Now you're seeing the rest, and you're learning that it's not simple. At all. And you're doing something about it." Owyn grimaced. "I learned that lesson really young. I don't think I'd know what to do with simple. Real simple."

"You could come back out to the deep with me," Aven offered. "I could show you."

Owyn laughed, sounding nervous. "Me? Out there? No, I can't do that." He shook his head. "I can't swim."

Aven joined Owyn at the table. "That's not a problem. I can teach you. I taught Aria."

Owyn shook his head again. "I... I don't know. Besides, would you be happy? Going back to the deep, knowing what you know now? Could you turn your back on this?" He made another expansive gesture. "On her?" He paused, and there was an odd note in his voice when he asked, "On me?"

Aven reached across the table and took Owyn's free hand. "I'm not turning my back on anyone, Mouse," he said. "Not you, and not Aria." He squeezed Owyn's fingers. "But I miss the sea."

Owyn nodded. "I understand that. I'm trying to get my brain around not being in the city anymore. I've never been more than a mile outside the walls, ever." He looked around. "After tomorrow, who knows if I'll ever be back?"

There was a knock on the door. Aven glanced at it, then at Owyn, who shook his head. He raised his voice. "Who's there?"

"It's me. It's Trey," Trey called.

"Gimme a minute, Trey!" Owyn called. He pointed at the bed. "Which pile is mine?"

"On the right," Aven answered. Owyn got up and grabbed his clean trousers, tugging them on. Once he'd fastened the waist, he called. "Come in."

The door opened, and Trey peered around the edge. He grinned when he saw Owyn. "You dressed for me? You don't need to be fancy, Wyn. I've seen you before."

"Fuck you, Trey," Owyn grumbled. "Did you find her?"

Trey came the rest of the way, kicking the door closed behind him. He had his hands cupped in front of him, and he opened them to reveal a flame-bright ball of fur. Owyn crowed with laughter.

"Trinket!" He scooped the fire mouse out of Trey's hands and sat down on the bed. Once he'd examined the mouse closely, he looked up, his expression gravely serious. "Thank you, Trey," he said softly. "I... she's important to me."

"I know, Wyn," Trey said. He sat down next to Owyn, and Aven felt for a moment as if he'd been forgotten. "I was there when you named her, remember?"

"Yeah," Owyn answered with a smile. He stroked his fingers over Trinket's fur. "Where was she?"

"Same place she used to hide. Under your bed," Trey answered. "Left slipper."

Owyn nodded. "If we had to go back, that would have been the first place I looked. Thank you, Trey." He looked up at Aven. "Oh. I... Aven, umm... Trey and I... did he tell you?"

"He didn't tell me anything," Aven said. "And I wouldn't have asked."

Trey sat up and smiled at Aven. "It didn't last long. Not even a season, really. We were both still figuring out how to be people and not things. And it was before we figured out that we could be friends without fucking each other."

"Which was really all we knew before that," Owyn added. "Trey, you could come with us, you know."

Trey shook his head. "I thought about it. Standing with the Heir? That's important. But then I thought about the people who need me here. Karse needs me. He needs someone at his back he can trust. Our squad needs me. And someone needs to stand up to the men like Fandor and say no. You go do your part to set things right. I'm staying here to do mine." He got up, turning to face Owyn. "You take care of yourself, Wyn."

Owyn looked up and smiled. "You, too."

Trey turned to Aven, nodded, and held his hand out. "It was good meeting you, Aven. Thank you, for everything."

"I should be thanking you," Aven said, taking Trey's hand. "I couldn't have done it without you."

Trey sniffed. "You would have. You'd have found a way." He squeezed Aven's hand. "Take care of him, all right?"

Aven smiled. He nodded. "Even if you hadn't asked."

Trey grinned. He let Aven's hand fall, stepped back, and looked around. "If you'd tell the Heir I sent my regards? And that I wish you all the best of luck."

"We'll tell her," Owyn said. "Be careful, Trey."

"You, too." Trey responded. He turned and left the room, closing the door behind him.

CHAPTER TWENTY-THREE

AVEN TOOK HIS TURN in the bath, coming out to find Owyn finishing his meal and sharing bits with Trinket. Aria was standing at the window, looking out into the night. She was wearing the wrapped coat, and trousers that made her legs look even longer. The new clothes suited her, and Aven admired her for a moment before picking up his new clothes — trousers, a long-sleeved shirt, and a vest that looked oddly familiar. He dressed quickly, but as he picked up the vest, he gasped and nearly dropped it. Aria turned to look at him.

"What is it?"

"Taipa," he stammered. "This is taipa cloth!"

"What's taipa?" Owyn asked.

"It's bark cloth. It's what we make our clothes from." Aven ran the fabric of the vest through his fingers. "This shouldn't be here. We don't trade taipa."

"Like my coat," Aria said. "They gave you something from your own people."

Aven pulled the vest on over his shirt, running one hand over the front. "It's... it's good," he said. "I'm not sure how to explain it. It's..."

"Comforting?" Owyn supplied. "You've got something familiar."

Aven nodded. "Yes. That's it."

"That's probably why she did it, then. Meris, I mean. She thinks of things like that," Owyn offered. "Since we're all ready, what's the plan? Are we staying here until they come for us, or are we going to go roust up the Council and tell them what we want?"

Aria looked thoughtful, then shook her head. "I will not dance to their tune. Let's go find them and get started."

Aven nodded and went to fetch his boots. He sat down to put them on, and jumped when something was lowered over his head from behind.

"It's me," Aria said. "Stay still." She adjusted the cord which held the water gem so that it sat at the hollow of Aven's throat. "There. Owyn, you're next."

"Yes, my Heir," Owyn said, sounding so serious that Aria stopped. He grinned. "What?"

"You didn't sound like you," Aria said. She looped the cord over his head and adjusted it. "There."

"Aven needs a scarf," Owyn said. "And, do I have boots? Shoes? Something?"

"We'll have to ask. I didn't see anything." Aven rose and picked up his swords and the shoulder harness that he was supposed to wear to carry them. He'd already worn them strapped to his back when he'd gone after Owyn, but it had felt unnatural — he'd never *worn* hook swords before. A club hanging from his belt? Of course. A knife strapped to his arm or hanging from his waist? Certainly. Swords? Swords were for dancing, and went back into their case when the dance was done.

"Something wrong?" Owyn asked.

Aven shrugged and put his carry-bag on, then slipped the harness on over his vest. "I'm not used to wearing these," he said. "And I don't like the idea that I'm going to get used to wearing them."

Owyn nodded. "I understand that. I'll be using my smoke blades to fight. I've never done that before. I know it's been done. It's part of the history I had to learn in my training. Smoke Dancers used to fight, too. But I've never done it." He looked down. "I don't know if I can. I mean, I've never fought like that before." He frowned. "I don't know if I can kill someone."

Aven met Aria's eyes. "Had you ever killed someone before tonight?"

She shook her head. "No. Hunted, certainly. Killed a person? No."

"Me either," Aven said. He turned back to Owyn, to find him staring at them.

"You... you killed someone?" Owyn whispered. He looked stunned. "For me?"

Aven nodded slowly. "Aria killed most of them," he said. "I only got two. But I didn't have proper weapons."

"You did fine with what you had," Aria assured him. "Owyn, you didn't realize?"

"No!" Owyn gasped. "I... I didn't. When I get... like that, I shut things out. When I panic like that, the world goes away. There's only the fear." He frowned. "Does that make sense?"

Aven nodded. "I think so. And you fell asleep before Memfis told me that we'd killed some of them." He looked down at the loose harness, then fastened the strap across his chest. "I didn't know I could kill someone. But I'd do it again to protect either of you. Or to get my parents back."

Aria put her hand on his arm and squeezed. "We'll find them."

"I really can't wait to meet them," Owyn added. He looked around. "I don't even know where my blades are."

"Memfis probably has them. Do you have Trinket?" Aria asked. Owyn patted his shirt pocket. "Good, then let's go find Memfis and finish this."

Aven hooked his swords into the harness and followed Aria to the door. As she opened it, two guards outside the door both jumped to attention.

"We're ready to meet with the Council," Aria announced. "But I wish to speak to Memfis and my grandmother first. Where are they?"

One of the guards nodded. "They're in the library, last I saw. Ah... I don't know what I should be calling you. I don't want to be rude."

Aria smiled. "I'm not entirely certain myself. I've had several people call me My Heir, but I don't know if that's correct. You may call me by name until we both know better. And what's your name?"

The guard nodded. "Very good, Lady Aria. And my name is Westir. Folks call me Wes."

"Thank you, Wes," Aria said. "Would you show us the way?"

Wes bowed and started down the corridor. Aria followed him, and Aven and Owyn fell in behind her, walking side by side.

"I feel unfinished," Owyn muttered. "No shoes, no weapons? You at least look the part."

"We'll find you shoes, and Memfis has your weapons," Aven answered, his voice low. "And it doesn't matter how you look. You're where you're supposed to be."

That drew a smile from Owyn, who didn't say anything more. They turned down another corridor, one that looked familiar, and Wes led them to the library door. He knocked, then opened the door.

"Begging your pardon, Lady Meris, but Lady Aria and her Companions are here," he said.

They heard Meris from inside the library. "Send them in!"

Meris met them halfway between the fireplace and the door, and completely ignored Aria and Aven both. She went straight to Owyn, and caught him in a fierce embrace that made Owyn squeak in surprise.

"My boy," she crooned, and from her raspy voice, it was clear that she'd been crying. "Oh, my boy. I'm sorry. I should have listened." She let Owyn go, backed up, and looked at him. "You weren't hurt?"

Owyn bit his lip, then shook his head. "Not... not really. Not that Aven couldn't fix." He tried to smile, but it slumped and faded from his face. "It's not your fault, Granna."

Meris blinked, and her mouth opened slightly. "Granna?" She looked back at Memfis. "You... you didn't tell me he calls me Granna!"

"Because that's the first time," Owyn said. "It's... you're his foster mother, really. Right? And... I'm his son. Well, going to be. So that makes you my grandmother."

"Not going to be," Memfis said. He came over and handed Owyn a folded bundle of paper. "Are."

Owyn's eyes widened, and he looked down at the bundle. His hands shook, and he couldn't break the wax seal holding the bundle closed. He stopped, closed his eyes, then turned to Aven. "Open this?" he asked, handing him the bundle. "Read it to me? I... I can't."

Aven took the bundle and stepped in close to Owyn, carefully breaking the seal and unfolding the papers. He held them in one hand, and put his arm around Owyn's shoulders. Aria crowded in on Owyn's other side as Aven started to read the ornately calligraphed letter.

"It is the decision of the Council of Forge, speaking for the Tribe of Fire, Children of Adavar, that the petition for adoption of the foundling Owyn, slave of unclaimed bloodline, be approved," he read. "Be it known that from this day forth, he shall be recognized as Owyn, son of Memfis, son of Trezi, of the line of Nerris, and a full member of the Tribe of Fire, with all rights, privileges, and responsibilities of such, as listed in the Codex. This adoption is so recorded in the *Book of Silver*, and renders all prior status null." He looked up. "Does that mean that Owyn isn't a slave anymore? That in their eyes, he never was?"

"That's what it means," Owyn said. "It means I get a fresh start." He smiled and looked at Aven. "It means my past was written in water." He pressed against Aven's side. "Is there more?"

"The rest is ruffles and flourishes, to impress on you how serious this is," Memfis said. "As if we'd do this for some silly reason. Most of that is a copy of the Tribal codex."

Owyn looked confused. "You taught me that. I can recite that from memory."

"What is it?" Aria asked. "Should we read it?"

"That bit about rights, privileges, and responsibilities?" Owyn answered. "That's all listed in the Codex. It's Fire tribe law, and some of it goes back to the beginning."

Aven nodded. He handed the bundle back to Memfis, then hugged Owyn tightly. "Congratulations," he said.

Owyn turned pink. "Thank you." He frowned. "I... we have things that need to be done. Aven needs a scarf. I need shoes. And are we going to the Council? When do we have to leave?"

"Aren't they here?" Aven asked. "I thought they were here."

"Not anymore," Meris answered. "We'd be up to our elbows in Councilors if they were. We'll leave for the meeting cavern as soon as you all are ready. Shoes. Memfis, how did I forget shoes?"

"I didn't think you had," Memfis answered. "They're probably still in the storeroom. And a scarf? We'll have to see what we can do about that."

Meris sniffed. "I can do something about that. Owyn, why don't you and Aria go see where I forgot the shoes, and see if there's anything else you need. Memfis, take them to the storeroom. Aven, come with me."

For a moment, Aven hesitated. He didn't want to let Aria or Owyn out of his sight. But they were with Memfis. And if he couldn't trust Meris, they were in far more trouble than they thought. Aria touched his arm, and Owyn grinned at him.

"We all thinking the same thing?" Owyn asked. "No splitting up?"

Aven nodded. "Yes. Which is—"

"Completely understandable," Meris said. "And I should have thought of that. You've all had a night of it. It's been horrible for us, but for you — it must have been torturous. We can all go to the storeroom, and then to my suite for the scarf."

Aria shook her head. "No, Grandmother. We'll be fine." She squeezed Aven's arm. "We will be fine."

Aven met her eyes and nodded, then turned to Meris. "Where are we going? Your suite, you said?"

Meris chuckled and took his arm. "You three. You're going to move mountains. I can't wait to meet your Earth and your Air." She led Aven out of the library and down the hall, going back the way they'd come, and past the room where Aven, Aria and Owyn had slept. At the very end of the corridor was a set of double doors; Meris opened them and led Aven inside.

"Have a seat, my dear," she said as she went to another door.

"Only if you want me to slice your furniture to ribbons," Aven called after her, and heard laughter. He looked around, seeing well-worn furnishings and a large bed piled high with blankets and pillows. There was a stack of books on a table next to the bed, and a small circle of fur that unwound into a sleek, four-legged animal with a long tail. It stretched, looked up at him with big, green eyes, and made an odd, mewling sound.

"Hello," Aven murmured. "What are you?" He moved closer to the bed. "Mother Meris, what is this?"

"What this?" Meris called back. She came out of the other room and laughed. "Oh, that's Patience. She keeps me company."

"And what is she?" Aven crouched to get a better look at the animal, who came closer and bumped her head against his chin. Her fur was soft, and she made a buzzing sound.

"You've never seen a cat before?" Meris asked. She came over and wiggled her fingers at Patience, who abandoned Aven and bounded over the bed to jump into Meris' arms. "Usually, she has the run of the house. But she hunts, and I didn't want her going after Owyn's Trinket."

"That's a cat?" Aven rose. "I was wondering what land cats were like. My father said that whoever named water-cats had clearly never seen a land cat. And Aria told me that land cats were small. But Patience is smaller than I thought a cat would be."

"There are larger ones," Meris told him. She stroked the cat in her arms, then scratched behind her ears. "Patience is still young."

Aven nodded and reached out to stroke the cat's head, rubbing her alongside the muzzle the way he would have done to Melody. Her buzz grew louder as her eyes closed. "What's that sound?" he asked.

"She's purring. Cats purr when they're happy. She likes you," Meris said. She nodded. "Hold your arms like this, like I am."

Aven did as she said, and froze when she poured the cat into his arms. "You just keep petting her," Meris said, and went back into the other room. Aven looked down at Patience, who looked up at him, then rested her head on his arm and closed her eyes. He scratched her behind the ears, the way Meris had done.

"What does she hunt?" he called.

"Small birds. Fire mice. Lizards. Crumpled pieces of paper tied to a string," Meris answered, coming back into the bedroom with an armload of multicolored scarves. "Let's see. Which one?"

"One that will hold up to wearing," Aven offered. Meris nodded, sorting through the colors. Occasionally, she'd look at one, then at him. She'd shake her head, and put the scarf aside, and go on to the next one.

"Blue, I think," she murmured. "Or green. Your coloring would take both. Not red. Red would be too garish."

"I like red," Aven protested. She acted as if she didn't hear him, holding a dark green scarf up to his chest. Patience batted at it, and Meris clicked her tongue at her. Aven grinned.

"I'd make the same sound at Melody when she was into something she shouldn't be," he said.

"It's universal. You make that sound to pets and small children." Meris picked out a second dark green scarf, then nodded. "These will do. They'll both hold up well. Put Patience on the bed, and we'll go find the others and be off."

Aven set the cat down on the bed and stroked her again, then took the scarves from Meris and followed her back out of the bedroom and down to the library. The room was empty, and Meris scowled at the open door.

"They're still in the storeroom," she said. "We'll meet them there."

"Mother Meris, why do we need to meet the Council?" Aven asked. "Is it just for supplies? Why can't we get those somewhere else?"

Meris looked up at him, then took his arm, leading him down the hall. "Supplies are only part of it. A minor part of it. The rest is to put a face to what we'll be fighting for. Aria's face, and yours, and Owyn's. The Council needs to know that this is real, and it's happening now. We took a chance on someone once, and it went badly."

Aven nodded. "You mean Yana? You said the name earlier, but we don't know who that is."

"Was. She disappeared some twenty years ago," Meris said. "And Memfis didn't tell you?"

"No, Mother," Aven answered. Meris sighed.

"He should have. I'll tell you in the carriage on the way."

IT WAS ONLY THE LURE of information that got Aria into the
carriage. She perched on the edge of the middle of the bench, her
wings pulled in tight to her body so that there was room next to
her. Owyn sat on her right, and Aven on her left. He considered the
bench before he sat, then unslung his swords from his back and held
them upright between his knees, mimicking the way that Owyn held
his smoke blades. Memfis and Meris faced them, and as the coach
started moving, Meris cleared her throat.

"Aven tells me that you've told them nothing about Yana," she
said to Memfis. "Memfis, we'll have no more of that. They need to
know everything that we know."

Memfis let out a long breath. "Yes, Meris. Yana—"

"You had your chance. Now I tell it," Meris interrupted. "Yana
was a daughter of Air. She came to Forge twenty years ago. And she
bore the Diadem, and carried the gems."

"What?" Aria gasped.

Meris nodded. "You were not the first Heir since your father
died. Yana was. At least, she was the first that we knew of. The
Mother chose Yana. But Yana refused to seek her Companions. She
would lead the rebellion against Mannon alone, to prove herself
as Heir. The Council gave her everything she asked for — men,
supplies, arms. She left with that army — a good number of our
young men and women. And none of them ever came back.
Mannon's forces slaughtered them. We don't know what happened
to Yana — her body was never found. There was a second, smaller
rebellion in Forge the following year, once it was clear that Yana had
fallen. They rose in her name, but that force failed as well." Meris
paused for a moment. "That's the reason that Mannon destroyed the
Temple. Because of Yana. Because she was the true Heir, and he knew
that since she had failed, there would be others behind her."

"So we're going to the Council why?" Aria asked. "If they've failed with Yana, and failed again in Yana's name, what makes you think that they'll try again?"

"You've got two of your four Companions," Memfis said. "And there's the vision of the dove—"

"Which we had with Yana," Meris interrupted. "But we were wrong to think it applied to her."

"What's the vision of the dove?" Aven asked. He looked at Aria. "I think I'm the only one who doesn't know it. Aria knows. Owyn, you said you knew it, too. You said you've had it."

"Yeah, I've had it," Owyn admitted. "All Smoke Dancers have seen it. We just aren't supposed to talk about it."

"Mannon takes exception to this particular vision," Memfis said. "Since it's the one that tells how he'll be overthrown. It's the reason that smoke dancing was banned, and if someone mentions the vision where one of Mannon's followers hears of it, well... it doesn't end well."

"So what is it?" Aven asked. For a moment, silence was his only answer. Then Meris nodded.

"We asked the question almost as soon as we found out what had happened in the Palace. How could we be rid of Mannon, and restore the Firstborn? So this vision has been part of our lives for longer than you've been alive. And when we asked, when any Smoke Dancer asked, the answer was always the same. We saw a dove, a water-cat, a flame, a flower, and a broken feather."

Aven frowned. "That's not a lot to go on."

"Considering that there wasn't anyone in Forge who knew what a water-cat was?" Memfis said. "It was nothing to go on for about five years. Then Yana showed up with the Diadem, and we realized that the next Firstborn was meant to be of Air. That was the dove. The rest fell into place after that."

"Memfis didn't trust Yana to be the right one," Meris said. "Because she was missing the Companions, and the vision showed all four with the dove. He was right." She smiled. "And now here you are with two. With your water-cat and your flame."

"I didn't make that connection until you said it, Aven," Owyn said. "You said that Melody tells her pod you're her boy. You were adopted by a water-cat."

"Which sort of makes me one?" Aven said slowly. He nodded. "It makes a weird sort of sense. But you should be a fire mouse, Mouse. Not a flame."

Owyn grinned, then looked back across the carriage. "What else is there that we don't we know? That we should know?"

Memfis looked thoughtful. He looked at Meris, who folded her hands in her lap and looked down at them. Aven went cold, and looked to his right at Aria and Owyn. Aria was frowning.

"What is it?" she demanded. "What is it that you do not want to say?"

"Nothing to do with you, my dear." Meris hesitated, then sighed. "I have searched the *Book of Silver* for two years now. There are... five possibilities, I think. Yes, that's it. Five." She looked up, looking at Owyn. "That's why I never said anything. I never could narrow it any further."

Owyn went pale. "You were looking at who I was?"

"My idea," Memfis said. "I thought you might want to know. I have the list, if you want it."

Owyn let out a slow breath, then shook his head. "You... you didn't have to do that," he said softly. "I mean, I appreciate it. But you didn't have to. Who I was doesn't matter to me. I know who I am." He grinned. "I'm Owyn. Son of Memfis, son of Trezi, son of... you never did tell me your grandfather's name, you know. Of the line of Nerris. And I'm the Heir's Fire companion. That's who I am."

CHAPTER TWENTY-FOUR

THE CARRIAGE STOPPED, and for a moment, no one moved. Aria looked from side to side, then across at Memfis and Meris. "Have we arrived?"

"Not quite," Memfis answered. As he spoke, there was a knock at the door to his right. He slid the curtain open and looked out. "Memfis and Lady Meris," he said. "And petitioners."

"I'll need to see them," a voice said from outside. "May I open the door?"

"Of course."

The door opened, and a man peered into the carriage. His eyes widened when he saw Aria, but he said nothing. Then he looked at Owyn, and his face went pale.

"Mother of us all," he murmured. "I..." He stopped, then bowed.

"May we pass?" Aria asked. He looked up; she smiled at him, and he blushed a brilliant red.

"Yes, my Heir," he said. "May the Mother guard and guide you." He stepped back and closed the carriage door, and the vehicle lurched forward.

"Where are we going?" Aria asked. "You said caverns. We'll be underground?"

"The Council — both Councils — meet in the cavern called the Heart of the Tribe," Meris answered. "It's believed to be the place where the first members of the tribe were born."

"Cave?" Aven swallowed, suddenly hot and cold all at once. "How small a cave?" he asked, trying to keep a quaver out of his voice.

"It's not," Memfis added. "It's not a small cave. There's plenty of space inside." He frowned and leaned forward. "Aven?"

Aven shook his head, leaning back in his seat. He rubbed his right palm against his thigh, then his left. "I... don't like caves," he said quietly. Mother, how *old* had he been? Five? Six? He couldn't remember. All he could remember was being alone in the tiny, pitch-black space, the cold, dark water, and the fear. "I don't have a problem with small spaces. But caves—" He shook his head again.

Aria took his hand. "What happened?"

Aven looked at her. "I don't remember how old I was. My mother and I were deep, in some of the caves near our island. Hunting lobster, probably. And looking for shark teeth. There was... a tremor. You get those, sometimes, underwater. Tremors you never feel on the land. Underneath, down deep, you're closer to the heart of Adavar. You can feel it when he rolls over in his sleep—"

"What?" Owyn interrupted.

Aven grinned, running his fingers through his hair. "That's what we call it, when the ground shakes. Father Adavar rolling in his sleep. You don't want Him to wake."

"He's precious close to it," Memfis muttered. "Go on."

Aven nodded. "There was a tremor, and the cave where we were hunting collapsed. When the rocks settled, Ama was on the other side of the fall." He swallowed. "The outside of the fall." He looked up at Aria, at Owyn. "I was trapped in the cave, in the dark and cold, for I don't know how long. Ama wouldn't tell me how long it was before she could dig me out. All I know is that when we finally reached the surface, when we finally got back to the canoe... it was weeks before I went back into the water."

"Does it help if I tell you that this cave is neither cold nor dark?" Memfis offered. "Or small, for that matter."

Aven tried to smile. "I don't know," he answered. Aria squeezed his hand tightly, and Owyn reached across her to rest his hand on Aven's knee.

"You're not alone," Owyn said. "We're here with you. You're not trapped in the dark alone."

"Memfis, how long will we be in this cave?" Aria asked.

"An hour?" Memfis said. "Maybe a little more, but I'm going to try and make it less. Much less. I want to be done as fast as possible. We need to be out of the city and as far as we can be by dawn."

"How close is dawn?" Owyn asked. "I have no idea how late it is. Or how early. It was dark when Fandor took us. I know that. But I'm not sure how long he had me."

"It had been about two hours, I think, when I took my bearings to try and find Meris' house," Aven said. "And another hour before we got to you, Mouse."

"Then however long we slept," Aria added. "We're on the far side of midnight now, aren't we?"

"Call it between three and four hours to dawn," Memfis said. "Closer to three."

Aven nodded. He closed his eyes and moved the hand that Aria held so that it rested on top of Owyn's hand. "I'm all right—"

"Liar," Owyn called, sounding incredibly cheerful. Aven opened his eyes and glared at him, then laughed when Owyn blew him a kiss.

"I'll try to be all right?" Aven offered. Owyn nodded.

"Better," he answered. "Just try to act normal. Sometimes, pretending to be all right helps you to be all right. If that makes sense?"

Aven frowned, thinking about it. He shook his head. "Not really."

"Just trust me on it." Owyn squeezed Aven's leg, then slipped his hand out from underneath Aven's and Aria's hands. "We're stopping."

Aven sat up as the carriage came to a shuddering stop. A door opened, and a guard looked in at them.

"Lady Meris, Memfis," he said. "And petitioners. If you'll come with me?"

Memfis stepped out first, and helped Meris out of the carriage. Owyn followed, then Aria, and Aven stepped out into the tunnel, moving away from the group so that he could slip his blades back into the harness. As he did, he looked around — the tunnel was large, wide and level, and lit every few feet with lamps that glowed without smoke or smell. It didn't feel like he was underground, or in a cave, and he relaxed a little as he rejoined the group, moving to stand next to Aria and Owyn. The guard studied him for a moment, looked as if he was going to say something, then turned abruptly and walked away to converse with a second guard.

"What was that?" Aria murmured.

"Usually, you can't bring weapons when you go before the Council," Owyn answered. "I think he decided that it wasn't worth fighting with the Heir over having her Companions disarmed."

Aria nodded slowly. "And it would have been a fight. I will not see you disarmed. Not after everything that's happened tonight."

The guard returned, bringing the second guard with him. He glanced at them briefly, then turned to Meris. "The Council is seated."

"I'm coming. Memfis, will you be taking your seat for this last time?"

Memfis frowned. He looked at Aria, then at Aven and Owyn. "No, Meris," he said. "I'll be petitioning with my son."

Owyn turned pink and smiled. Meris nodded and followed the guard down the tunnel.

"What do I do now?" Aria asked. "All we want is supplies and to be out of the city, correct?"

"And to let them see us," Aven added. "Meris told me that. To give them a face and a name, for when we need them later."

Aria nodded. She drew herself up, reached up and touched the Diadem on her brow. Then she studied Owyn and Aven in turn. She nodded, and looked back at Memfis. "Will you go ahead of us, or follow?"

Memfis smiled. "I'll follow, my Heir."

"Then let us proceed." Aria turned to the second guard. "I am ready. Will you show us the way?"

The guard bowed slightly. "A moment, my Heir," he said. "The Council will signal when they're ready. There's a procedure—" A soft bell interrupted him, and he nodded. "That's the signal. If you'll follow me?"

Aria nodded, and started forward, following the guard. Aven and Owyn fell in behind her — Aven on her left, Owyn on her right. Aven didn't look to see, but he could feel Memfis behind them. The tunnel narrowed slightly as they walked, the ceiling growing lower as they approached a large set of closed double doors. There were four guards at the doors, and they opened the doors as the group approached. The guard leading them stepped out of the way and bowed.

"Just go straight ahead, my Heir," he said softly. "The Council will be in front of you."

"Thank you," Aria answered. She took a deep breath, drew herself up to her full height, and glanced back at them. Aven nodded, and Owyn grinned. She smiled, faced forward, and started walking. They followed, into the Heart of the Tribe.

Memfis had been right — the cave wasn't dark, or cold. Nor could it ever have been called small. It was, Aven thought, like being inside an enormous bubble. He tried to keep his eyes forward, but he really wanted to look around and gape; if this had been underwater, there was room in here for at least two great gray whales to swim freely.

"You okay?" Owyn whispered.

"This is huge," Aven whispered back, hearing the awe in his own voice. He heard Owyn snort, but didn't look at him. If he had, he might have started laughing. He kept his eyes forward, looking at the Council. At the end of the hall, there was a long table that looked to have been carved out of the stone itself. The table was divided into three sections — a long table, a short one, and another long one. At the short table at the center was Meris, flanked by two men who were easily as old as she. The seats at the other tables were divided into four groups of three, except for two. Those seats were empty. One of those empty seats, Aven knew, belonged to Memfis. The other must have been Fandor's.

There was a railing in front of the table, and a space where Melody could have stretched out without touching either. It was at the railing that Aria stopped. She rested her fingers lightly on the stone and waited. Aven stayed back, standing clear of Aria's wings, and saw Meris smile at them.

"Identify yourselves for the Dark Council," one of the men sitting with Meris said.

"I am Aria, daughter of Milon and his Air Companion Liara," Aria answered, her clear voice ringing out in the cavern. "I bear the Diadem of Axia, and stand as Heir to the Firstborn." She paused, then glanced over her left shoulder.

"I am Aven, son of Water Companion Aleia and Earth Companion Jehan," Aven announced. "I bear the Water gem."

"I am Owyn—" Owyn announced, only to be interrupted.

"Slave, slut, whore!"

Aven spun, drawing his swords at the sound of Fandor's voice. The disgraced Loremaster stalked past them, past the railing, and up to the center table. He threw something down on the table top and stepped back, his arms folded over his chest. Meris scowled at him, picking up what appeared to be a rolled scroll. She unfurled it, and her eyes widened.

"Where the fuck did he come from?" Memfis growled. "Meris—"

Meris took a deep breath. "He... appears to have every right to be here," she said slowly. "This is a full pardon, of all charges levied by the Council, and a reappointment to the Council." She rolled the scroll up and set it gently down on the table. "Signed and sealed by Mannon's own hand."

"Can he do that?" Owyn demanded. "After everything Fandor did to me, and to Aven? Is the Council just going to let him walk away?"

Meris met his eyes, and shook her head. She started to speak, but Fandor cut her off. "There's nothing they can do. I told you, boy. You're mine."

Aven stepped between Fandor and Owyn. "Do you want me to quarter him lengthwise? Or across his width?" he asked.

"Aven, stand down," Aria murmured. "This isn't your fight."

Aven turned, his eyes wide. "Owyn—"

"Can fight his own battles," Aria said calmly. She reached out and rested her hand on Owyn's chest, her fingertips touching the gem at his throat, and lowered her voice. "And defend his own honor. Can't you, son of Memfis, son of Trezi, of the line of Nerris?"

Owyn blinked. He blinked again. Then, to Aven's shock, he smiled. "Yes, I can. My Heir, do I have your leave?"

Aria stepped in closer and kissed Owyn on the lips. "My very enthusiastic leave, my Fire."

Memfis chuckled. "You're devious, Aria. I like it. Owyn, remember your lessons."

"Yes, Mem," Owyn said.

Aven moved in close. "Are you doing what I think you're doing?" he whispered.

"You'll see in a minute," Owyn said. "I'm naming you second, Fishie."

Aven blinked. "Naming me what?"

"Oh?" Owyn breathed. "You don't have that part? In your tribal laws?"

"I'll explain," Aria said. "Go on."

Owyn nodded. He moved away from them, walking around the railing, idly twirling one of his smoke blades. He stopped just out of reach of Fandor and cocked his head to the side. "So, you've been pardoned," he said. "And you've had all your rights restored. Now what?"

"Oh, should I tell them all what I have planned for you?" Fandor said with a laugh. "Or should I just tell Fisher?"

"I think they have a good idea, considering that tonight you've what? Kidnapped me, poisoned me, tortured me, and were going to rape me to death?" Owyn looked thoughtful. "To say nothing of the assault and kidnapping of a scion of the Water tribe. Everyone here knows what you did." Owyn looked down. He took a deep breath, then looked up and met Fandor's eyes. "What you've been doing. For years. How many other boys like me, hm? I bet you know. You know every name, every face. You remember all of us. And you love it, knowing that you had the power of life and death over us, and no one would ever stop you. You know, that's why your lady left you. What was her name? Melisant? She found out you couldn't keep it up unless you were fucking a little boy. That you got your rocks off on hurting kids, and that you paired with her young because she was little, and you could pretend that she was a boy. It's in the separation decree." He paused, and his brows rose, as if he was surprised. "You know, I just remembered. No one knows where Melisant went when she left you. I mean, she went home to her family. But then she vanished. I wonder... was that one more body in the lime pit, Fandor?"

The slap rang out through the caves, hard enough that Owyn's head whipped to the side, and he staggered back a pace before he recovered. He spat, and Aven saw the blood on the floor. Aven stepped forward, only to stop with Aria's hand on his arm.

"Watch, Aven," she murmured. "Let him do this."

Owyn touched his lip, looked down at his bloody fingers, and nodded.

"Well, now that we've got that out of the way," he said, sounding pleased. He smiled, and for a moment, Aven thought of sharks. "You are not a man's equal, and you are not a man at heart."

Fandor caught his breath. "What?"

"You heard me," Owyn said, then repeated, "You are not a man's equal, and you are not a man at heart."

Fandor laughed. "Is this a joke?" he demanded. "Is this supposed to be funny? A slave, demanding an honor challenge?"

"Oh," Owyn breathed. "Oh, that's right. You missed it. You weren't on the Council when it happened." He glanced back at Aven. "Do you still have it? Would you mind reading it to Fandor here? He missed it."

Aven nodded, turning to take the bundle of papers from Memfis. He unfolded them, and once more read the words, "It is the decision of the Council of Forge, speaking for the Tribe of Fire, Children of Adavar, that the petition for adoption of the foundling Owyn, slave of unclaimed bloodline, be approved. Be it known that from this day forth, he shall be recognized as Owyn, son of Memfis, son of Trezi, of the line of Nerris, and a full member of the Tribe of Fire, with all rights, privileges, and responsibilities of such, as listed in the Codex. This adoption is so recorded in the *Book of Silver*, and renders all prior status null." Aven finished and folded the papers, then handed them back to Memfis. Owyn nodded and turned back to Fandor.

"So, now that we're all on the same page," he said. "You're *still* not a man's equal, and you are not a fucking man at heart. Or anywhere else, for that matter." He looked toward the center table. "Lady Meris, as the challenger, I have the right to say time and place, don't I?"

Meris looked practically giddy. "You do, Owyn."

"Then I say here and now," Owyn said. He stepped back, and raised one of his smoke blades. "Right here, and right fucking now."

"Memfis?" Fandor stammered. "What... Memfis died in the Palace..." his voice trailed off, and he turned to stare at Memfis. "Fisher."

"Memfis," Memfis corrected. "And I'm still breathing, last I checked."

"I... I have no weapons, no..." Fandor sputtered and coughed, then turned to the Council. "As challenged, I have the choice of weapons."

The man sitting to Meris' left nodded. "You do. Name your weapon."

Fandor scowled. He glanced at Owyn, and his scowl deepened. He pointed at Owyn. "He cannot use those. They're proscribed weapons."

"Wasn't going to," Owyn announced. "Stop fussing and pick. Or refuse the challenge."

"I know what happens in the deep when a challenge is refused," Aven whispered to Memfis. "What happens here?"

"Fandor is cast out of the tribe, and anyone who wants to can kill him," Memfis answered. His voice carried through the cave, and Aven saw Fandor shudder. Next to Aven, Aria nodded.

"I hope he refuses," she said, her voice carrying just as well as Memfis' did. "I will enjoy turning him into a pincushion."

"Oh, I don't get a turn?" Aven asked.

"Perhaps, my Water. Perhaps."

Aven bit back a smile. He could see Fandor listening to them, growing more and more agitated. "Swords," he snapped. "I choose swords."

The man at the table nodded, then turned to Owyn. "And your weapon?"

"Swords, I said!" Fandor snapped.

"You choose for yourself, Fandor," the man said. "As Loremaster, you know the law. You don't have any say over what weapon Owyn uses, save only that he may not use the proscribed smoke blades." He smiled at Owyn. "Your weapon?"

"Whip chain, Senior Loremaster," Owyn answered. "And I allow Fandor a quarter of an hour to fetch his weapon and change his trousers." He glanced sideways at Fandor. "And to make his peace with the Mother."

CHAPTER TWENTY-FIVE

OWYN HAD STRIPPED OFF his shirt and his boots, and was stretching when Fandor returned. Aven glanced over at where the Loremaster stood, then turned his focus back to Owyn.

"What does a second do?" he asked. Owyn frowned slightly, twisting at the waist.

"They don't have seconds in the Water tribe?"

"No," Aven said. He leaned against the rail, thinking about it. "I know the rules of challenge among my tribe, but I've never heard of it actually happening. But if it did, then the two would go out onto a canoe alone with their weapons. They either settled their differences or they didn't come back."

"Wait, at all?"

Aven shook his head. "When you live at the mercy of the deep, there's no time for feuding or petty squabbles. So... we don't have them."

Owyn nodded. "Interesting. Here, it's first blood." He nodded to where a long square of some kind of leather had been laid on the ground. "First blood on the hide ends the fight. If it's his, then he loses everything. Status, name, everything. There's no coming back from an honor challenge."

"And what if it's yours?" Aven asked.

Owyn gave a weak smile. "And if it's mine, then my challenge was rejected by the Mother, and I lose everything. But since I've only had everything for about an hour, it's not as much for me to lose."

"And you are not losing," Aria said. She moved up behind Owyn and slipped her arms around him, resting her cheek on his bare shoulder. "You will win, and it will be magnificent."

Owyn rested his arms over Aria's, turning his head to rub his cheek against her hair. "Keep telling me that, will you?" he murmured. "I'm terrified."

"You aren't showing it," Aven said, keeping his voice low. He stepped closer. "May I?"

Owyn looked puzzled, then snorted. "Get over here, Fishie."

Aven grinned and moved in close, putting his arms around both of them. "Beat him like a drum, Owyn," he said, making Aria and Owyn both laugh.

"Owyn," Memfis called, coming toward them. "I have the whip chain."

Owyn shifted, and Aven let him and Aria go. Owyn drew out of Aria's arms and held his hand out, taking the long length of metal from Memfis. He examined it, section by section, then stopped and looked at Memfis. "Where's the tip?"

"Do you want the ball or the blade?"

Owyn snorted. "What do you think? The blade!" Memfis just looked at Owyn, who grimaced and ducked his head. "Sorry, Mem."

Memfis just snorted. He reached out and ruffled Owyn's hair. "You're growing, Fire Mouse. I like it. Give it back, and I'll put the blade in place." He took the whip chain, and sat down to work. As he did, he nodded toward the rail and Fandor. "I've no idea how he fights. I've never seen him."

"Doesn't matter," Owyn answered. He rolled his shoulders, and Aven heard the muscles pop.

"How are your shoulders, Owyn?" he asked. "You had your arms tied behind you for a long time. And when I healed you, I was looking for poisons, not muscle damage."

"I'm a little stiff," Owyn said with a shrug. "I'll be fine. Once the chain is ready, I can finish loosening up."

"It's ready," Memfis said. He held the chain up. "Be careful, Fire Mouse."

Owyn took the chain and draped it around his neck. "Right. You all stay here. Don't come any closer than the rail." He looked seriously at Aria and Aven. "You can't see the chain when it's in motion. And I can't stop it if you step into the wrong place. So stay here."

"We understand," Aria said. She stepped forward, took Owyn's face between her hands and kissed him. Then she smiled at him. "Win."

"As you wish, my Heir," Owyn answered. He kissed her on the tip of the nose, then turned to Aven. "Kiss for luck?"

Aven smiled and leaned down. He meant for it to be a brief kiss, but Owyn had other ideas, catching the back of Aven's neck in one hand and holding him close with the other, kissing him passionately. He heard Aria laughing, then nothing but the sound of his own heartbeat hammering in his ears. He pulled Owyn closer, running his hands over his back....

And Owyn let him go. He pulled back slightly, then tucked his head and rested his forehead on Aven's chest. He was, Aven realized, giggling.

"What's so funny?" Aven asked.

"Just that I'm realizing that there aren't any beds where we're going. At least, not for a while," Owyn answered, his voice low. "Starting to regret making us wait."

Aven laughed and put his arms around Owyn. "We'll make do. Or we'll wait."

"Yeah, yeah, we will." Owyn looked up and grinned. "Got all the luck I need now, don't I?"

Aven kissed him on the forehead. "And a little more. Can't hurt."

Owyn nodded. "Right. Let me go finish warming up." He smiled, then walked around the railing to one side of the hide. He picked up the ends of the chain where they draped over his shoulders, and in one fluid move, started to spin the chain over his head. The whip-chain almost immediately vanished from sight, but there was a slight whistling sound as the metal segments cut the air.

"I thought he was exaggerating when he said that the chain would disappear," Aria murmured. "How can you defend against something like this?"

"That's the point," Memfis said, coming up behind him. "And Owyn's surprisingly good with it, for all that he hasn't been training with it for long."

"How long?" Aven asked, not looking away from Owyn. His movements looked familiar, and Aven realized that they were similar to the way he handled his hook swords.

"A little over a year," Memfis answered. Aven turned to stare at him, and Memfis smiled. Then he nodded across the cave. "Fandor is warming up. Tell me what you think."

Aven nodded and looked over to where Fandor was swinging a pair of short swords. After a moment, Aven coughed. "I don't think he has any idea what he's doing," he said, his voice low.

"That's what I was thinking. And it can't be. He wouldn't have chosen an unfamiliar weapon for an honor challenge," Memfis said. "Something isn't right here."

"What can we do?" Aria asked. "I don't think there is anything, is there?"

"No. We have to let it play out, and hope for the best," Memfis answered. "The Council is ready."

Aven nodded, watching as the seats at the table were filled, watching as Owyn brought the chain slowly to a stop and draped it once more over his shoulders. There was a slight sheen of sweat on his skin, but his breathing was normal. He smiled at them, then moved to stand in front of the center table, where Meris was taking her seat.

"Owyn, is it your intent to proceed with the challenge?" she asked. The question sounded almost ritualistic. Owyn's answer did not.

"Yes, Granna," he replied, and Meris struggled not to smile. She looked at Fandor instead, and her expression hardened.

"And do you refuse the challenge?" Meris asked. "Keeping in mind that doing so forfeits your place in the tribe?"

"I do not refuse," Fandor growled. He turned and glared at Owyn, and Aven frowned. Fandor's voice sounded wrong, and his eyes seemed too bright, too glassy. There was something–

"Lady Meris!" he shouted. "Is there a healer present? An unbiased healer?"

Meris frowned. "Aven, this is highly irregular—"

"I understand that," Aven replied. He pointed at Fandor. "It is my opinion as a healer that Fandor has drugged himself."

A hiss went up from around the Council table, and Meris raised her hand until there was silence. "That's a grim accusation, Aven," she said.

"I'm aware," Aven said. "And I know that he will not accept any report I make as a healer. So I ask, is there a healer present who can confirm that he is not fit to enter this challenge?"

This time, Meris' raised hand wasn't enough to silence the buzz of conversation around the table. It took one of the men seated with her standing and raising his voice to quiet the others. "Enough!" he snapped. "Aven, son of Earth and Water, you are a trained healer?"

"Trained, but not formally recognized by the Earth tribe," Aven answered. "I was trained by my father, but we lived at sea. I've never been on land before."

The man nodded. "And, if you had to guess, what level healer would you be?"

"My father judged me to be second level, perhaps, sir," Aven answered. The man nodded.

"You may call me Oppa. And would you swear to the Council that your report would be factual and unbiased?"

Aven licked his lips and considered the question. "I would swear to be factual, Lord Oppa," he said slowly. "But I am not unbiased. Fandor assaulted Owyn and me both tonight, and would have handed me over to Mannon to be killed. He attempted to murder Owyn. I cannot forget that."

"A fair answer, Healer Aven," Oppa said. "I see why you requested a second healer to evaluate him. In your opinion, what sort of drug is in use here?"

Aven frowned, studied Fandor, who glared at him. "Without touching him? I would say that I think it's some sort of stimulant. Possibly something to dull pain and increase his stamina. But I'm not familiar with everything you might have at hand here in Forge. I didn't know what Rut was, for example."

Oppa blinked. "Rut?" he repeated.

"It's what Fandor gave to Owyn," Aven answered.

Oppa looked at Meris. "And this young healer defeated *Rut*?"

"We think that perhaps Aven is a better healer than he knows," Meris said. "I would accept his report without question. But I know the young man, and I knew his parents."

Oppa nodded. "I yield to the opinion of Lady Meris, and request that Healer Aven report on Fandor. Has the challenged attempted to pervert these proceeding?"

"Why not?" Owyn muttered, loud enough to be heard throughout the cave. "He perverts every other fucking thing he touches."

A ripple of laughter, and Aven fought to keep a straight face. It took him a minute to be able to answer, "I cannot examine Fandor without his consent."

Fandor turned and looked at him, his expression oddly blank. Aven had the distinct feeling that he was swimming into a trap, but there wasn't any way around it as Fandor nodded. "I will allow it," he announced, and held his arms wide.

Aven hesitated, then came around the railing. He was on the far side when he realized that Fandor hadn't lowered his arms... or his swords. Aven stopped.

"Put the swords down," he said. Fandor looked puzzled. He looked at each of his hands, as if he'd forgotten he was carrying his weapons.

"Oh?" he said. Then he smiled and lunged at Aven. Aven jumped back, slamming into the railing, and pulled his own swords free. He blocked, feeling the impact all the way up his arm, and pushed back, trying to get off the rail. He'd been wrong — Fandor definitely knew what he was doing with a sword. Aven blocked again, catching the blade of Fandor's left hand sword in the hooks of his own swords. He twisted, and Fandor's blade shattered, metal clattering to the ground. Losing the blade had no effect on Fandor — he just lunged again, using the jagged, broken blade. Aven slashed, and saw the blood well up across Fandor's abdomen. But still Fandor kept coming, seeming not to feel the pain as he drove Aven back against the railing. Aven heard shouting, heard the Council clamoring, heard Aria and Memfis from behind him. But Owyn's voice cut through the din like a blade.

"Get down!"

Aven dropped, hearing a whistling sound as he sprawled on the floor. From above him, he heard a wet sound and something ripping. He felt something splatter the back of his arm and his hand. He saw Fandor staggering away, and saw Owyn following. The whip-chain was still whistling, so Aven stayed where he was.

"Aven, are you all right?" Aria crouched on the other side of the rail.

"I think so," Aven answered.

"There is blood on your arm."

Aven shook his head. "It's not mine."

"Owyn's far enough away," Memfis said. "You can get up."

Aven got to his feet, moving behind the railing and watching the fight. Fandor was covered in blood from a multitude of wounds, but whatever drug he'd taken seemed to be keeping him from feeling the pain. He kept lunging, slashing, trying to get through Owyn's guard, trying to get past the chain, failing every time, leaving a bloody trail that marked the steps of the gruesome dance. He was panting, a mad light in his face. Owyn, on the other hand, somehow was managing to look both completely calm, and absolutely furious.

Aven frowned. "Memfis, should I—"

"No," Memfis answered before Aven had a chance to finish the question. "Owyn needs to finish this on his own."

Owyn apparently had the same idea — he started moving faster, spinning the whip chain harder. The whistle grew more high pitched as he closed the distance between himself and Fandor. Fandor went pale and staggered backwards, stumbling out of range. Then he turned, and sprinted toward the rail.

His target was clear. Aria.

It was over before Aven could react — Owyn dashed after Fandor and whipped the chain forward, so that it wrapped around Fandor's neck. As soon as the loop closed, Owyn stopped and planted himself, jerking back hard on the chain. The crack as

Fandor's neck broke was loud enough to echo; he dropped like a stone and didn't move.

Owyn stood for a moment, panting, looking down at the body. He jerked the whip chain free, and slowly began folding the sections up until he could hold them in one hand. Then he turned to the Council members, who were huddled against the farthest wall.

"Now," Owyn announced. "Speaking as Fire companion, you all are going to give my Heir exactly what she asks for, and every damned thing that she asks for. Immediately. Is that understood?" He scowled. "Well?"

Meris stepped out of the group. "Yes, Companion."

"Thank you, Lady Meris," Owyn answered with a nod. "As a personal request, will someone take that—" he pointed at Fandor's body. "And pitch it into the volcano?"

"At first light, Companion," Oppa said. "Are you hurt?"

"Me?" Owyn shook his head. "Nah. I'm good. He never touched me. However, while you do whatever it is that my Heir tells you to do, I'm going to go find a nice, quiet place to throw my guts up. Excuse me."

THEY WERE GOING TO leave Forge from the northern gate, following what Memfis called the old trade road. The supplies would be waiting for them there — riding horses, a pack-horse, food and clothes and supplies they'd need on the road. Meris insisted on bringing them to the gate herself, so they all crowded back into the carriage.

"You're sure you're all right?" Aven asked as Owyn settled onto the bench. "You look pale."

"Right now? I feel pale," Owyn said with a chuckle. "I'm surprised my bones aren't on the outside with as hard as I puked." He shook his head. "It's over. He's not hanging over me anymore."

"You did the entire city a service, Owyn," Meris said. "But there are many who won't see it that way."

"Oh, I know," Owyn said with a nod. He looked out the carriage window. "Sorry you're going to have to deal with that. But not much."

Meris laughed. "Nor am I, to be honest." Meris said. She looked to her side, to Memfis. "What's your next step?"

"The main healing center in the Earth tribal lands," Memfis answered. "Raise some troops, get Aria's name out there. Then... I'm not sure. Maybe the coastal towns and contact with Water before we head north for Air."

"How are we going to reach the Air tribes?" Owyn asked. "You told me that you can't get further than the village at the base of the mountains. Not without wings."

"That's where I will go on alone," Aria answered. "But first we have to get there." She took Owyn's hand, then Aven's. "This will not be easy. Mannon will know where we're going. He'll try to stop us."

"Are you saying that to try and scare us off?" Owyn asked. "Because I don't scare easy." He paused. Frowned. "Well, I do, but not over that. It's scarier to think about leaving you."

Aven squeezed Aria's hand until she looked at him. He smiled. "I promised you. Where you fly, I follow." He raised her hand to his lips and kissed her fingers, and saw her blush.

"The Mother chose well, when She chose you three," Meris said softly. "You're dangerous, you know. The three of you together. Mannon knows you're a threat, but I don't think he realizes how much of one."

Aria frowned slightly. She looked at Owyn, then at Aven. Then she looked back to Meris. "Grandmother? Why?"

"Because for the first time in a very long time, I'm seeing a chance that this nightmare will end. That Mannon will be overthrown, and the Firstborn restored," Meris answered. "You three, together, bring me hope. And others see it, too. People are going to follow you. And that makes you dangerous. Mannon will do whatever he can to stop you."

The carriage bumped along in silence for a few minutes, then Owyn cleared his throat. "Ah... thought of something. Aven, you don't ride, do you?"

"I rode with Trey," Aven answered. "But by myself? No."

"Aria?"

"I've never been on a horse," Aria answered. "I thought I would fly."

"In the dark?" Memfis asked. "No, you ride with me for now. Aven, you can ride with Owyn. You'll learn as we go."

"We're all going to learn as we go," Aria said. "And we're not going to stop until we're done."

"Sounds like a plan," Aven said, as the carriage rolled to a stop. He looked at Aria, at Owyn. At his future. And he smiled. "Let's go."

Also by Elizabeth Schechter

Heir to the Firstborn
Worlds Begin
Written in Water
Forged in Fire
Bones of Earth

Rebel Mage
Counsel of the Wicked
Haven's Fall
Where Home Lies

Swords of Charlemagne
Hidden Things
The Lady and the Sword
Ashes and Light
Table of Stone
Swords of Charlemagne: The Complete Series

Standalone
The Rape of Persephone
Fools Rush In
Her Captive
To Market
Infernal Machine
Chains of Light

Watch for more at elizabethschechterwrites.com.

About the Author

Elizabeth Schechter has been called one of the top erotica and alternative sexuality writers in the world. Her writing credits include the award-winning steampunk erotic romance *House of Sable Locks*, the Celtic fantasy *Princes of Air*, and the dystopian fantasy *Rebel Mage* trilogy. Her shorter work has appeared in anthologies edited by D.L King (*Carnal Machines*), Laura Antoniou (*No Safewords*), and Cecilia Tan (*Jingle Balls*; *Like a Prince*).

With *Written in Water*, the first in the *Heir to the Firstborn* series, Elizabeth is exploring new ground, with her first new adult romance that was written entirely in real time on Patreon.

She was born in New York at some point in the past. She is officially old enough to know better, but refuses to grow up. She lives in Central Florida with her husband and son.

Elizabeth can be found online at http://elizabethschechterwrites.com, or on Facebook at https://www.facebook.com/Elizabeth.A.Schechter. You can also find her on Patreon, at https://www.patreon.com/EASchechter.

Subscribe to Elizabeth's newsletter at https://www.subscribepage.com/k4u7k2

Read more at elizabethschechterwrites.com.